Anna Letitia Barbauld

Tales, poems and essays

Anna Letitia Barbauld

Tales, poems and essays

ISBN/EAN: 9783337174781

Printed in Europe, USA, Canada, Australia, Japan

Cover: Foto ©Andreas Hilbeck / pixelio.de

More available books at **www.hansebooks.com**

EMS AND ESSAYS

BY

ANNA LETITIA BARBAULD

WITH A

Biographical Sketch

BY GRACE A. OLIVER

———◆———

BOSTON

ROBERTS BROTHERS

1884

CONTENTS.

MEMOIR.

ANNA LÆTITIA (AIKIN) BARBAULD was born at the
little village of Kibworth-Harcourt, Leicestershire,
England, in 1743. This admirable and gifted woman,
whose name has long been dear to those who, as children, have read her "Hymns in Prose," with the "Early
Lessons," in short words, and then passed to her
essays and fables for the young, will be gratefully remembered by many who have passed into middle life.
To an earlier generation of readers this name was as
well known as that of any writer in the language.
Then came a time when the literature for children
assumed a different aspect, and floods of trivial, light,
and sometimes very inferior books were prepared for
the young.

Amidst the thousands of such books put before the
public in the last fifty years, how few survive even the
first decade, and how rarely one finds a story — a book
— worthy of preservation or purchase. Some are unob-
jectionable in their tone, but many more are positively
hurtful in their influence. We have stories for little
children which are exciting,— inciting them to mischief,
or rousing their minds to fear and dangers which they

ought not to experience until years have brought discretion and strength of character.   Then, for boys and
girls of larger growth, the tales of thrilling adventure
which are constantly appearing, give them a distaste
for quiet pleasures, home life, and domestic virtues.
A buffalo hunt, an escape from Indians, or frightful sea
tales furnish the ordinary food for growing boys, while
many books for girls fill their minds too soon with a
desire for society and gaiety.   Notable exceptions to
this class of literature are to be found, and should be
named if space allowed.

The peculiar mission of Mrs. Barbauld as a teacher,
writer, and inspirer of the young may be briefly expressed by a view of the work she did in reforming
literature for the children of England.

When the darkness of the middle ages became illuminated by the dawn of a new era, and the influences
of Eastern literature were gradually felt, after the returning Crusaders introduced a glimpse of Oriental
warmth and vivifying power among the nations of
Western Europe, the renaissance of popular learning
progressed rapidly and with a wonderful result.

The imagination of the East acted like a magic
power upon the dead literature of the Western world.
It can only be compared to the softening influence of
spring rains upon the ice-bound fields left by winter's
frost.

The learning of Europe — the literature of the ancients — was almost entirely confined to the monas-
teries and palaces of the dignitaries of the Roman

Church. That great power held all the important
offices in Church and State, and science and literature
crouched helpless in the chains imposed upon them by
the religious autocrats. Justice should be done to the
Church of Rome, for, while it held the power in its
own hands, it did take the charge of the bodies and
souls of its people ; but monks and nuns were unfitted
by their life and vocation to carry the beneficent work
of teacher and writer beyond their own narrow horizon.
To the East, therefore, we owe that flood of warm light
and life which came with resistless force, sweeping away
the old fancies and conventionalities, and preparing the
way for the thinker, the student, the poet, and the artist
of modern times. Works of imagination held the field
and supplied the need of generations of young readers,
till the immense revulsion of opinion and feeling which
preceded the French Revolution. The encyclopedists
in France, with the new views put before the world
by a race of educators, among whom may be named
Rousseau, De Genlis, the Edgeworths, Mrs. Barbauld,
Pestalozzi, Jacotot, Froebel, and Diesterweg, completely
altered the old style of writing for children, and revolu-
tionized the process of instruction all over the world.

Mrs. Barbauld may be justly ranked among the bright
and shining names of the great leaders in this educational movement. She was descended from a stock
of teachers, married a clergyman in charge of an academy, in the management of which she assisted for
years, and her practical knowledge was of great value
to a large number of scholars, and by her writings she

drew an immense circle of little minds within the range
of her powerful influence.

While many who love the name of Barbauld associate it with the exquisite hymns still sung in our
churches, and others rank her among the essayists
of our language, for her clear impartial thought and
elegant style, it is as a writer of admirable works for
the young that she will be long remembered. The
names of Barbauld, Ann and Jane Taylor, and Maria
Edgeworth will bring back many recollections to older
readers, and their works may still be read with pleasure
and advantage by our children.

With genius and powers of mind uncommon in her
sex, cultivation of the highest order, womanly charms
and accomplishments which fitted her for the most brilliant society and the highest walks of literature, what
Dr. Johnson said of Dr. Watts' character and writings
is not less true of Mrs. Barbauld, — that she " conde-
scended to lay aside the scholar, the philosopher, and
the wit, and write little poems of devotion and systems
of instruction adapted to their wants and capacities,
from the dawn of reason through its gradations of advance in the morning of life."

Mrs. Barbauld was descended on her father's side
from a Scotch family, her father, John Aikin, D. D.,
being the son of a Scotchman who was settled in London as a shopkeeper. Mr. Aikin was originally intended
by his father for a business life, but after some time
spent in a city counting-room, his health was so seriously affected by the confinement to a desk, that he

was sent into the country. Dr. Doddridge, who was
well known in devotional literature, had succeeded Dr.
Jennings in his academy at Kibworth-Harcourt, was
his teacher, and influenced by him he sought and
obtained his father's permission to engage in the
ministry.

After becoming Dr. Doddridge's assistant in his
academy at Northampton, he married Jane Jennings,
the daughter of the Rev. Mr. Jennings, and, again obliged by ill-health to give up his occupation, he resigned
all hope of the ministry which he had entered, and
giving up his congregation at Leicester, he opened a
school of his own at Kibworth. Mr. Aikin was an
accomplished scholar and a worthy man. It was said
of him by one capable of judging, " Every path of
polite literature had been traversed by him, and traversed with success. He understood the French and
Hebrew languages to perfection, and had an intimacy
with the best authors of Greece and Rome superior to
what I have ever known in any dissenting minister
from my own experience."

On her maternal side Miss Aikin was descended
from an ancient and respectable family of some importance in Bedfordshire. Her grandmother was Anne
Laetitia, one of the daughters of Sir Francis Wingate,
of Harlington Grange, Bedfordshire, by his wife Lady
Anne, daughter of Sir Arthur Anglesey, First Earl of
Anglesey, and Lord Privy Seal under Charles II. One
of the family held the exalted office of " Master of the
Bears," to Queen Elizabeth. Miss Aikin says : —

"Sir Francis, in his elaborate letter of declaration to the Lady Anne, still preserved, I think, values his estate at £1000 per annum, and promises to keep a coach and six. The Earl, her father, gave her several thousand pounds. Bishop Burnet writes of this noble lord, that he had sold himself so often that at length no party thought him worth buying. He seems indeed to have feathered his nest pretty well, but was certainly an able man. We may take comfort, roguery is not hereditary, folly often is.

"Grand were the preparations made at poor Harlington for the reception of the bride. The hall, and *state bedchamber* over it, were fitted up on the occasion. The chamber was hung with tapestry, 'disfiguring and representing' the judgment of Paris, and other classical stories; the bed was of crimson damask, richly adorned with fringe and gilding; there was a handsome Japan cabinet, heavy arm chairs, and toilet ornaments to match, and a dressing-room within; splendors which excited my youthful awe and veneration, decayed and faded as they were, — but as for Lady Anne, tradition says that she sat her down and cried, when she saw to how poor a place she had been brought as her future home. Her husband looks in his portrait very good natured, but heavy enough; the Lady Anne — let us hope she was of a sweeter temper than she looks in hers. She was a stiff Presbyterian, her husband a jolly Episcopalian, who said, somewhat bitterly, that when he was gone she would certainly turn his great hall into a conventicle. Perhaps this thought had set an edge on his zeal, when, in the character of a Justice of the Quorum, he committed John Bunyan to Bedford gaol for unlicensed preaching, — the only memorable action of his life, as far as I am aware.

"But that an old family mansion must absolutely have a ghost,—in fact, it would be almost as disgraceful to the race to be without one as to want a coat of arms,—I would not be so undutiful to my great-great grandmother as to tell the tale; but it is a matter of necessity, so here it is. The lady Anne had a friend who, unknown to her husband, had made up a purse, the contents of which she destined to be shared among her children by a former marriage. On her deathbed she entrusted to her this deposit. Lady Anne, I dare not say with what thoughts, she being then a widow, and hard pressed enough, *delayed* to deliver over the money. One night, she was startled by a mysterious rustling in a certain long, dark, crooked passage into which her chamber opened; the rustling — yes, she could not be mistaken — of a silk gown, the very gown of her departed friend. It passed on to a certain narrow door, at which *something* seemed to enter, and the rustling ceased. Her ladyship paid the money next day, and nothing was ever heard or seen more; but some people had an odd feeling as they passed that door, leading only to the china-closet, within my memory.

"A more favorable trait of Lady Anne has been pre-served. She possessed two beautiful miniatures, evidently a pair; one represented her brother, Lord Altham, the other a lady, so lovely in feature, and still more in ex-pression, one was never weary of gazing upon it. Lady Anne was accustomed often to take it out of her cabinet and weep tenderly over it; so far her daughters could attest from their own knowledge, but she would never inform them whom it represented, or what had been her story. Lord Altham, worthy to shine amongst the court-iers of Charles II., had three wives living at the same time; the first of these deceived and unhappy ladies was

probably his sister's friend; yes, it must have been her
wrongs over which she shed these frequent tears; and
shame at her brother's treachery and wickedness doubtless tied her tongue.

"Sir Francis died in middle age, leaving his lady with
three sons, and six ill-portioned daughters. Some few
notices have reached me of all the six sisters. Mr. Moore,
the husband of the eldest, was a clergyman, very poor,
very honest, and the simplest of the simple. He would
sometimes borrow a trifle of his mother-in-law, giving her
an acknowledgment in these. cautious terms, 'I promise
to pay, if I am able.' 'My dear' he once cried out to his
wife, 'a great rude girl came and robbed our apple-tree
while I was in the garden.' 'And did you let her?'
'How could I help it?' Neither could he help his sons'
going to ruin. Another sister married a Dr. Hay, a Scotch
physician.

"The sons all possessed the estate in succession. . . .
By way of retaliation, I suppose, for his persecution of
Bunyan, two of the daughters of Sir Francis married dissenting ministers, — not in his lifetime, however. One was
Mrs. Norris, the other was Anna Letitia, my great grandmother. One died single, aunt Rachel, of whom all I
know is that she had the honor to have Rachel, lady
Russell, for her godmother, — the families being in some
way related."

Mrs. Barbauld's mother "was presented at court by a
lady of the Annesley connection, no small distinction in
those days. She was sprightly, not without personal
charms, and had a natural talent for singing. The result
of the whole was, that her honored tutor[1] was moved to
indite an elaborate epistle, still preserved, in which he

---

[1] Dr. Doddridge.

labored to convince her that it was actually possible for a grave divine of thirty years to experience the passion of love for a little gentlewoman of fiftcen. The converse of the problem he seems to have taken for granted; not so the young lady, who steadfastly refused to become the Eloise of such an Abelard."

Dr. Aikin was more successful in his suit, and married the charming young Miss Jennings.

·After a while Dr. Aikin was called to a professorship at the little academy of Warrington. While there his University of Aberdeen conferred on him the degree of D. D.

Mrs. Aikin was much struck with the early promise of Laetitia, and wrote of her: "I once, indeed, knew a little girl who was as eager to learn as her instructors could be to teach her, and who, at two years old, could read sentences and little stories in her *wise* book roundly, without spelling, and in half a year more could read as well as most women; but I never knew such another, and I believe, never shall."

Only one son and daughter were born to Dr. and Mrs. Aikin. The son was Dr. John Aikin, who is well known for his critical work and essays, and that valuable book for children, " Evenings at Home." Dr. Aikin practised medicine at Yarmouth, and later in London, where he was long settled, till he moved to Stoke Newington, a little village, now lost in London.

Anna received a fine classical education from her father, and under her mother's devoted care grew to womanhood. Others observed the remarkable genius

of the child. One day a student of Dr. Aikin's was
conversing with him on the passions. Dr. Aikin remarked to Mr. Cappe, that "joy accurately defined
could not have a place in a state of perfect felicity, since
it supposed an accession of happiness." "I think you
are mistaken, papa," said a little voice from the opposite side of the table. "Why so, Laetitia?" "Because in the chapter I read to you this morning in the
Testament, it is said, there is more joy in heaven over
one sinner that repenteth than over ninety and nine
just persons that need no repentance." Mr. Cappe in
recording this incident, says that she was but five years
old.

When Miss Aiken was fifteen years old her father
became classical instructor at the academy lately
founded by Dissenters in Warrington. This academy numbered among its trustees, tutors, and scholars
names celebrated in literature, art, and the sciences.
Lord Willoughby of Parham, was for a time President
of the Board of Trustees, and the trustees were men
of position and respectability, who gave largely towards
its first endowment and support. The tutors or professors included Dr. Taylor of Norwich, author of a
Hebrew Concordance which received the cordial en-
dorsement of the bishops of the Established Church,
whose names were among its first subscribers. Dr.
Enfield, Gilbert Wakefield, and Mr. Holt were among
the other tutors, and the celebrated Dr. Priestley,
the "Patriot, and Saint, and Sage" of Coleridge,
first displayed his great mental endowments and be-

gan his original investigations in science during his residence at Warrington. He wrote of his residence there : " The tutors in my time, lived in the most perfect harmony. We drank tea together every Saturday, and our conversation was equally instructive and pleasing. We were all Arians, and the only subject of much consequence on which we differed respected the doctrine of the Atonement, concerning which Dr. Aikin held some obscure notions."

The little academy drew to Warrington distinguished visitors and pupils from the best dissenting families in the kingdom.

Howard, the philanthropist, was a visitor there, that Mrs. Barbauld's brother, John Aikin, might revise his MSS. and correct his proofs which were being struck off at the Warrington press. Roscoe of Liverpool, the botanist, Pennant the naturalist, Currie the biographer of Burns, and other names of local repute in that day, were among those who visited there more or less frequently, attracted by the talents and learning of the professors. Miss Aikin wrote : " I have often thought with envy of that society. Neither Oxford nor Cambridge could boast of brighter names in literature or science than several of these dissenting tutors — humbly content, in an obscure town and on a scanty pittance, to cultivate in themselves, and communicate to a rising generation, those mental acquirements and moral habits which are their own exceeding great reward. They and theirs lived together like one large family, and in the facility of their intercourse they found large compensation for its deficiency in luxury and splendor. Such days, are past; whom have we now 'content with science in a humble shed?'"

Kibworth was a very small village, and probably Mrs. Barbauld had a very monotonous life there; though she was able to recall the excitement and anxiety felt in the family when the news of the advance of the Pretender's army on London reached Kibworth in 1745. The town was on the high-road to London, and the three-year child could vividly recall the commotion caused by the approach of the rebels, and the relief felt when the news came of their defeat at Derby.

Always brilliant in beauty, Anna had admirers in Kibworth, and one of these suitors was desperately in love with the young girl. She was full of life and untamed spirits, though her mother was even rigorous in exacting all the details of a household training from her, and made her a proficient in the usual feminine accomplishments. Her severe classical training, thorough course of reading, and intense love of books and nature, did not prevent her from a very lively enjoyment of the pleasures of youth. "Great bodily activity, and a lively spirit struggled hard against the tight rein" which her mother held over her. In later years she told her niece that she had never been placed in a situation thoroughly congenial to her. This undoubtedly was true, if we except the fifteen years at Warrington, which were certainly full of promise and brilliant with intellectual and social attractions. It was a limited circle, it is true, but exceptionally endowed with social and mental attractions for one of Miss Aikin's powers. In after life she undoubtedly realized more fully that she had not had the full advantages of a worldly career; but the very attitude of dissent precluded all hopes of an introduction among the first literary circles in London, until she had won recognition by her talents and gentle womanly charms. Her life was then settled beyond a hope of material alteration, and her position as the wife of a dissenting clergyman was too clearly defined to afford her the opportunities she must have much desired. Dissent was respectable but very un- fashionable in England, and all the legal privileges granted Dissenters in later years have not entirely removed this stigma. Mrs. Aikin was "neat, punctual, strict;" and though of cultivated mind and polished manners, it is said by those who knew best, that Anna and her mother were not in any respect congenial.

Mrs. Barbauld was described at this time by an observer as follows : —

"She was possessed of great beauty, distinct traces of which she retained to the latest period of her life. Her person was slender, her complexion exquisitely fair with the bloom of perfect health; her features regular and elegant, and her dark blue eyes beamed with the light of wit and fancy."

"London cousins wondered sometimes at the gymnas- tic feats of the country lass. It was these perhaps, added to the brightness of her lilies and roses which sunk so deep into the heart of Mr. Haynes, a rich farmer of Kib- worth. He followed this damsel of fifteen to Warrington and obtained a private audience of her father, and begged

his consent to make her his wife. My grandfather answered that his daughter was then walking in the garden,
and he might go and ask her himself. With what grace
the farmer pleaded his cause I know not; but at length,
out of all patience at his unwelcome importunities, she
ran nimbly up a tree which grew by the garden wall, and
let herself down into the lane beyond, leaving her suitor
'*planté là*.' The poor man went home disconsolate; he
lived and died a bachelor; though he was never known to
purchase any other book whatever, 'the works of Mrs.
Barbauld,' splendidly bound, adorned his parlor to the
end of his days."

At Warrington, stimulated by the affectionate admiration she received from the society which surrounded her, Miss Aikin began to write; and the interest
which Dr. Priestley and his wife, with other friends,
showed in her work, encouraged her to continue labors
first assumed to amuse and enliven social gatherings.
Both "*bout rimes*" and "*vers de société*" were in fashion
in the set which gathered there. Anonymous poems
were often read, and excited much comment and admiration. The authorship of these poems was often
very puzzling to the hearers, and many were the
guesses made. Once a' very brilliant copy of verses
was slipped into Mrs. Priestley's work-bag, a favorite
place with these players at hide and seek. After long
consideration it was finally traced to Dr. Priestley
himself.

Simple pleasures, and an elevated social and literary
taste characterized the life at Warrington. The inspiration of such minds as Priestley gave the opening years

of this academy much activity; and the educational advantages of the place were combined with such moderate expenses of living that many scholars were drawn there from the remote parts of Great Britain and her dependencies.

After a time, as the students were lodged in buildings arranged for them, and no longer under the personal care of the tutors, at whose houses they had previously lived, they had more freedom, and the West Indian scholars became very troublesome. They shocked the tutors by their violence and lawlessness. They were wont to bewail their native islands, and say that the earliest request of the planter's children was for "a young nigger to kick." This set of unruly spirits finally ruined the academy by their insubordination, and it was merged in another institution.

In the palmy days of Warrington Academy, Miss Aikin was the centre of all that was brightest in the little town. In 1773, John Aikin, who had recently returned from his medical studies, persuaded his sister to allow him to print and publish her poems. She had been writing more or less for some years. Dr. Priestley says that some of her first poems were written during a visit at his house in Leeds. Mrs. Barbauld herself stated that her first poems were written after reading some verses of Dr. Priestley's, which interested her so much that she began to write in verse.

She began to write early in life, and on various occasions showed her facility in the range of thought and style, which varied happily from " grave to gay, from lively to severe." Riddles, *jeux d'esprit*, letters in verse, alternated with the noble "Address to the Deity," inspired by a sermon of Dr. Priestley's, and the "Invitation to Miss Belsham," containing the fine lines often quoted, —

> "Man is the nobler growth our realms supply,
> And souls are ripened in our northern sky."

There is a very affectionate address to Dr. Aikin, when he left the family to pursue his studies at Aberdeen ; and verses thrown into Dr. and Mrs. Priestley's chaise when they left Warrington show her playful fancy. She was blessed with a fine imagination and nice sense of the ridiculous, blended with the highest capacity for sublime and devotional thought. How impressive are the following lines from " A Summer Evening's Meditation," which are written by the same hand that penned the sportive " Lines from A Mouse," " Washing Day " and the " Inventory of the Furniture in Dr. Priestley's Library," —

> "How deep the silence, yet how loud the praise !
> But are they silent all ? — or is there not
> A tongue in every star, that talks with man,
> And woos him to be wise ?   Nor woos in vain :
> This dead of midnight is the noon of thought,
> And Wisdom mounts her zenith with the stars."

Dr. Aikin's publication of his sister's poems was attended with results which justified his opinion of their merits. The public and the critics received them well, and four editions were called for during the year 1773. Encouraged by success of the poems Dr. Aikin urged his sister to print some essays in prose, and added some of his own pieces to the collection. Lucy Aikin, his daughter, does not repeat the good story about the reception of his essays.

She very bitterly says that, as the authors did not put their names to each essay, some were credited wrongly ; "and the fragment of 'Sir Bertrand,' in particular, though alien from the character of that brilliant and airy imagination which was never conversant with terror, and rarely with pity, has been repeatedly ascribed to Mrs. Barbauld, even in print."

The truth was quite evident at the time, that Dr. Aikin's portion of the book he would have been wise to confine to editing. At a London dinner table where Samuel Rogers was, C. J. Fox met Aikin. "I am greatly pleased with your *Miscellaneous Pieces*, Mr. Aikin," said Fox (alluding to this collection of Essays). Aikin bowed. "I particularly admire," continued Fox, "your essay *Against Inconsistency in Our Expectations*." "That," says Aikin, "is my sister's." "I like much," returned Fox, "your essay *On Monastic Institutions*." "That," answered Aikin, "is also my sister's." Rogers adds, "Fox thought it best to say no more about the book." Miss Aikin never alluded to this little incident.

The essay "*On Romances*" was an imitation of Dr. Johnson's style. Boswell, in talking with Dr. Johnson, spoke of Hugh Blair's comments on his style, which he had deprecated as too pompous, and he had attempted to imitate it by giving a sentence of Addison, in Johnson's peculiar manner. Boswell repeated the passage and the changes made by Blair, when Johnson replied, " Sir, these are not the words I should have used. No. sir. the imitators of my style have not hit it. Miss Aikin has done it the best. for she has imitated the sentiment as well as the diction."

Surrounded by a small but congenial circle of friends, Miss Aikin was not without admirers who desired to take the first place in her affections. She had many suitors for her hand. and among them Archibald Hamilton Rowan. the notorious Irish rebel. was classed by himself. While being rusticated at the University for misconduct. he was sent to Warrington, and in after years he often declared. in recalling his sojourn there. that " Lætitia Aikin, afterwards Mrs. Barbauld, was his first love."

This remarkable man, in whose defence Curran made his famous eulogium of the British law. — " The law which proclaims even to the stranger and sojourner. the moment he sets his foot on British earth. that the ground he treads is holy. and consecrated by the genius of universal emancipation," — was only one of several ardent admirers of Miss Aikin.

Among the Warrington students there was a young man of French descent. Rochemont Barbauld. He was grandson of a French Huguenot. During the persecution of the Protestants by Louis XIV.. his grandfather, " then a boy. was carried on board a ship, enclosed in a cask, and conveyed to England." He settled in that country, married there, and had a son who took orders in the Established Church. On the marriage of one of the daughters of George II. to the Elector of Hesse, he received an appointment as chaplain in her household; and at Cassel his son Rochemont was born and passed his early years. When the household of the Electress was broken up, he accompanied his father to Paris, remaining there a year. After his return to England his father sent him to Warrington. It was Mr. Barbauld's intention that his son should enter the English establishment, but his life at Warrington and his intimacy with Miss Aikin so altered his views that he began to fit himself for the Presbyterian ministry. For some time want of occupation prevented his marriage, but finally, in May, 1774, he married Miss Aikin.

Anna, or " Nancy," Aikin, as her family and the friends of her youth called her, had one among other lifelong friends, " Betsey " Belsham, afterwards Mrs. Kenrick. To this lady she poured out all the joys and sorrows of her lot. These letters began in 1768. Sometimes, in the gayety of youth, it was lively chatter about a " beau," as girls then designated their admirers. Of one, " I talked to him, smiled upon him, gave him my fan to play with. Nothing would do ; he was grave as a philosopher. I tried to raise a conversation : ' 'T was fine weather for dancing.' He agreed to my observation. ' We had a tolerable set this time.' Neither did he contradict that. Then we were both silent. Stupid mortal ! thought I. But, unreasonable

as he appeared to the advances that I made him, there
was one object in the room, a sparkling object, which
seemed to attract all his attention, on which he seemed
to gaze with transport, and which he hardly took his
eyes off the whole time. The object I mean was his
shoe-buckle."

Early in 1774, came the eventful news to the beloved
Betsey of the approaching marriage of her friend, for
some time expected but necessarily deferred by the
uncertain prospects of Mr. Barbauld.

" I should have written to you sooner had it not been
for the uncertainty and suspense in which for a long time
I have been involved, and, since my lot has been fixed, for
many busy engagements which have left me few moments
of leisure. They hurry me out of my life. It is hardly
a month that I have certainly known I should fix on
Norfolk, and now next Thursday they say I am to be
finally, irrevocably married. Pity me, dear Betsy: for on
the day, I fancy, when you will read this letter will the event
take place which is to make so great an era in my life.
I feel depressed, and my courage almost fails me. Yet
upon the whole, I have the greatest reason to think I shall
be happy. I shall possess the entire affection of a worthy
man, whom my father and mother now entirely and heartily approve. The people where we are going, though
strangers, have behaved with the greatest zeal and affection: and I think we have a fair prospect of being useful,
and living comfortably in that state of middling life to
which I have been accustomed and which I love."

This depression was not unnatural for a woman past
her first youth entering on the uncertain venture of

matrimony. Then came a word about John Howard, the Christian philanthropist, the friend of her father, and always her hero.

" It was too late, as you say, or I believe I should have been in love with Mr. Howard. Seriously, I looked upon him with that sort of reverence and love which one should have for a guardian angel. God bless him, and preserve his health for the health's sake of thousands. And now, farewell," she writes in conclusion ; " I shall write to you no more under this name ; but under any name, in every situation, at any distance of time or place, I shall love you equally, and be always affectionately yours, tho' *not* always, A. AIKIN."

Dr. John Kenrick of York, a very dear friend, in speaking of Mrs. Barbauld's regard for her future husband, said he was slow to believe that her attachment to him was not of the truest and tenderest kind. He added that he knew she described her future husband to the friend to whom " he had before referred," who warned her that Mr. Barbauld had already had an attack of insanity, " as little in stature *but all over heart;* " and Mr. Kenrick, from his intimate and long acquaintance with her, judged that " the extreme sensibility of her own heart would make the manifestation of such feeling on his part irresistible."

Miss Lucy Aikin, who was of a remarkably bitter disposition, joined to a considerable literary skill and power, has left so sharp a picture of Mr. Barbauld that it is fair to qualify it somewhat after quoting it. Miss Aikin did not like to print this in the lifetime of the relations of Mr. Barbauld ; Mrs. Le Breton the great-niece of Mrs. Barbauld, has recently published it.

Miss Lucy Aikin says : —

"Her attachment to Mr. Barbauld was the illusion of a romantic fancy— not of a tender heart. Had her true affections been early called forth by a more genial home atmosphere, she would never have allowed herself to be caught by crazy demonstrations of amorous rapture, set off with theatrical French manners, or have conceived of such exaggerated passion as a safe foundation on which to raise the sober structure of domestic happiness. My father ascribed that ill-starred union in great part to the baleful influence of the 'Nouvelle Heloise,' Mr. B. impersonating St. Preux. She was informed by a true friend that he had experienced one attack of insanity, and was urged to break off the engagement on that account. 'Then,' answered she, 'if I were now to disappoint him, he would certainly go mad.' To this there could be no reply ; and with a kind of desperate generosity, she rushed upon her melancholy destiny. It should however in justice be said, that a more upright, benevolent, gener-ous, or independent spirit than Mr. Barbauld's did not exist, as far as his malady would permit ; his moral char-acter did honor to her choice, but he was liable to fits of insane fury, frightful in a schoolmaster. Her sufferings with such a husband, who shall estimate ? Children this pair seemed immediately to have despaired of. My brother Charles, born only one year after their marriage, was bespoken by them almost directly. They took him home with them before he was two years old. She en-joyed in his dutiful affection, in the charms of his de-lightful disposition, his talents and his accomplished mind, her pride, her pleasure, the best solace of her lonely age. Mrs. Barbauld's indolence was a standing subject of regret and reproach with the admirers of her genius. But those who blamed her, little knew the daily and hourly miseries of her home; they could not compute the amount of hindrances proceeding from her husband's crazy habits, and the dreadful apprehensions with which they could not fail to inspire her.

"At length the blow fell, — Mr. B.'s insanity became manifest, undeniable ; and it took the unfortunate form of a quarrel with his wife. Well for her that she had the protection of an opposite neighbor in her brother ! We were all of us constantly on the watch as long as she persisted in occupying the same house with the lunatic. Her life was in perpetual danger. Then shone forth the nobleness of her spirit. She had a larger share than any woman I ever knew of the great quality of courage, — courage both physical and moral. She was willing to expose herself to really frightful danger from the madman's rage, rather than allow him to be irritated by necessary restraint. When all was over, and this miserable chapter of her history finally closed, her genius reasserted its claims. Her best poems, her noble, though not appreciated, "1811," all those evincing a tenderness she had never before been known to possess, bear date from her widowhood."

Miss Lucy Aikin was certainly too severe in her statements when she wrote these words. Mrs. Barbauld's own words and the devotion of her lifetime are a strong refutation of parts of this description of Mr. Barbauld. To the last she tenderly loved Mr. Barbauld, and trying as his eccentricities were, she must have deeply loved her husband and respected his

character.   In the "*Dirge*" written November, 1808,
she makes touching allusion to his sufferings and rest :—

> " Pure Spirit! Oh, where art thou now!
>   Oh, whisper to my soul!
> Oh, let some soothing thought of thee,
>   This bitter grief control!

> "'T is not for thee the tears I shed,
>   Thy sufferings now are o'er ;
> The sea is calm, the tempest past,
>   On that eternal shore.

> .   .   .   .   .

> " Farewell! With honor, peace, and love,
>   Be thy dear memory blest!
> Thou hast no tears for me to shed,
>   When I too am at rest."

In the sketch written by Mrs. Barbauld after her
husband's death, for the " Monthly Repository of The-
ology and General Literature," she expressed herself
so clearly that it is well to allow her opinion to decide
us in our estimate of Mr. Barbauld's character.

" The scenes of life Mr. Barbauld passed through were
common ones, but his character was not a common one.
His reasoning powers were acute, and sharpened by exercise ; for he was early accustomed to discussion, and
argued with great clearness, — with a degree of warmth,
indeed, but with the most perfect candor towards his
opponent.   He gave the most liberal latitude to free inquiry, and could bear to hear those truths attacked which
he most steadfastly believed ; the more *because* he steadfastly believed them ; for he was delighted to submit to

the test of argument those truths, which he had no doubt could, by argument, be defended. He had an uncommon flow of conversation on those points which had engaged his attention, and delivered himself with a warmth and animation which enlivened the driest subject. He was equally at home in French and English literature ; and the exquisite sensibility of his mind, with the early culture his taste had received, rendered him an excellent judge of all those works which appeal to the heart and the imagination. His feelings were equally quick and vivid; his expressive countenance was the index of his mind, and of every instantaneous impression made upon it. Children, who are the best physiognomists, were always attracted to him, and he delighted to entertain them with lively narratives suited to their age, in which he had great invention. The virtues of his heart will be acknowledged by all who knew him. His benevolence was enlarged : it was the spontaneous propensity of his nature, as well as the result of his religious system. He was temperate, almost to abstemiousness ; yet without any tincture of ascetic rigor. A free, undaunted spirit, a winning simplicity. a tendency to enthusiasm, but of the gentle and liberal kind, formed the prominent lineaments of his character. The social affections were all alive and active in him. His heart overflowed with kindness to all, — the lowest that came within his sphere. There never was a human being who had less of the selfish and worldly feelings ; they hardly seemed to form a part of his nature. His was truly the charity which thinketh no ill. Great singleness of heart, and a candor very opposite to the suspicious temper of worldly sagacity, made him slow to impute unworthy motives to the actions of his fellow-men ; yet his candor by no means sprung from indifference to moral rectitude, for

when he could no longer resist conviction, his censure
was decided and his indignation warm and warmly expressed. His standard of virtue was high, and he felt no
propensities which disposed him to lower it. His religious sentiments were of the most pure and liberal cast;
and his pulpit services, when the state of his spirits sec-
onded the ardor of his mind, were characterized by the
rare union of a fervent spirit of devotion with a pure,
sublime philosophy, supported by arguments of metaphysical acuteness. He did not speak the language of
any party, nor exactly coincide with the systems of any.
He was a believer in the pre-existence of Christ, and, in
a certain modified sense, in the atonement ; thinking those
doctrines most consonant to the tenor of scripture ; . . .
but he was too sensible of the difficulties which press
upon every system not to feel indulgence for all, and he
was not zealous for any doctrine which did not affect the
heart. Of the moral perfections of the Deity he had the
purest and most exalted ideas ; on these was chiefly
founded his system of religion, and these, together with
his own benevolent nature, led him to embrace so warmly
his favorite doctrine of the final salvation of all the
human race, and indeed, the gradual rise and perfectibility
of all created existence. . . . His latter days were oppressed by a morbid affection of his spirits, in a great
degree hereditary, which came gradually upon him, and
closed the scene of his earthly usefulness ; yet in the
midst of the irritation it occasioned, the kindness of his
nature broke forth, and some of his last acts were acts of
benevolence."

In the *jeu d'esprit* of Mrs. Barbauld, called the
"Map of Matrimony," which she addressed to Mr.
Barbauld some years after their marriage, she concluded

with the following lines, after speaking of the fickleness
of man, and his love of change : —

> " So shalt not thou, for no returning prow
> E'er cut the ocean which thy bark has past ;
> Too strong relentless Fate has fixed her bars,
> And I my destined captive hold too fast."

While Mr. and Mrs. Barbauld were undecided as to
their plans for the future, and considering how they
might increase Mr. Barbauld's small income as a
preacher, a proposal was made by Mrs. Montague, and
some other friends of Mrs. Barbauld, to her of the
plan of a college or academy for young ladies. No
better idea can be gained of Mrs. Barbauld's views
on the higher education of women, and the changes
which have occurred in the last hundred years, in this
respect, than by reading her reply to these ladies. She
gave them her views on the subject in a letter which
contains so much good sense and sound reasoning that
her statement is worthy of note as the opinion of one
who was an ornament to her age and sex. With some
modifications, which a century with its inevitable
changes brings, the reasoning is as sound to-day as it
was then, and it is worthy of attention as the view of a
cultivated woman, and also something of a picture of
her own early training. She says : —

"A kind of Literary Academy for ladies (for that is
what you seem to propose), where they are to be taught
in a regular, systematic manner the various branches of
science, appears to me better calculated to form such

characters as the *'Précieuses'* or the *'Femmes sçavantes'* of Moliere, than good wives or agreeable companions. . . . The best way for women to acquire knowledge, is from conversation with a father, a brother, or friend, in the way of family intercourse and easy conversation, and by such a course of reading as they may recommend. . . . Perhaps you may think, that having myself stepped out of the bounds of female reserve in becoming an author, it is with an ill grace I offer these sentiments : but though this circumstance may destroy the grace, it does not the justice of the remark ; and I am full well convinced that to have a too great fondness for books is little favorable to the happiness of a woman, especially one not in affluent circumstances. My situation has been peculiar, and would be no rule for others.

"I should likewise object to the age proposed. Their knowledge ought to be acquired at an earlier period ; geography, those languages it may be proper for them to learn, grammar, etc., are best learned from about nine to thirteen or fourteen, and will then interfere less with other duties. I should have little hopes of cultivating a love of knowledge in a young lady of fifteen, who came to me ignorant and untaught. . . . It is too late then to *begin* to learn. The empire of the passions is coming on ; a new world opens to the youthful eye ; those attachments begin to be formed which influence the happiness of future life : — the care of a mother, and that alone, can give suitable attention to this important period. At this period they have many things to learn which books and systems never taught, — the grace and ease of polished society, with the established modes of behavior to every different class of people ; the detail of domestic economy, to which they must be gradually introduced ; the duties, the proprieties of behavior which they must practise in their own family, in the families where they visit, to their friends, to their acquaintance ; lastly, their behavior to the other half of their species, with whom before they were hardly acquainted, and who then begin to court their notice. . . . These are the accomplishments which a young woman has to learn from fourteen or fifteen till she is married, or fit to be so ; and surely these are not to be learned in a school. They must be learned partly at home, and partly by visits. . . . For all these reasons, it is my full opinion that the best public education cannot at that period be equally serviceable with — I had almost said — an indifferent private one.

"My next reason is, that I am not at all qualified for the task. I have seen a good deal of the manner of educating boys, and known pretty well what is expected in the care of them ; but in a girl's boarding-school I should be quite a novice : I never was at one myself, have not even the advantage of younger sisters, which might have given me some notion of the management of girls ; indeed, for the early part of my life I conversed little with my own sex. In the village where I was, there were none to converse with ; and this, I am very sensible, has given me an awkwardness in many common things, which would make me most peculiarly unfit for the education of my own sex. But suppose I were tolerably qualified to instruct those of my own rank ; — consider, that *these* must be of a class far superior to those I have lived amongst and conversed with. Young ladies of that rank ought to have their education superintended by a woman perfectly well-bred, from whose manner they may catch that ease and gracefulness which can only be learned from the best company ; and she should be able to direct them, and

judge of their progress in every genteel accomplishment.
I could not judge of their music, their dancing: and if I
pretended to correct their air, they might be tempted to
smile at my own : for I know myself to be remarkably deficient in gracefulness of person, in my air and manner.
I am sensible the common schools are upon a very bad
plan, and believe I could project a better ; but I could
not execute it."

Soon after the marriage of Mrs. Barbauld, her husband received a call from the little dissenting society of
Diss, near Palgrave in Suffolk.   After a visit in London,
where they saw something of the social and literary life
of the day, and visited the various places of interest in
and around the metropolis, they settled at Palgrave.
One call they made on Horace Walpole, who, in writing the Countess of Ossory, says : " Miss Aikin has
been here this morning (she is just married) ; she
desired to see the Castle of Otranto (Strawberry Hill) ;
I let her see all the antiquities of it."   Among the first
letters from Palgrave is one beginning : " The 14th of
July, in the village of Palgrave (the pleasantest village
in all England), at ten o'clock, all alone in my great
parlor, Mr. Barbauld being studying a sermon, do I
begin a letter to my dear Betsy."

The school for boys, which Mr. Barbauld opened at
Palgrave, was soon a great success.   The names of the
first Lord Denman, Sir William Gell, Dr. Sayers and
William Taylor of Norwich, Basil, Lord Daer, the Earl
of Selkirk, and two of his brothers, sons of Lord Tem-
pledown, and Lord More, Lord Aghrim, and others

were among the roll at Palgrave, — names distinguished
in the professions, and among the best in Great Britain.
William Taylor of Norwich, afterwards celebrated as
one of England's first German scholars, always called
Mrs. Barbauld "the mother of his mind." He recalled
with gratitude her instruction, and the way in which
she encouraged his talent for poetry. He wrote long
afterwards of the school : —

"On Wednesdays and Saturdays the boys were called
in separate classes to her apartment : she read a fable, a
short story, or a moral essay, to them aloud, and then
sent them back into the school-room to write it out on the
slates in their own words. Each exercise was separately
overlooked by her ; the faults of grammar were obliterated,
the vulgarisms were chastised, the idle epithets were can-
celled, and a distinct reason was always assigned for every
correction ; so that the arts of enditing and of criticising
were in some degree learnt together. Many a lad from
the great schools, who excels in Latin and Greek, cannot
write properly a vernacular letter, for want of some such
discipline."

Sir William Gell, afterwards the explorer of Pompeii,
was among the youngest scholars in her infant-class, for
whom she wrote the beautiful "Hymns in Prose."
Lord Denman, who was Chief Justice of England,
meeting Lucy Aikin years after, went up to her at a
great public entertainment, and said, with a look of
delight, "I dreamed of Mrs. Barbauld last night." With
all his legal learning Lord Denman cherished a love for
literature and poetry, and he always ascribed to his
beloved teacher his taste for belles lettres.

The " Prose Hymns " of Mrs. Barbauld are really remarkable for the spirit of pure devotion, simple beauty, and absolute perfection of form and idea. Called prose by their gifted author, they abound in the most harmonious periods, and pure, elevating ideas of true poetry; written for the very young, they cannot fail to affect the intelligent, cultivated, and developed mind by their pure simplicity of style, their elevation of thought, and devotional spirit which they display.

The " Early Lessons " were written for the use of little Charles Aikin, son of Mrs. Barbauld's brother, John Aikin, M.D., author of most of the charming tales in " Evenings at Home," " Essays on Song Writing," and many other valuable works and compilations, including his "Biographical Dictionary." Fifty large publications are numbered among Dr. Aikin's literary works.

Mrs. Barbauld took little Charles at his birth, and never having any children of her own, both Mr. and Mrs. Barbauld gave him most devoted care. For him she wrote " Early Lessons," with the desire to facilitate his first reading, and make less painful those difficult steps on the ladder of learning which all beginners must take.

Her practical experience in teaching very little children led her to say of this little book and her purpose in preparing it : —

" It was found that amidst the multitude of books professedly written for children, there is not one adapted to the comprehension of a child from two to three years old.

A grave remark or a connected story, however simple, is above his capacity, and *nonsense* is always below it, for folly is worse than ignorance. Another defect is the want of *good paper*, a *clear and large type*, and large spaces. Those only who have actually taught young children can be sensible how necessary these assistances are. The eye of a child cannot catch a small obscure ill-formed word amidst a number of others, all equally unknown. To supply these deficiencies is the object of this book. The task is humble, but not mean; for to lay the first stone of a noble building and to plant the first idea in a human mind can be no dishonor to any hand."

Of the "Hymns in Prose for Children," perhaps the best known of all her writings, she says in her preface her " peculiar object was to impress devotional feelings as early as possible on the infant mind, — to impress them, by connecting religion with a variety of sensible objects, with all that he sees, all he hears, all that affects his young mind with wonder and delight; and thus, by deep, strong, and permanent associations, to lay the best foundation for practical devotion in future life."

Mrs. Barbauld kept all the school and family accounts during these very busy years at Palgrave, lectured to the boys, wrote "Hymns in Prose" and " Early Lessons," " Devotional Pieces," with " Thoughts on Devotional Taste," and in answer to her brother, who was continually urging her to greater literary efforts, she replied, — " Now to prove to you I am not lazy, I will tell you what I have been about. First, then, making up beds; secondly, scolding my maids, preparing for

company; and lastly, drawing up and delivering lectures on geography. Give me joy of our success, for
we shall have twenty-seven scholars before the vacation,
and two more have bespoke places at midsummer; so
that we do not doubt of being soon full."

Dr. Johnson was very severe on Mrs. Barbauld's little
books, and was once heard to say, "Miss Aikin was
an instance of early cultivation, but in what did it terminate? In marrying a little Presbyterian parson, who
keeps an infant boarding-school; so that all her employment now is 'to suckle fools, and chronicle small beer.'
She tells the children, 'This is a cat, and this is a dog,
with four legs and a tail. See there! You are much
better than a cat or a dog, for you can speak.' If I
had bestowed such an education on a daughter, and
had discovered that she thought of marrying such a
fellow, I would have sent her to the Congress." In
another mood the famous grumbler said better things
of her, for Mrs. Piozzi says, "Mrs. Barbauld, however,
had his best praise, and deserved it. No man was ever
more struck than Mr. Johnson with voluntary descent
from possible splendor to painful duty."

During the eleven years passed at Palgrave, Mr. and
Mrs. Barbauld were often in London, and at the hospi-
table house of her publisher, Joseph Johnson of St.
Paul's Churchyard, she saw many celebrated literary
people. The more fashionable circles of the West End
were not unknown to her, and at the house of Mrs.
Montague she met many distinguished men and women.
Hannah More, in her poem on "Sensibility," alludes to

the famous literary and social queens of the day. In her *Bas Bleu* she had already celebrated Mrs. Elizabeth Montague, Mrs. Boscawen, and Mrs. Vesey, as leaders of society.

In Miss More's eulogy of woman's friendship, which contains beautiful tributes to the distinguished women of her day, including Mrs. Boscawen, Vesey, Delany, Montague, Chapone, and others, she addressed the following fine lines to Mrs. Barbauld, whose friendship she valued much, though their opinions differed on many subjects : —

" Nor, Barbauld, shall my glowing heart refuse
Its tribute to thy virtues or thy Muse ;
This humble merit shall at least be mine,
The poet's chaplet for thy brow to twine;
My verse thy talents to the world shall teach,
And praise the genius it despairs to reach.
Yet what is wit, and what the poet's art ?
Can genius shield the vulnerable heart ?
Ah, no ! where bright imagination reigns,
The fine-wrought spirit feels acuter pains ;
Where glow exalted sense and taste refined,
There, keener anguish rankles in the mind ;
There, feeling is diffused through every part,
Thrills in each nerve, and lives in all the heart;
And those whose generous souls each tear would keep
From others' eyes, are born themselves to weep.
Can all the boasted powers of wit and song,
Of life one pang remove, one hour prolong?
Fallacious hope ! which daily truths deride ;
For you, alas ! have wept, and Garrick died ! "

During the holidays the Barbaulds made excursions to
Warrington, Norwich, and London, pleasantly relieving
the tedium of teaching by such jaunts.

Soon after their marriage, in a visit to Warrington,
the lively lady found that her friend "Dr. Enfield's
face is grown half a foot longer since I saw him, with
studying mathematics, and for want of a game of
romps ; for there are positively none now at Warrington
but grave matrons. I, who have but half assumed the
character, was ashamed of the levity of my behavior."

Mr. James Martineau inherited a friendship and
respect for Mrs. Barbauld, and told me many little
anecdotes of her early years, gathered from her own lips
in after life. Once, perhaps during this very visit, the
lively school-mistress who so sadly felt the want of a
"game of romps,"—imagine her usher and scholars
hearing of this confession ! —went to ride with her husband and Dr. and Mrs. Estlin. They were travelling
on pillions, as was customary at that time in the country roads of England, where travelling could only be
accomplished on horseback. Dr. Estlin had Mrs.
Barbauld with him, and the other lady rode with Mr.
Barbauld. Dr. Estlin's horse made some sudden violent bounds, which threw Mrs. Barbauld off. Mr. Barbauld, on seeing his wife fall, sprang off his own horse
regardless of his fair companion, and thus threw her off.
Neither of the four were hurt, but the horse ran off
before he could be caught, and two of the party were
obliged to walk ignominiously home.

In 1784, during one of these London visits, Mrs.

Barbauld wrote she began "to be giddy with the whirl of London, and to feel my spirits flag. There are so many drawbacks, from hair-dressers, bad weather, and fatigue, that it requires strong health greatly to enjoy being abroad." She was beginning to feel the tremendous strain ón mind and body which her years of teaching, active housekeeping, and thought of Mr. Barbauld caused her. In this last London visit she felt the fatigue more fully than before, and in 1785 an entire change of scene was decided to be necessary for both Mr. and Mrs. Barbauld. They gave up the school, and Mr. Barbauld resigned his church ; which allowed them perfect freedom, and this they determined to enjoy in a continental tour. They left England in September, 1785, and were absent until the following June ; which time they passed very agreeably in France and Switzerland.

While the Barbaulds were absent, Mrs. Barbauld sent home many bright and witty letters to her family and friends. They saw much to interest them, and found a cordial reception in many places. Geneva, where they made something of a stay, attracted them by its social charms, and there Mr. Barbauld found relations among the Rochemonts, "amiable and respectable people." Geneva was a literary centre then and for many years, and the names of Necker, Minister of France, father of Madame de Staël, Madame Necker (*neé* Curchod), the early love of Gibbon, De Saussure, De Candolle, Sismondi, Bonstetten, M. Dumont, the Pictets, Marc Auguste and his brother M. Pictet de Rochemont, worthily sustained the reputation of Geneva, which had long been an educational centre for the Protestant youth of Great Britain, France, Germany, and Spain. The college founded by Calvin in 1558, with the *Académie* of earlier date which was reorganized by him and Beza in 1539, with many other public institutions conducted on the most liberal principles, had made Geneva, in the course of centuries, a place of enviable importance, an abode of science and literature. Visits at Aix, Nismes, Carcassone, Marseilles, and many other interesting spots in France occupied their time very pleasantly. In one letter descriptive of their summer's journey, Mrs. Barbauld sent the following little summary of her views on travelling : —

Advantages of Travelling.	*Per Contra.*
A July sun and a southern breeze.	Flies, fleas, and all Pharaoh's plague of vermin.
Figs, almonds, etc., etc.	No tea, and the very name of a teakettle unknown.
Sweet scents in the fields.	Bad scents within doors.
Grapes and raisins.	No plum-pudding.
Coffee as cheap as milk.	Milk as dear as coffee.
Wine a demi-sous the bottle.	Bread three sous the halfpenny roll.
Provençal songs and laughter.	Provençal roughness and scolding.
Soup, salad, and oil.	No beef, no butter.
Arcs of triumph, fine churches, stately palaces.	Dirty inns, heavy roads, uneasy carriages.
A pleasant and varied country.	But many, many, a league from those we love.

At Marseilles they bought a comfortable English chaise for their return journey, — at that time this was the only pleasant way of making long journeys, — and posting with their own carriage was much more agreeable to them than a diligence.

In this manner they saw Toulon, crossed the mountains of the South of France, making excursions aside as objects of interest were thought of. Hieres they visited on foot, and returned to Toulon in a primitive fashion, Mrs. Barbauld probably to her own amazement, on the *bourrique* of a *paysanne*, as the nine mile road was so steep that she was glad of a change and rest.

Mrs. Barbauld was troubled to see that at Nismes, the very centre of Protestantism in France, the congregation, some thirty thousand people, assembled in what they called the *desert*, a place " in the open air, surrounded by rocks which reverberate the voice," a few stones served as seats for the elders, and with a movable pulpit made up the furnishing of this singular place of worship. Their.great festivals conducted in this place were most striking. " No church, not even a barn," was theirs to use, and yet they were supposed to be wealthy, and only persecutions of the government prevented their building for religious purposes.

Some little time was passed at Paris, which was just then all excitement over the affair of the Diamond Necklace.

After the Barbaulds' return to England they passed some months in London, lodging in Caroline street, seeing their friends and enjoying very much the attrac-

tions of the social atmosphere and literary life. Mrs.
Barbauld could greatly add to the pleasure of any social
gathering by her conversational powers. Miss Aikin
says, from her own recollections of her aunt in the maturity of her powers, " Her conversation in her happiest
moods had a charm inexpressible : wit, playful wit,
tempered with true feminine softness and the gentle
dignity of a high mind, unwont to pour forth its hidden
treasures on all demands." Mr. John Kenrick, whose
wife was a life-long friend of Mrs. Barbauld, wrote
recently that "her conversational powers were best
seen when, in a circle of friends of cultivated minds,
some topic of literary, historical, or moral interest was
started, and the ball was thrown freely from hand to
hand. She could maintain her place against the most
fluent and subtle of the party."

Sometimes, perhaps, she offended by this spirit of
argument ; for Mrs. Opie wrote to Mrs. Barbauld's very
dear friend, Mrs. John Taylor of Norwich, that she had
a talk with Mrs. Barbauld, who maintained " that reading was an indolent way of passing the time," and took
that view of what she probably thought was reading in
a desultory manner without an object. Mrs. Opie "was
extremely surprised, as you may think, and began," she
adds, "to combat her assertions ; but I recollected
that I had heard it said that Mrs. Barbauld, like Mr.
Taylor, often contradicted for the sake of argument,
and when I feel this, as it is a proceeding which I
thoroughly disapprove, I am too angry to keep up the
ball."

In 1787 Mr. Barbauld received a call from the Hampstead dissenting chapel, and the move there was made in the spring of that year. Hampstead was a very rural suburb of London, and most inconvenient of access from the metropolis, but it was a little centre of a delightful society. The Carrs, the sisters Agnes and Joanna Baillie, the Hoares, and other delightful neighbors were near them; and at Hackney, near by, lived Dr. Priestley and Gilbert Wakefield, both endeared to Mrs. Barbauld by many tender associations of her happy years at Warrington.

She described her new home to her brother, who was settled in London, in a note which I extract from : —

"Hampstead is certainly the pleasantest village about London. The mall of the place, a kind of terrace, which they call *Prospect Walk*, commands a most extensive and varied view over Middlesex and Berkshire, in which is included, besides many inferior places, the majestic Windsor and lofty Harrow, which last is so conspicuously placed that, you know, King James called it 'God's visible church upon earth.' Hampstead and Highgate are mutually objects to each other, and the road between them is delightfully pleasant, lying along Lord Mansfield's fine woods, and the Earl of Southampton's *ferme ornée*. Lady Mansfield and Lady Southampton, I am told, are both admirable dairy-women, and so jealous of each other's fame in that particular that they have had many heart-burnings, and have once or twice been very near a serious falling-out, on the dispute which of them could make the greatest quantity of butter from such a number of cows.

"As we have no house, we are not visited except by those with whom we have connections; but few as they

are, they have filled our time with a continual round of
company; we have not been six days alone. This is a
matter I do not altogether wish, for they make very long
tea-drinking afternoons, and a whole long afternoon is
really a piece of life. However, they are very kind and
civil. I am trying to get a little company in a more im-
proving way, and have made a party with a young lady to
read Italian together."

Church Row was a green avenue of quaint old Dutch-
built houses, which led to the old church tower, which
guards the graves of old Hampstead worthies.

On a visit in Hampstead in 1873, I saw the house
described by Mrs. Barbauld as "standing in the high-
road, at the entrance of the village, quite surrounded by
fields." The house is much dilapidated, and the fields
quite built over now. After a time they chose a delightful old house on Rosslyn Hill, and this was their
home till the move was made to Newington. There
came parishioners and friends, and they in their turn
made excursions which varied the year's occupations.

A stage-coach was the only means of communication
between the "village revelling in varieties," as Leigh
Hunt named it in his sonnet, and the hill was so steep
which had to be surmounted to reach their abode that
the passengers were always obliged to walk up the hill.
The state of the roads was such, too, that Mr. Barbauld
was often kept at home when he wished to go to town.

At Hampstead Mrs. Barbauld did some literary
work. The stories for "Evenings at Home," and several prose essays, were written there. The spirited

poem addressed to the champion of the West Indian blacks, William Wilberforce, was also composed there, and Mrs. Hannah More thanked Mrs. Barbauld most cordially for it in July, 1791, saying that she had repeated parts of it to Mr. Wilberforce, who was visiting her, "and he did full justice to the striking picture" of the barbarity of the West Indian women, in the lines : —

> "Lo ! where reclined, pale Beauty courts the breeze
> Diffused on sofas of voluptuous ease ;
> With anxious awe her menial train around
> Catch her faint whispers of half-uttered sound ;
> See her in monstrous fellowship unite
> At once the Scythian and the Sybarite !
> Blending repugnant vices, misallied,
> Which frugal nature purposed to divide ;
> See her, with indolence to fierceness joined,
> Of body delicate, infirm of mind,
> With languid tones imperious mandates urge ;
> With arm recumbent wield the household scourge ;
> And with unruffled mien, and placid sounds,
> Contriving torture, and inflicting wounds."

Among the cares of housekeeping, anxious watchfulness of her husband's mental condition, and her interest in literature, Mrs. Barbauld found time to enjoy society. In writing Samuel Rogers, the banker-poet, then a young man, whose career was watched by Mrs. Barbauld with motherly affection, she says : —

"We are to have an assembly at the Long Room, on Monday next, the 22nd, which they say will be a pretty

d

good one ; I take the liberty to ask whether it will be agreeable to you to be of our party, and in that case we have a bed at your service. I could, I am sure, have my petition supported by a round robin of the young ladies of Hampstead, which would act like a spell to oblige your attendance, but not being willing to make use of such compulsory methods I will only say how much pleasure it will give to, Sir,

"Your obliged and obedient servant,

"A. L. BARBAULD.

" Our dinner hour, if you can give us your company to dinner, is half after three.

" Hampstead, October " (about 1788).

In 1790 Mrs. Barbauld was roused by the rejection of the bill for the repeal of the Corporation and Test Acts, and she produced her eloquent and impressive address to the opposers of the repeal. By this act, passed in the reign of Charles II., no person was eligible to any position, either civil or military, under the crown, without the acceptance of the Lord's Supper according to the forms of the Church of England. The act was finally repealed in 1828.

The high spirit of Mrs. Barbauld, her broad and liberal views, and earnest advocacy of all measures of progress made her some enemies among the ranks of the conservative party. She was without a shadow of party feeling, and her whole aim was to elevate the cause of humanity.

The spirited " Lines of the Rising of the French Nation," with the prose essays already named, and " Re-

marks on Mr. Wakefield's Inquiry into the Expediency
and Propriety of Public or Social Worship," a discourse
for the Fast in 1793, with the " Epistle to William Wilberforce," made her enemies.   Horace Walpole called
her *Deborah*, and Helen Maria Williams *Jael*, and in
writing constantly was abusing her even to her friends.
To Hannah More he wrote, " Deborah may cant rhymes
of compassion — she is a hypocrite ; and you shall not
make her real, nor with all your sympathy and candor
can you esteem her.   *Your* compassion for the blacks
is genuine, sincere from your soul, most amiable ; hers,
a measure of faction."   Deep indignation against her
" Address on the Corporation and Test Acts " made
him forget himself so far to call her " the virago
Barbauld," and class her among the lowest pamph-
leteers, " who spit their rage at eighteen pence a
head."   ·

Meantime the disinterested spirit of Mrs. Barbauld,
and her real love of freedom and humanity, upheld her
under the rising storm of scorn and ridicule.   Her
heart always beat true for mankind, for every class
and nation, in their struggles for freedom and right.
Her pen and voice were ever ready for the defence of
what she felt was the true cause.   Her gaze was ever
turned to the brightening future, to which she confi-
dently looked forward.

Diffident, modest by nature, and distrusting always
her own powers, it required great firmness to espouse
the unpopular side.   Her first ambitious effort was
the generous appeal for Corsica, which she wrote

when only twenty-six, in the seclusion of her country home.

She realized from the first the true meaning of the French Revolution, and braved the displeasure of Burke and many other friends to uphold her opinions.

She encouraged Priestley when mob law drove him from his home with brutal violence ; saw the desecration which the rigid enforcement of the Test Act caused, and the hypocrisy, also, which grew out of it ; spoke a brave and timely word in the lines to Wilberforce, then at the outset of his work for the slaves ; and even in her much-abused poem of " 1811 " showed she had the " courage of her convictions," when she re-encountered voluntarily such attacks as that made on her by " the Wicked Wasp," J. W. Croker.

In 1793 the memorable visit was made to Scotland, when Mrs. Barbauld, while at Dugald Stewart's, drew from her pocket-book the spirited verses of Bürger's " Lenore," and read the "composition to the company, who were electrified by the tale. It was the more successful," adds Sir Walter Scott, "that Mr. Taylor had boldly copied the imitative harmony of the German, and described the spectral journey in language resembling that of the original."

" Bürger had thus painted the ghastly career : —

'Und hurre, hurre, hop, hop, hop !
Ging's fort in sausendem Galopp,
Dass Ross und Reiter schnoben,
Und Kies und Funken stoben.'

" The words were rendered by the kindred sounds in English : —

'Tramp, tramp, across the land they speed ;
Splash, splash, across the sea ;
Hurrah! the dead can ride apace,
Dost fear to ride with me ? '

" When Miss Aikin had finished her recitation, she replaced in her pocket-book the paper from which she had read it, and enjoyed the satisfaction of having made a strong impression on the hearers, whose bosoms thrilled yet the deeper as the ballad was not to be more closely introduced to them. The author was not present on this occasion, although he had then the distinguished advantage of being a familiar friend and frequent visitor of Professor Stewart and his family. But he was absent from town while Miss Aikin was in Edinburgh, and it was not until his return that he found all his friends in rapture with the intelligence and good sense of their visitor, but in particular with the wonderful translation from the German, by means of which she had delighted and astonished them. The enthusiastic description given of Bürger's ballad and the broken account of the story, of which only two lines were recollected, inspired the author, who had some acquaintance, as has been said, with the German language, and a strong taste for popular poetry, with a desire to see the original."

Miss Cranstoun, afterwards Countess of Purgstall, who was present that evening, described the scene to Captain Basil Hall many years after. Scott was so much interested in his translation that he sat up very late finishing it, and carried it next morning to Miss Cranstoun who was delighted and wrote to a country friend, "Upon my word, Walter Scott is going to turn out a poet, — something of a cross, I think, between Burns and Gray."

In 1795 the Essays prefixed by Mrs. Barbauld to illustrated editions of Akenside's "Pleasures of the Imagination" and Collins's "Odes" were published. They show her usual critical taste and nice discrimination.

In 1796 Mrs. Barbauld met Paoli, whom she had so warmly eulogized in her poem on Corsica thirty years before. She said herself, "Had it been thirty years ago, it would have made my heart beat stronger."

Visits at various pleasant country places varied the suburban life of Hampstead ; and South Wales, Surrey, and the region about Bristol were familiar to them.

While at Bristol, in 1797, Mrs. Barbauld became better acquainted with Hannah More, whom she had long known as a correspondent after meeting her in London. A day was passed at the little cottage of the Mores', Cowslip Green. The Estlins, who were intimate friends of the Barbaulds, kept a large boarding school in Bristol, and with them many pleasant days were spent. Delightful walks and drives varied the time, and new acquaintances were made among the literary and scientific men of the town. Dr. Beddoes was then at the height of his fame and practising at the "Pneumatic Institution" his various hobbies in gas inhalation, and making his patients inhale the breath of cattle.

While at Dorking in Surrey they made one visit to

Madame D'Arblay, Fanny Burney, which that lady chronicles as follows : —

"I was extremely surprised to be told by the maid a gentleman and lady had called at the door, who sent in a card and begged to know if I could admit them, and to see the names on the card were Mr. and Mrs. Barbauld. I had never seen them more than twice : the first time, by their own desire, Mrs. Chapone carried me to meet them at Mr. Burrow's ; the other time, I think, was at Mrs. Chapone's. You must be sure I could not hesitate to receive with thankfulness this civility from the authoress of the most useful books, next to Mrs. Trimmer's, that have been yet written for children ; though this with the world is probably her very secondary merit, her many pretty poems, and particularly songs, being generally esteemed. But many more have written those as well, and not a few better ; for children's books she began the new walk which has since been so well cultivated, to the great information as well as utility of parents.

" Mr. Barbauld is a Dissenting minister, — an author also, but I am unacquainted with his works. They were in our little dining-parlor, — the only room that has any chairs in it, — and began apologies for the visit ; but I interrupted, and finished them with my thanks." (Madame D'Arblay had just moved into her new cottage, named by her, after her last novel, Camilla Cottage ; and it was in much disorder, for her marriage with M. D'Arblay had been one of affection, hardly of prudence, and they were very much straitened in their income.) " She is much altered, but not for the worse to me, though she is for herself, since the flight of her youth, which is evident, has also taken with it a great portion of an almost set smile, which had an air of determined complacence and prepared acquiescence that seemed to result from a sweetness which never risked being off guard. I remember Mrs. Chapone's saying to me, after our interview, 'She is a very good young woman, as well as replete with talents ; but why must one always smile so ? It makes my poor jaws ache to look at her.' We talked, of course, of that excellent lady ; and you will believe I did not quote her notions of smiling. . . . Her brother, Dr. Aikin, with his family, were passing the summer at Dorking on account of his ill health, the air of that town having been recommended for his complaint. The Barbaulds were come to spend some time with him, and would not be so near without renewing their acquaintance. They had been walking in Norbury Park, which they admired very much ; and Mrs. Barbauld very elegantly said, 'If there was such a public officer as Legislator of Taste, Mr. Lock ought to be chosen for it.' They inquired much about M. D'Arblay, who was working in his garden, and would not be at the trouble of dressing to appear. They desired to see Alex " (her son), "and I produced him ; and his orthographical feats were very well timed here, for, as soon as Mrs. Barbauld said, 'What is your name, you pretty creature?' he sturdily answered, 'BOY.'

" Almost all our discourse was upon the Irish rebellion. Mr. Barbauld is a very little, diminutive figure, but well-bred and sensible. I borrowed her poems afterwards, of Mr. Daniel, who chanced to have them, and have read them with much esteem of the piety and worth they exhibit, and real admiration of the last amongst them, which is an epistle to Mr. Wilberforce in favor of the demolition of the slave-trade, in which her energy seems to spring from the real spirit of virtue, suffering at the luxurious depravity which can tolerate in a free land, so unjust, cruel, and abominable a traffic.

"We returned their visit together in a few days, at Dr. Aikin's lodgings at Dorking, where, as she permitted M. D'Arblay to speak French, they had a very animated discourse upon buildings, French and English, each supporting those of their own country with great spirit, but my monsieur, to own the truth, having greatly the advantage, both in manner and argument. He was in spirits, and came forth with his best exertions. Dr. Aikin looks very sickly, but is said to be better; he had a good countenance."

In Rogers's "Table-Talk" there is an anecdote related by him of Madame D'Arblay in her old age, which is not out of place here. He says: "I know few lines finer than the concluding stanza of 'Life' by Mrs. Barbauld, who composed it when she was very old.

> 'Life! we've been long together,
>   Through pleasant and through cloudy weather;
>   'T is hard to part when friends are dear;
>   Perhaps 't will cost a sigh, a tear;
>   Then steal away, give little warning,
>   Choose thine own time;
>   Say not Good Night, — but in some brighter clime
>   Bid me Good Morning.'

Sitting with Madame D'Arblay some weeks before she died, I said to her, 'Do you remember those lines of Mrs. Barbauld's "Life" which I once repeated to you?' 'Remember them!' she replied; 'I repeat them to myself every night before I go to sleep.'"

In a visit of 1799 at Clifton, Mrs. Barbauld, by the invitation of Mr. Edgeworth made the acquaintance of

his interesting family. Maria and she became life-
long friends. Some criticism courted by Mr. Edgeworth, on " Practical Education," the joint work of his
daughter and himself, was graciously received by him
and adopted in a later edition, though at the time Mrs.
Barbauld made it, it was evidently distasteful to him.
After several pertinent suggestions, " Mrs. Barbauld was
further well prepared," says Maria, " to urge against
his plan the tendency to foster aristocratic pride and
perhaps ingratitude. The one and twenty other good
reasons she said could be given, my father spared her."
As she was the first person to make' some unanswerable
objections to Mr. Edgeworth's peculiar system of education he found it difficult to hear her, but the practical
views of Mrs. Barbauld had their effect.

Mrs. Edgeworth gave a little account of their new
friends in a letter to her family in Ireland : —

" Mr. Barbauld was an amiable and benevolent man, so
eager against the slave-trade that when he drank tea with
us he always brought some East India sugar, that he
might not share our wickedness in eating that made by
the negro slave. Mrs. Barbauld, whose ' Evenings at
Home ' had so much delighted Maria and her father was
very pretty, and conversed with great ability in admirable
language."

One story told me in London of Mr. Barbauld
while minister at Hampstead gives one a funny impression of the little man. He visited an old lady who had
recently joined his society, accompanied by his wife.
He was exceedingly restless and fidgety, and moved

about a good deal. Finally the lady turned to Mrs.
Barbauld and said, "Would not your little boy like to
go and play in the garden, and then we can have a nice
long talk !"

Among other Hampstead friends were two young ,
Scotch women, who came to "Mr. Barbauld's meeting," and were kindly greeted and welcomed as household friends by the pastor and his wife. A volume of
anonymous tragedies which appeared at the close of
the last century was much admired by Mrs. Barbauld,
and one morning she praised the plays "with all her
heart" to Miss Baillie. Lucy Aikin was struck by the
coincidence, — Mrs. Barbauld had no knowledge of the
authorship, — and says, "I well remember the scene.
She and her sister arrived on a morning call at Mrs.
Barbauld's. My aunt immediately introduced the topic
of the anonymous tragedies, and gave utterance to her
admiration with the generous delight in the manifesta-
tions of kindred genius which distinguished her."
The "sudden delight" which she thinks the author
must have felt, did not tear the veil of reserve in which
she had shrouded her plays, and Mrs. Barbauld must
have learned elsewhere her young friend's secret. Years
after, she addressed her in the poem "1811" : —

" Then, loved Joanna, to admiring eyes,
Thy storied groups in scenic pomp shall rise :
Their high-souled strains and Shakespeare's noble rage
Shall with alternate passion shake the stage."

In 1802 Mr. Barbauld received a call from the society at Newington Green, which had been under the

pastoral care of Dr. Price. The fact that Dr. Aikin had permanently fixed his abode in this village, which was quiet and yet convenient of access to London, was a great inducement to Mrs. Barbauld, and caused her to leave the many dear Hampstead friends with less reluctance. William Howitt, some years since, said of the Green, "It is one of the oldest places of the parish, and has had ancient houses and distinguished inhabitants. It had, till of late years, a still, out-of-the-way look, surrounded in most parts by large trees, and green lanes to it on all sides." One of her letters to Mrs. Kenrick gives a description of what might have been a happy home: "We have a pretty little back parlor that looks into our little spot of a garden," she says, "and catches every gleam of sunshine. We have pulled down the ivy, except what covers the coach-house. We have planted a vine and a passion-flower, with abundance of jasmine, against the window, and we have scattered roses and honey-suckle all over the garden. You may smile at me for parading so over my house and domains." In May she writes a pleasant letter, in good spirits, comparing her correspondence with her friend to the flower of an aloe, which sleeps for a hundred years, and on a sudden pushes out when least expected. "But take notice, the life is in the aloe all the while, and sorry should I be if the life were not in our friendship all the while, though it so rarely diffuses itself over a sheet of paper."

The writer saw it much changed a few years since. The quaint houses are now crowded by suburban villas

bearing the usual flowery inscriptions over their preten-
tious gates, and Newington is no longer the sequestered
and rural place it was when good Mrs. Barbauld settled
herself in her quaint little home next that occupied by
John Aikin. This happy family reunion had its sad
drawback in the shape of the ill health and increasing
irritability of Mr. Barbauld. The wearing life led by
Mrs. Barbauld, and the overshadowing anxiety, made
itself felt when she wrote an old friend in 1802, just
after this change of home, " My enthusiasm is all gone,
— not for Buonaparte, for with regard to him I never
had any, — but for most things. I wish there were any
process, electric, galvanic, or through any other me-
dium, by which we might recover some of the fine feelings which age is so apt to blunt ; it would be the true
secret of growing young."

For the "Annual Review," edited by her nephew
Arthur Aikin, Mrs. Barbauld prepared some reviews of
the poetry and polite literature of the day for the earlier
volumes, and among these may be mentioned the cri-
tique on the " Lay," named by Scott as the review of
it which he "approved and admired the most."

The year 1804 was a happier period, and we read a
lively letter written from Tunbridge Wells, describing
the various diversions of the crowds who walked the
Pantiles for health or pleasure.

In this year Mrs. Barbauld was asked to prepare a
selection from the "Spectator," "Tatler," "Guardian,"
and " Freemen," with an essay on the various writers
whose papers are there embalmed for the edification of

the future student of the finest English style.   This
essay has been considered by many critics as Mrs.
Barbauld's finest piece of work.   The genius and power
of Addison has never been more ably displayed than in
the nice and discriminating study of his works here
offered by Mrs. Barbauld.   Steele, and other writers of
the day, contributors to these periodicals, are briefly
but carefully and judiciously reviewed by her skilful
hand.   The essay opens with the observation that " it
is equally true of books as of their authors, that one
generation passeth away and another cometh."   The
mutual influence exerted by books and manners on
each other is then remarked ; and the silent and gradual declension from what might be called the active
life of an admired and popular book to the honorable
retirement of a classic is briefly but impressively traced ;
the essay being closed by remarks on the mutations and
improvements which have particularly affected the
works in question.

During the same year Mrs. Barbauld, having been
asked to prepare a life of Richardson and edit his letters, began the work.   The real value of the work lies
in her biography, and the dull, prolix letters of the
publisher-novelist are very uninteresting.   The bright
and pleasant account of his life, his stories, and his
friends and home makes modern readers for Richardson.   Many excellent critics thought the " Life of
Richardson " Mrs. Barbauld's best work.   Charles
James Fox told Samuel Rogers he thought it " admirable, and regretted that she had wasted her talents on

writing books for children (excellent as those books might be) now that there were so many pieces of that description."

One day, as Mrs. Barbauld was going home from London in the stage-coach she had a Frenchman for her companion, and upon entering into conversation with him she found that he was making an excursion to Hampstead for the express purpose of *seeing the house in the Flask Walk* where Clarissa Harlowe lodged. Rogers, in telling this anecdote, adds, " What a compliment to the genius of Richardson ! "

Mrs. Barbauld was much struck with the enthusiasm of the foreigner, and he for his part "was surprised," she says, "at the ignorance or indifference of the inhabitants on that subject. The *Flask Walk* was to him as classic ground as the rocks of *Meilirie* to the admirers of Rousseau."

Henry Crabbe Robinson wrote : —

" In December I formed a new acquaintance, of which I was reasonably proud, and in the recollection of which I still rejoice. At Hackney I saw repeatedly Miss Wakefield,[1] a charming girl. And one day at a party, when Mrs. Barbauld had been the subject of conversation, and I had spoken of her in enthusiastic terms, Miss Wakefield came to me, and said, ' Would you like to know Mrs. Barbauld?' I exclaimed, ' You might as well ask me whether I should like to know the Angel Gabriel ! ' ' Mrs. Barbauld is, however, more accessible. I will introduce you to her nephew.' She then called to Charles Aikin, whom she soon after married ; and he said : ' I dine every Sun-

[1] Daughter of Gilbert Wakefield.

day with my uncle and aunt at Stoke Newington, and I
am expected always to bring a friend with me.   Two
knives and forks are laid for me.   Will you go with me
next Sunday?'   Gladly acceding to the proposal, I had
the good fortune to make myself agreeable, and soon
became intimate in the house.

"Mr. Barbauld had a slim figure, a meagre face, and a
shrill voice.   He talked a great deal, and was fond of
dwelling on controversial points in religion.   He was by
no means destitute of ability, though the afflictive disease
was lurking in him, which in a few years broke out, and,
as is well known, caused a sad termination to his life.

"Mrs. Barbauld bore the remains of great personal
beauty.   She had a brilliant complexion, light hair, blue
eyes, a small, elegant figure, and her manners were very
agreeable, with something of the generation then depart-
ing.   She received me very kindly, spoke very civilly of
my aunt, Zachary Crabbe, and said she had herself once
slept at my father's house.   In the estimation of Wordsworth she was the first of our literary women, and he was
not bribed to this judgment by any especial congeniality
of feeling, or by concurrence in speculative opinions.   I
may here relate an anecdote concerning her and Wordsworth :   It was after her death that Lucy Aikin published
Mrs. Barbauld's collected works, of which I gave a copy
to Miss Wordsworth.   Among the poems is a stanza on
Life, written in extreme old age.   It had delighted my
sister, to whom I repeated it on her death-bed.   It was
long after I gave these works to Miss Wordsworth that
her brother said, 'Repeat me that stanza by Mrs. Barbauld.'   I did so.   He made me repeat it again.   And so
he learned it by heart.   He was at the time walking in
his sitting-room at Rydal, with hands behind him ;   I

heard him mutter to himself, 'I am not in the habit of grudging other people their good things, but I wish I had written those lines,' and repeated to himself the stanza which I have already quoted : —

'Life we 've been long together,' etc."

In naming a number of poetesses, Wordsworth himself, in writing to Mr. Dyce in 1830, put Mrs. Barbauld at the head of the list. He mentions Helen Maria Williams, Charlotte Smith, Anna Seward, and others, and adds of Mrs. Barbauld, that, "with much higher powers of mind," she "was spoiled as a poetess by being a Dissenter, and concerned with a Dissenting Academy. . . . One of the most pleasing passages in her poetry is the close of the lines on ' Life,' written, I believe, when she was not less than eighty years of age," and he quotes it to his friend. "He much admired Mrs. Barbauld's ' Essays,' and sent a copy of them, with a laudatory note, to the then Archbishop of Canterbury, his friend," says the biographer of the poet.

The great Lake Poet appears to have disregarded the fact that his own father was an attorney, and acted as agent to a nobleman, and he himself consented to hold an office of small honor but fair salary, — that of stamp distributor, — and later receive a pension from government ; all of which makes it rather unjust in him to blame Mrs. Barbauld for the position in life to which she was born.

Mrs. Barbauld made some little journeys during the year 1805. We hear of a visit at Dorking and some weeks spent in London lodgings, where she offered to

take Lucy Aikin, but she refused, saying to a correspondent: "The Barbaulds are going next week to
lodgings in town, which they have taken for a few
weeks, in order to see everything and everybody with
little trouble. They wish me to go and share their
gayety, but I feel by no means equal to racketing at
present, and my father shows little inclination to in-
trust me to the prudence of my aunt, who is at least
forty years younger than I am."

What poor Mrs. Barbauld could have done with her
niece, beyond giving her many desirable introductions,
it is hard to see.

The condition of her husband must have been
enough to steady the gayest nature. A sudden outburst
of violence, in which he threatened Mrs. Barbauld's
life put an end to the long restraint the devoted wife
had put on her nerves and heart. For years his temper
had been very trying, and sudden outbreaks of fury
even at Palgrave made her cares very great; but this
attack was accompanied by such hallucinations regard-
ing his wife and Dr. Aikin that he was removed to a
house next that of Dr. C. R. Aikin, in the care of a
keeper.

For several years his eccentricities had been very
trying to his wife. He would spend whole days washing himself. A lady whom the Barbaulds visited a few
years before his death wrote of this peculiar craze that
frequently at six o'clock in the afternoon, after all day
had been passed by him bathing, Mrs. Barbauld would
urge him to walk with them. Again and again she

would ask him if he was ready, calling in her kindest
tones, " Rochemont, Rochemont, are you coming? We
are all waiting for you to walk with us ! " " Yes, my
dear," the little man would reply, " I am just washing
myself, and will soon be ready to go with you."

It became a very dangerous position, however, for
his wife, some time before she consented to give up
her brave and self-sacrificing devotion ; but at last, frequent attempts upon her life brought about a necessary
change in their relations. After his removal to London
she did not give up all hopes for his recovery, though
his disease was hereditary, and she tried to cheer herself as well as she could with thoughts of old friends.
She wrote briefly of the sad condition of Mr. Barbauld,
urging her old friend "Betsy " to visit her. " An alienation from me has taken possession of his mind,"
she says, in a letter to Mrs. Kenrick ; " my presence
seems to irritate him, and I must resign myself to a
separation from him who has been for thirty years the
partner of my heart, my faithful friend, my inseparable
companion."

A little later, after Mrs. Kenrick had made her a
visit, and comforted her in her desolate home, she
wrote, when again alone, to her of Mr. Barbauld.

" He is now at Norwich, and I hear very favorable accounts of his health and spirits ; he seems to enjoy himself very much among his old friends there, and converses
among them with his usual animation. There are no
symptoms of violence or of depression ; so far is favorable ;
but this cruel alienation from me, in which my brother is

included, still remains deep-rooted, and whether he will
ever change in this point Heaven only knows ; the medical men fear he will not. If so, my dear friend, what
remains for me but to resign myself to the will of Heaven,
and to think with pleasure that every day brings me
nearer a period which naturally cannot be very far off,
and at which this as well as every temporal affliction must
terminate ?

" ' Anything but this ! ' is the cry of weak mortals when
afflicted ; and sometimes I own I am inclined to make it
mine ; but I will check myself."

The improvement in the sufferer's health and spirits
was such that he was allowed more freedom, and being
trusted with money, he bribed his keepers to let him
walk out.   He disappeared, and being looked for, was
found dead in the New River, attracted doubtless by
his singular fancy for bathing at all times and places.

As before said, Mrs. Le Breton having published
what was known generally, though not publicly stated,
concealment is no longer necessary, and one can only
revere and admire the more the fortitude and courage,
and the true wifely devotion of Mrs. Barbauld to her
husband.   It is no longer a matter of surprise that she
did so little literary work after her marriage ; the wonder
is that she lived so calm and beautiful a life, full of the
noblest silence about her cruel lot.

One better understands that mind which wrote what
Sir James Mackintosh calls as fine a piece of mitigated
and rational stoicism as our language can boast of, — the
observations on the moral of Clarissa Harlowe.   It is but
simple justice to name the great trial of Mrs. Barbauld's

life, as a better evidence of the powers of her mind than all her writings, grand and powerful as all the great minds of England pronounce them.

In the year 1809, Mrs. Barbauld had the strength of mind to turn her attention to literary work ; and receiving an offer to prepare a " Collection of the British Novelists," she edited, with introductions, lives, and notes, the fifty charming volumes which appeared in the year 1810, an edition highly valued now as then. Sir Walter Scott acknowledged his indebtedness to Mrs. Barbauld for some material he used on Ballantyne's " Novelists " which he received from her.

In 1811, appeared from her hand the selection of prose and verse known to the scholars of the day as the " Enfield Speaker," a work in one volume, intended for the use of young ladies.

The year 1811 was a memorable one for Mrs. Barbauld. For years she had felt the apathy which open or concealed grief and distress causes the strongest mind, the bravest heart. The work of biographer, editor, or annotator was sufficiently easy to her well-trained mind and vigorous reasoning powers to afford her relaxation, not exhilaration or inspiration. At last she felt a stirring of the old poetic fire which blazed in the "Corsica," the "Epistle on Slavery," addressed to William Wilberforce, the "Summer Evening's Meditation," and the noble "Address to the Deity," with the soul-inspiring hymns. The subject of her poem was the luxury and ambition of Great Britain, and the warning conveyed to the nation was, that unbounded ambition and unjustifiable wars must finally destroy the noblest government.

> " Arts, arms, and wealth destroy the fruits they bring ;
> Commerce, like beauty, knows no second spring."

She may justly claim the simile used by many later writers, and by none more grandly than by Macaulay in his sonorous prose, — that of the New Zealander who " shall, in the midst of a vast solitude, take his stand on a broken arch of London Bridge to sketch the ruins of St. Paul's." The youth from Ontario's shore was no more objectionable than Macaulay's New Zealander, but the indignation of the critics at the thought was most violent. The visit to the former seat of a grand empire upon which the sun never set was as follows : —

> " Pensive and thoughtful shall the wanderers greet
> Each splendid square, and still untrodden street ;
> Or, of some crumbling turret, mined by time,
> The broken stairs with perilous step shall climb;
> Thence stretch their view the wide horizon round,
> By scattered hamlets trace its ancient bound,
> And, choked no more with fleets, fair Thames survey
> Through reeds and sedge pursue his idle way."

A singularly offensive article in the " London Quarterly " for 1812, noted for its bitterness towards women, attacked the venerable lady. It was not known till long after that this was the work of Southey. He descends to personal insult in the attack, knocking even her spectacles and knitting-needles about in the assault. There was a good deal of scurrility written and printed in the letters which come to us from Coleridge, Lamb, Godwin and others of that set, — literary men of a certain school. During their lives they were very glad, as we learn, to accept the friendship and hospitality of Mrs. Barbauld. Jealousy, or disappointed literary aspirations, often had a part in these gentle personalities, as when Lamb called Mrs. Inchbald and Mrs. Barbauld "his *bald* women," nicknamed her *Bare bald* and the like. At another time Charles wrote to Coleridge : "'Goody Two Shoes' is almost out of print. Mrs. Barbauld's stuff has banished all the old classics of the nursery, and the shopmen at Newberry's hardly deigned to reach them off an old shelf when Mary asked for them. Mrs. Barbauld's and Mrs. Trimmer's nonsense lay in piles around." More of this he added, ending, "Hang them ! I mean the cursed reasoning crew, those blights and blasts of all that is human in man and child."

It is not wonderful that Southey wished Lamb to "declare war upon Mrs. *Bare*bold. He should singe her flaxen wig," he adds, "with squibs, and tie crackers to her petticoats till she leaped about like a parched pea for very torture. There is no man in the world who could so well revenge himself." This extraordinary tirade on the part of the poet-laureate was provoked by the rejection of an article he sent Arthur Aikin for his magazine. The revenge he took was most brutal, and the pain inflicted was never forgotten by Mrs. Barbauld. She never printed anything after the appearance of this poem and the abusive criticism of the "Quarterly."

She wrote, however, occasionally, and the exquisite lines on "Life," the ode which Wordsworth wished he had written, and Tennyson called "sweet verses," were composed after this.

Mr. Murray was known to regret exceedingly the appearance of Southey's article in the "Review," of which he was then the publisher. He said he was more ashamed of it than of anything that had ever been published in that periodical.

To the quiet little home at Newington came many distinguished men and women. Earnest thinkers, learned men and women, clever and appreciative of the talents of others were often seen at the door, and the little parlor of Mrs. Barbauld was frequently the meeting-place of England's men of mark. Here came Mackintosh and Macaulay, Coleridge and Charles Lamb, Sir Henry Holland, Dr. Channing, the Edgeworths, Sir John Bowring, Sir James Smith. Samuel Rogers, and Joanna Baillie, with her sister Agnes, were among the old Hampstead friends. In 1815 one reads of a day at Hampstead at the Carrs, "a charming day," when Sir Walter Scott told the old lady her reading of Taylor's "Lenöre," "Tramp, tramp, splash, splash," "made him a poet."

One gets a glimpse of her taking up a little girl into her lap and asking her if she could read, and what book she was then reading. "I answered, 'Barbauld's Lessons,' quite unconscious I was sitting in the lap of their author. She then said, 'I suppose you study geography, and can tell me what ocean is between England

and America?'" Mrs. Farrar adds that her mother having relatives in America, to whom she wrote often, she was able to answer this question; but fearing that the next might be more difficult, she slid down from the perch, where she was very comfortable, and ran off. She says, "I often met her after I was grown up, and remember her as a sweet-looking, lively old lady, wearing her gray hair, which was then uncommon, reading aloud to a circle of young people on a rainy morning in the country. She read well; the book was 'Guy Mannering,' then just published." Mrs. Barbauld then made them all draw their impressions of the witch, and kept that done by Mrs. Farrar's sister. "The kind old lady" and her pleasant manners made much of an impression on the youthful mind of Mrs. Farrar, who long after recalled with pleasure her venerable friend.

In the summer of 1812 Mrs. Barbauld, who always enjoyed a journey, made a visit to Hannah More, while she was with the Estlins at Bristol. It was thirty years since the two had met, — thirty years of change and sorrow for Mrs. Barbauld, but Miss More she found very much as she left her. "Nothing could be more friendly than their reception, and nothing more charming than their situation." The thatched cottage overlooking the lovely view of Wrington and the Mendip Hills, and standing on a slight declivity, they had planted and made "quite a little paradise." She adds, "The five sisters, all good old maids, have lived together these fifty years, without any break having been made in their little community, by death or any other

cause of separation. Hannah More is a good deal
broken by illness, but possesses fully her powers of
conversation, and her vivacity. We exchanged riddles
like the wise men of old."

Dr. Channing, who saw Mrs. Barbauld in her old age,
was much struck with her mental vigor and the interest
she felt in daily events. He said to a friend, afterwards, " I recollect with much pleasure the visit which
we paid with you to Mrs. Barbauld. It is rare to meet
with such sensibility, mildness, and I may say sweetness, united with the venerableness of old age ; and I
was particularly gratified with seeing, in a woman so
justly distinguished, such entire absence of the consciousness of authorship." And after her death, in
writing Lucy Aikin, he said, " I remember my short
interview with her with much pleasure. Perhaps I
never saw a person of her age who had preserved so
much of youth, — on whom time had laid so gentle a
hand. Her countenance had nothing of the rigidness
and hard lines of advanced life, but responded to the
mind like a young woman's. I carry it with me as
one of the treasures of memory."

Mrs. Barbauld visited more or less in the later years
of her life. One letter of 1819, from Miss Aikin, in
speaking of their home-circle says, " We are all quite
well here ; my Aunt Barbauld hears as quick as ever,"
and " though complaining a little, occasionally, has
continued to make many visits, and enjoy, I think, a
great deal of pleasure this summer." She herself wrote
of the season, and her visiting one friend's house :

"Our weather is still pleasant. I am going to spend two or three days at ——, Mr. and Miss B. and myself in a post-chaise. An agreeable companion in a post-chaise — though I would not advertise for one — is certainly an agreeable thing. You talk, and yet you are not bound to talk; and if the conversation drops, you may pick it up again at every brook, or village, or seat you pass, — 'What's o'clock?' and 'How's the wind?' 'Whose chariot's that we left behind?' You may sulk in a corner if you will; nay, you may sleep, without offence."

The sketches of Mr. Murch, president of the Bath Literary Association, contain a pleasant reminiscence of the eloquent praise bestowed by Walter Savage Landor on Mrs. Barbauld at a dinner. Mr. Murch says: "He spoke of her as 'the first writer of the day,' and became so enthusiastic in her praise that he ended by gaining the attention of the entire company. His good memory enabled him to repeat his favorite passages. After quoting the following passage from the 'Summer Evening's Meditation' he turned in his well-known manner, and asked, 'Can you show me anything finer in the English language?' —

> "'But are they silent all? — or is there not
> A tongue in every star that talks with man,
> And woos him to be wise? Nor woos in vain:
> This dead of midnight is the noon of thought,
> And Wisdom mounts her zenith with the stars.
> At this still hour the self-collected soul
> Turns inward; and behold! a stranger there,

Of high descent and more than mortal rank, —
An embryo God ! — a spark of fire divine,
Which must burn on for ages, when the sun —
Fair transitory creature of a day —
Has closed his golden eye, and, wrapt in shades,
Forgets his wonted journey through the east.'

" The very impressive manner of the speaker heightened the effect of the words intended to convey the deep, solemn, awful silence of the stars."

It was to this poem Leigh Hunt made allusion in his lines on Mrs. Barbauld, in the " Blue Stocking Revels," published in 1837 in the " Monthly Repository," where he says, after naming other poetesses and novelists of the day : —

" Then Barbauld, fine teacher, correcting impatience,
Or mounting the stars in divine meditations."

The ode " Life " was written after Mrs. Barbauld was seventy years old ; and there is another impressive poem, "Octogenary Reflections," a touching bit of personal experience.   It begins : —

" Say ye, who through this round of eighty years
Have proved its joys and sorrows, hopes and fears,
Say, what is life, ye veterans who have trod,
Step following step, its flowery, thorny road?
Enough of good to kindle strong desire ;
Enough of ill to damp the rising fire ;
Enough of love and fancy, joy and hope,
To fan desire and give the passions scope ;
Enough of disappointment, sorrow, pain,
To seal the wise man's sentence — 'All is vain.' "

One observer, who saw her often, said, only a short time before she died, "She is now the confirmed old lady. Independently of her fine understanding, and literary reputation, she would be interesting. Her white locks, fair and unwrinkled skin, brilliant starched linen, and rich silk gown, make her a fit object for a painter. Her conversation is lively, her remarks judicious, and always pertinent." The usual fate of those who live long was hers. She saw her brother suffer much and long, and then, as he himself said, —

"From the banquet of Life rise a satisfied guest,
    Thank the Lord of the Feast, and in hope go to rest."

Mrs. Kenrick, a very dear and life-long friend, was lost in 1819. A few months later came the tidings of the death of Mrs. John Taylor, of Norwich, perhaps her most near and sympathetic friend in spirit, though always more separated by distance than some others. For her she always cherished peculiarly tender feelings. To this lady she wrote, after the tragic death of Mr. Barbauld, "A thousand thanks for your kind letter, still more for the very short visit that preceded it. Though short — too short — it has left indelible impressions on my mind. My heart has truly had communion with yours ; your sympathy has been balm to it ; and I feel that there is *now* no one on earth to whom I could pour out that heart more readily."

Some striking lines were found among her papers, written not many months before her death. One, a fragment in which she likens herself to a schoolboy who is left forgotten, and hears no wheels to bear him to his father's home : —

> " To him alone no summons comes.
>   Thus I
>   Look to the hour when I shall follow those
>   That are at rest before me."

Another is a natural and simple comparison of herself to a leaf left alone : —

> " Fall, fall ! poor leaf, that on the naked bough,
>   Sole lingering spectacle of sad decay,
>   Sits shivering at the blasts of dark November.
>   Thy fellows strew the ground ; not one is left
>   To grace thy naked side.   Late, who could count
>   Their number multitudinous and thick,
>   Veiling the noon-day blaze ?   Behind their shade,
>   The birds half-hid disported ; clustering fruit
>   Behind their ample shade lay glowing ripe.
>   No bird salutes thee now ; nor the green sap
>   Mounts in thy veins: thy spring is gone, thy summer ;
>   Even the crimson tints,
>   Thy grave but rich autumnal livery,
>   That pleased the eye of contemplation.
>   Some filament perhaps, some tendril stronger
>   Than all the rest, resists the whistling blast.
>   Fall, fall, poor leaf !
>   Thy solitary, single self shows more
>   The nakedness of winter.
>   Why wait and fall, and strew the ground like them ? "

She welcomed the approaching change with composure and relief, as a release from weakness and suffering ; consented to change her home to that of her nephew

and adopted son Charles, and was so little distressed
by her decline of strength that she was visiting her
sister-in-law, Mrs. Aikin, when she very rapidly failed,
and passed away gently from earth on the 9th of
March, 1825, in the eighty-second year of her age.

For this noble heart, with its life-long burden grandly
borne, what more appropriate words than her own
beautiful lines on the death of the virtuous? —

> " So fades a summer cloud away ;
>   So sinks the gale when storms are o'er ;
> So gently shuts the eye of day ;
>   So dies a wave along the shore.

> " Farewell, conflicting joys and fears,
>   Where light and shade alternate dwell ;
> How bright the unchanging morn appears !
>   Farewell, inconstant world, farewell !

> . . . .

> " While heaven and earth combine to say,
>   'Sweet is the scene when virtue dies !' "

THE HILL OF SCIENCE.

A VISION.

In that season of the year when the serenity of the
sky, the various fruits which cover the ground, the
discolored foliage of the trees, and all the sweet but
fading graces of inspiring autumn open the mind to
benevolence, and dispose it for contemplation, I was
wandering in a beautiful and romantic country, till
curiosity began to give way to weariness; and I sat
me down on the fragment of a rock overgrown with
moss, where the rustling of the falling leaves, the
dashing of waters, and the hum of the distant city
soothed my mind into the most perfect tranquillity,
and sleep insensibly stole upon me, as I was indulging
the agreeable reveries which the objects around me
naturally inspired.

I immediately found myself in a vast extended
plain, in the middle of which arose a mountain higher
than I had before any conception of. It was covered
with a multitude of people, chiefly youth; many of
whom pressed forwards with the liveliest expression
of ardor in their countenance, though the way was in
many places steep and difficult. I observed that those
who had but just begun to climb the hill thought themselves not far from the top; but, as they proceeded,
new hills were continually rising to their view; and
the summit of the highest they could before discern
seemed but the foot of another, till the mountain at
length appeared to lose itself in the clouds. As I was
gazing on these things with astonishment, my good

Genius suddenly appeared. "The mountain before thee," said he, "is the Hill of Science. On the top is the temple of Truth, whose head is above the clouds, and whose face is covered with a veil of pure light. Observe the progress of her votaries; be silent and attentive."

I saw that the only regular approach to the mountain was by a gate, called the Gate of Languages. It was kept by a woman of a pensive and thoughtful appearance, whose lips were continually moving, as though she repeated something to herself. Her name was Memory. On entering this first enclosure I was stunned with a confused murmur of jarring voices and dissonant sounds, which increased upon me to such a degree that I was utterly confounded, and could compare the noise to nothing but the confusion of tongues at Babel. The road was also rough and stony, and rendered more difficult by heaps of rubbish, continually tumbled down from the higher parts of the mountain, and by broken ruins of ancient buildings, which the travellers were obliged to climb over at every step; insomuch that many, disgusted with so rough a beginning, turned back, and attempted the mountain no more; while others, having conquered this difficulty, had no spirits to ascend further, and, sitting down on some fragment of the rubbish, harangued the multitude below with the greatest marks of importance and self-complacency.

About half-way up the hill, I observed on each side the path a thick forest, covered with continual fogs, and cut out into labyrinths, cross-alleys, and serpentine walks, entangled with thorns and briars. This was called the Wood of Error; and I heard the voices of many who were lost up and down in it, calling to one another and endeavoring in vain to extricate themselves. The trees in many places shot their boughs over the path, and a thick mist often rested on it; yet never so much but that it was discernible by the light which beamed from the countenance of Truth.

In the pleasantest part of the mountain were placed the bowers of the Muses, whose office it was to cheer the spirits of the travellers, and encourage their fainting steps with songs from their divine harps. Not far from hence were the Fields of Fiction, filled with a variety of wild flowers springing up in the greatest luxuriance, of richer scents and brighter colors than I had observed in any other climate. And near them was the Dark Walk of Allegory, so artificially shaded that the light at noonday was never stronger than that of a bright moonshine. This gave it a pleasingly romantic air for those who delighted in contemplation. The paths and alleys were perplexed with intricate windings, and were all terminated with the statue of a Grace, a Virtue, or a Muse.

After I had observed these things I turned my eyes towards the multitudes who were climbing the steep ascent, and observed amongst them a youth of a lively look, a piercing eye, and something fiery and irregular in all his motions. His name was Genius. He darted like an eagle up the mountain, and left his companions gazing after him with envy and admiration; but his progress was unequal, and interrupted by a thousand caprices. When Pleasure warbled in the valley, he mingled in her train. When Pride beckoned towards the precipice, he ventured to the tottering edge. He delighted in devious and untried paths; and made so many excursions from the road that his feebler companions often outstripped him. I observed that the Muses beheld him with partiality; but Truth often frowned and turned aside her face. While Genius was thus wasting his strength in eccentric flights, I saw a person of a very different appearance, named Application. He crept along with a slow and unremitting pace, his eyes fixed on the top of the

mountain, patiently removing every stone that ob-
structed his way, till he saw most of those below him
who had at first derided his slow and toilsome progress.   Indeed there were few who ascended the hill
with equal and uninterrupted steadiness ; for, beside
the difficulties of the way, they were continually so-
licited to turn aside by a numerous crowd of Appetites,
Passions, and Pleasures, whose importunity, when they
had once complied with, they became less and less
able to resist; and, though they often returned to the
path, the asperities of the road were more severely
felt, the hill appeared more steep and rugged, the
fruits, which were wholesome and refreshing, seemed
harsh and ill-tasted, their sight grew dim, and their feet
tripped at every little obstruction.

I saw with some surprise that the Muses, whose
business was to cheer and encourage those who were
toiling up the ascent, would often sing in the bowers
of Pleasure, and accompany those who were enticed
away at the call of the Passions.   They accompanied
them, however, but a little way, and always forsook
them when they lost sight of the hill.   Their tyrants
then doubled their chains upon the unhappy captives,
and led them away without resistance to the cells of
Ignorance or the mansions of Misery.   Amongst the
innumerable seducers who were endeavoring to draw
away the votaries of Truth from the path of Science,
there was one, so little formidable in her appearance,
and so gentle and languid in her attempts, that I
should scarcely have taken notice of her but for the
numbers she had imperceptibly loaded with her chains.
Indolence (for so she was called), far from proceeding
to open hostilities, did not attempt to turn their feet
out of the path, but contented herself with retarding
their progress ; and the purpose she could not force
them to abandon she persuaded them to delay.   Her
touch had a power like that of the torpedo, which

withered the strength of those who came within its influence. Her unhappy captives still turned their faces towards the temple, and always hoped to arrive there ; but the ground seemed to slide from beneath their feet, and they found themselves at the bottom before they suspected that they had changed their place. The placid serenity which at first appeared in their countenance changed by degrees into a melancholy languor, which was tinged with deeper and deeper gloom as they glided down the Stream of Insignificance, — a dark and sluggish water, which is curled by no breeze, and enlivened by no murmur, till it falls into a dead sea, where the startled passengers are awakened by the shock, and the next moment buried in the Gulf of Oblivion.

Of all the unhappy deserters from the paths of Science none seemed less able to return than the followers of Indolence. The captives of Appetite and Passion could often seize the moment when their tyrants were languid or asleep, to escape from their enchantment ; but the dominion of Indolence was constant and unremitted, and seldom resisted till resistance was in vain.

After contemplating these things I turned my eyes towards the top of the mountain, where the air was always pure and exhilarating, the path shaded with laurels and other evergreens, and the effulgence which beamed from the face of the Goddess seemed to shed a glory round her votaries. Happy, said I, are they who are permitted to ascend the mountain ! But while I was pronouncing this exclamation with uncommon ardor, I saw standing beside me a form of diviner features and a more benign radiance. " Happier," said she, " are those whom Virtue conducts to the mansions of Content !" " What !" said I, " does Virtue then reside in the vale ? " " I am found," said she, " in the vale, and I illuminate the mountain. I cheer the cottager at his toil, and inspire the sage at his meditation. I mingle in the crowd of cities, and bless the hermit in his cell. I have a temple in every heart that owns my influence ; and to him that wishes for me I am already present. Science may raise you to eminence, but I alone can guide you to felicity." While the Goddess was thus speaking I stretched out my arms towards her with a vehemence which broke my slumbers. The chill dews were falling around me, and the shades of evening stretched over the landscape. I hastened homeward, and resigned the night to silence and meditation.

AGAINST INCONSISTENCY IN OUR EXPECTATIONS.

"What is more reasonable, than that they who take pains for any thing, should get most in that particular for which they take pains? They have taken pains for power, you for right principles ; they for riches, you for a proper use of the appearances of things : see whether they have the advantage of you in that for which you have taken pains, and which they neglect. If they are in power, and you not, why will not you speak the truth to yourself, that you do nothing for the sake of power, but that they do every thing? No, but since I take care to have right principles, it is more reasonable that I should have power. Yes, in respect to what you take care about, your principles. But give up to others the things in which they have taken more care than you. Else it is just as if, because you have right principles, you should think it fit that when you shoot an arrow, you should hit the mark better than an archer, or that you should forge better than a smith."   Carter's Epictetus.

As most of the unhappiness in the world arises rather
from disappointed desires than from positive evil, it is
of the utmost consequence to attain just notions of the
laws and order of the universe, that we may· not vex
ourselves with fruitless wishes, or give way to ground-
less and unreasonable discontent.   The laws of natural
.philosophy, indeed, are tolerably understood and attended to ; and though we may suffer inconveniences,
we are seldom disappointed in consequence of them.
No man expects to preserve orange-trees in the open
air through an English winter ; or when he has planted
an acorn, to see it become a large oak in a few
months.   The mind of man naturally yields to necessity ; and our wishes soon subside when we see the
impossibility of their being gratified.   Now, upon an
accurate inspection, we shall find, in the moral government of the world, and the order of the intellectual
system, laws as determinate, fixed, and invariable as
any in Newton's Principia.   The progress of vegetation
is not more certain than the growth of habit ; nor is
the power of attraction more clearly proved than the
force of affection or the influence of example.   The
man therefore who has well studied the operations of
nature in mind as well as matter, will acquire a certain
moderation and equity in his claims upon Providence.
He never will be disappointed either in himself or
others.   He will act with precision ; and expect that
effect and that alone from his efforts, which they are
naturally adapted to produce.   For want of this, men
of merit and integrity often censure the dispositions of
Providence for suffering characters they despise, to run
away with advantages which, they yet know, are purchased by such means as a high and noble spirit could
never submit to.   If you refuse to pay the price, why
expect the purchase ?   We should consider this world as
a great mart of commerce, where fortune exposes to
our view various commodities, riches, ease, tranquillity,

fame, integrity, knowledge. Every thing is marked at
a settled price. Our time, our labor, our ingenuity, is
so much ready money which we are to lay out to the
best advantage. Examine, compare, choose, reject;
but stand to your own judgment; and do not, like children, when you have purchased one thing, repine that
you do not possess another which you did not purchase. Such is the force of well-regulated industry,
that a steady and vigorous exertion of our faculties,
directed to one end, will generally insure success.
Would you, for instance, be rich? Do you think that
single point worth the sacrificing every thing else to?
You may then be rich. Thousands have become so
from the lowest beginnings by toil, and patient diligence, and attention to the minutest articles of expense
and profit. But you must give up the pleasures of
leisure, of a vacant mind, of a free, unsuspicious temper. If you preserve your integrity, it must be a
coarse-spun and vulgar honesty. Those high and lofty
notions of morals which you brought with you from
the schools must be considerably lowered, and mixed
with the baser alloy of a jealous and worldly-minded
prudence. You must learn to do hard, if not unjust
things; and for the nice embarrassments of a delicate
and ingenuous spirit, it is necessary for you to get rid
of them as fast as possible. You must shut your heart
against the Muses, and be content to feed your understanding with plain, household truths. In short, you
must not attempt to enlarge your ideas, or polish your
taste, or refine your sentiments; but must keep on in
one beaten track, without turning aside either to the
right hand or to the left. " But I cannot submit to
drudgery like this — I feel a spirit above it." 'T is well;
be above it then; only do not repine that you are not
rich.

Is knowledge the pearl of price? That, too, may be
purchased — by steady application, and long solitary

hours of study and reflection. Bestow these, and you shall be wise. " But," says the man of letters, "what a hardship is it that many an illiterate fellow who cannot construe the motto of the arms on his coach, shall raise a fortune and make a figure, while I have little more than the common conveniences of life." *Et tibi magna satis !*—Was it in order to raise a fortune that you consumed the sprightly hours of youth in study and retirement? Was it to be rich that you grew pale over the midnight lamp, and distilled the sweetness from the Greek and Roman spring? You have then mistaken your path, and ill employed your industry. "What reward have I then for all my labors?" What reward ! A large comprehensive soul, well purged from vulgar fears, and perturbations, and prejudices ; able to comprehend and interpret the works of man — of God. A rich, flourishing, cultivated mind, pregnant with inexhaustible stores of entertainment and reflection. A perpetual spring of fresh ideas ; and the conscious dignity of superior intelligence. Good heaven ! and what reward can you ask besides?

"But is it not some reproach upon the economy of Providence that such a one, who is a mean, dirty fellow, should have amassed wealth enough to buy half a nation?" Not in the least. He made himself a mean, dirty fellow for that very end. He has paid his health, his conscience, his liberty for it ; and will you envy him his bargain? Will you hang your head and blush in his presence because he outshines you in equipage and show? Lift up your brow with a noble confidence, and say to yourself, I have not these things, it is true ; but it is because I have not sought, because I have not desired them ; it is because I possess something better. I have chosen my lot. I am content and satisfied.

You are a modest man ; you love quiet and independence, and have a delicacy and reserve in your temper which renders it impossible for you to elbow your way in the world, and be the herald of your own merits. Be content then with a modest retirement, with the esteem of your intimate friends, with the praises of a blameless heart, and a delicate, ingenuous spirit; but resign the splendid distinctions of the world to those who can better scramble for them.

The man whose tender sensibility of conscience and strict regard to the rules of morality makes him scrupulous and fearful of offending, is often heard to complain of the disadvantages he lies under in every path of honor and profit. " Could I but get over some nice points, and conform to the practice and opinion of those about me, I might stand as fair a chance as others for dignities and preferment." And why can you not? What hinders you from discarding this troublesome scrupulosity of yours, which stands so grievously in your way? If it be a small thing to enjoy a healthful mind, sound at the very core, that does not shrink from the keenest inspection; inward freedom from remorse and perturbation; unsullied whiteness and simplicity of manners; a genuine integrity

" Pure in the last recesses of the mind; "

if you think these advantages an inadequate recompense for what you resign, dismiss your scruples this instant, and be a slave-merchant, a parasite, or — what you please.

" If these be motives weak, break off betimes; "

and as you have not spirit to assert the dignity of virtue, be wise enough not to forego the emoluments of vice.

I much admire the spirit of the ancient philosophers, in that they never attempted, as our moralists often do, to lower the tone of philosophy, and make it consistent with all the indulgences of indolence and sensuality. They never thought of having the bulk of mankind for their disciples ; but kept themselves as distinct as possible from a worldly life. They plainly told men what sacrifices were required, and what advantages they were which might be expected.

> " Si virtus hoc una potest dare, fortis omissis
> Hoc age deliciis————— "

If you would be a philosopher, these are the terms. You must do thus and thus ; there is no other way. If not, go and be one of the vulgar.

There is no one quality gives so much dignity to a character, as consistency of conduct. Even if a man's pursuits be wrong and unjustifiable, yet if they are prosecuted with steadiness and vigor, we cannot withhold our admiration. The most characteristic mark of a great mind is to choose some one important object, and pursue it through life. It was this made Cæsar a great man. His object was ambition ; he pursued it steadily, and was always ready to sacrifice to it, every interfering passion or inclination.

There is a pretty passage in one of Lucian's dialogues, where Jupiter complains to Cupid that though he has had so many intrigues, he was never sincerely beloved. In order to be loved, says Cupid, you must lay aside your ægis and your thunder-bolts, and you must curl and perfume your hair, and place a garland on your head, and walk with a soft step, and assume a winning, obsequious deportment. But, replied Jupiter, I am not willing to resign so much of my dignity. Then, returns Cupid, leave off desiring to be loved. He wanted to be Jupiter and Adonis at the same time.

It must be confessed, that men of genius are of all others most inclined to make these unreasonable claims. As their relish for enjoyment is strong, their

views large and comprehensive, and they feel themselves lifted above the common bulk of mankind, they
are apt to slight that natural reward of praise and
admiration which is ever largely paid to distinguished
abilities ; and to expect to be called forth to public
notice and favor : without considering that their talents
are commonly very unfit for active life ; that their ec-
centricity and turn for speculation disqualifies them for
the business of the world, which is best carried on by
men of moderate genius ; and that society is not
obliged to reward any one who is not useful to it.
The poets have been a very unreasonable race, and
have often complained loudly of the neglect of genius
and the ingratitude of the age.   The tender and pensive Cowley, and the elegant Shenstone, had their
minds tinctured by this discontent ; and even the
sublime melancholy of Young was too much owing to
the stings of disappointed ambition.

The moderation we have been endeavoring to inculcate, will likewise prevent much mortification and disgust in our commerce with mankind.   As we ought not
to wish in ourselves, so neither should we expect in
our friends contrary qualifications.   Young and san-
guine, when we enter the world, and feel our affections
drawn forth by any particular excellence in a character,
we immediately give it credit for all others ; and are
beyond measure disgusted when we come to discover,
as we soon must discover, the defects in the other side
of the balance.   But nature is much more frugal than
to heap together all manner of shining qualities in one
glaring mass.   Like a judicious painter, she endeavors
to preserve a certain unity of style and coloring in her
pieces.   Models of absolute perfection are only to be
met with in romance ; where exquisite beauty, and
brilliant wit, and profound judgment, and immaculate
virtue, are all blended together to adorn some favorite
character.   As an anatomist knows that the racer can-

not have the strength and muscles of the draught-horse ; and that winged men, griffons, and mermaids must be mere creatures of the imagination ; so the philosopher is sensible that there are combinations of moral qualities which never can take place but in idea. There is a different air and complexion in characters as well as in faces, though perhaps each equally beautiful ; and the excellencies of one cannot be transferred to the other. Thus, if one man possesses a stoical apathy of soul, acts independent of the opinion of the world, and fulfils every duty with mathematical exactness, you must not expect that man to be greatly influenced by the weakness of pity, or the partialities of friendship : you must not be offended that he does not fly to meet you after a short absence ; or require from him the convivial spirit and honest effusions of a warm, open, susceptible heart. If another is remarkable for a lively, active zeal, inflexible integrity, a strong indignation against vice, and freedom in reproving it, he will probably have some little bluntness in his address not altogether suitable to polished life ; he will want the winning arts of conversation ; he will disgust by a kind of haughtiness and negligence in his manner, and often hurt the delicacy of his acquaintance with harsh and disagreeable truths.

We usually say, that man is a genius, *but* he has some whims and oddities ; such a one has a very general knowledge, *but* he is superficial, etc. Now in all such cases we should speak more rationally did we substitute *therefore* for *but*. He is a genius, *therefore* he is whimsical ; and the like.

It is the fault of the present age, owing to the freer commerce that different ranks and professions now enjoy with each other, that characters are not marked with sufficient strength : the several classes run too much into one another. We have fewer pedants, it is true, but we have fewer striking originals. Every one is expected to have such a tincture of general knowledge as is incompatible with going deep into any science ; and such a conformity to fashionable manners, as checks the free workings of the ruling passion, and gives an insipid sameness to the face of society, under the idea of polish and regularity.

There is a cast of manners peculiar and becoming to each age, sex, and profession ; one, therefore, should not throw out illiberal and common-place censures against another. Each is perfect in its kind, — a woman as a woman ; a tradesman as a tradesman. We are often hurt by a brutality and sluggish conceptions of the vulgar ; not considering that some there must be, to be hewers of wood and drawers of water, and that cultivated genius, or even any great refinement and delicacy in their moral feelings, would be a real misfortune to them.

Let us then study the philosophy of the human mind. The man who is master of this science, will know what to expect from every one. From this man, wise advice ; from that, cordial sympathy ; from another, casual entertainment. The passions and inclinations of others are his tools, which he can use with as much precision as he would the mechanical powers ; and he can as readily make allowance for the workings of vanity, or the bias of self-interest in his friends, as for the power of friction, or the irregularities of the needle.

TO-MORROW.

Sᴇᴇ where the falling day
In silence steals away
Behind the western hills withdrawn;
Her fires are quenched, her beauty fled,
While blushes all her face o'erspread,
As conscious she had ill fulfilled
The promise of the dawn.

Another morning soon shall rise,
Another day salute our eyes,
As smiling and as fair as she,
And make as many promises;
But do not thou
The tale believe,
They're sisters all,
And all deceive.

RIDDLE.

Fʀᴏᴍ rosy bowers we issue forth,
From east to west, from south to north,
Unseen, unfelt, by night, by day,
Abroad we take our airy way:
We foster love and kindle strife,
The bitter and the sweet of life:
Piercing and sharp, we wound like steel;
Now, smooth as oil, those wounds we heal:
Not strings of pearl are valued more,
Or gems enchased in golden ore;
Yet thousands of us every day,
Worthless and vile are thrown away.
Ye wise, secure with bars of brass
The double doors through which we pass;
For, once escaped, back to our cell
No human art can us compel.

ON EDUCATION.

THE other day I paid a visit to a gentleman with whom, though greatly my superior in fortune, I have long been in habits of an easy intimacy. He rose in the world by honorable industry; and married, rather late in life, a lady to whom he had been long attached, and in whom centered the wealth of several expiring families. Their earnest wish for children was not immediately gratified. At length. they were made happy by a son, who, from the moment he was born, engrossed all their care and attention. — My friend received me in his library, where I found him busied in turning over books of education, of which he had collected all that were worthy notice, from Xenophon to Locke, and from Locke to Catherine Macauley. As he knows I have been engaged in the business of instruction, he did me the honor to consult me on the subject of his researches, hoping, he said, that, out of all the systems before him, we should be able to form a plan equally complete and comprehensive; it being the determination of both himself and his lady to choose the best that could be had, and to spare neither pains nor expense in making their child all that was great and good. I gave him my thoughts with the utmost freedom, and after I returned home, threw upon paper the observations which had occurred to me.

The first thing to be considered, with respect to education, is the object of it. This appears to me to have been generally misunderstood. Education, in its largest sense, is a thing of great scope and extent.

It includes the whole process by which a human being is formed to be what he is, in habits, principles, and cultivation of every kind. But of this, a very small part is in the power even of the parent himself; a smaller still can be directed by purchased tuition of any kind. You engage for your child masters and tutors at large salaries; and you do well, for they are competent to instruct him: they will give him the means, at least, of acquiring science and accomplishments; but in the business of education, properly so called, they can do little for you. Do you ask, then, what will educate your son? Your example will educate him; your conversation with your friends; the business he sees you transact; the likings and dislikings you express; these will educate him; — the society you live in will educate him; — your domestics will educate him; above all, your rank and situation in life, your house, your table, your pleasure-grounds, your hounds, and your stables will educate him. It is not in your power to withdraw him from the continual influence of these things, except you were to withdraw yourself from them also. You speak of *beginning* the education of your son. The moment he was able to form an idea his education was already begun; the education of circumstances — insensible education — which, like insensible perspiration, is of more constant and powerful effect, and of infinitely more consequence to the habit, than that which is direct and apparent. This education goes on at every instant of time; it goes on like time; you can neither stop it nor turn its course. What these have a tendency to make your child, that he will be. Maxims and documents are good precisely till they are tried, and no longer; they will teach him to talk, and nothing more. The *circumstances* in which your son is placed will be even more prevalent than your example; and you have no right to expect him to become what you yourself are, but by the same means. You, that have toiled during youth to set your son upon higher ground, and to enable him to begin where you left off, do not expect that son to be what you were, — diligent, modest, active, simple in his tastes, fertile in resources. You have put him under quite a different master. Poverty educated you; wealth will educate him. You cannot suppose the result will be the same. You must not even expect that he will be what you now are; for though relaxed perhaps from the severity of your frugal habits, you still derive advantage from having formed them; and, in your heart, you like plain dinners, and early hours, and old friends, whenever your fortune will permit you to enjoy them. But it will not be so with your son : his tastes will be formed by your present situation, and in no degree by your former one. But I take great care, you will say, to counteract these tendencies, and to bring him up in hardy and simple manners; I know their value, and am resolved that he shall acquire no other. Yes, you make him hardy; that is to say, you take a country-house in a good air, and make him run, well clothed and carefully attended, for, it may be, an hour in a clear, frosty winter's day upon your gravelled terrace; or perhaps you take the puny shivering infant from his warm bed, and dip him in an icy cold bath, — and you think you have done great matters. And so you have; you have done all you can. But you were suffered to run abroad half the day on a bleak heath, in weather fit and unfit, wading barefoot through dirty ponds, sometimes losing your way benighted, scrambling over hedges, climbing trees, in perils every hour both of life and limb. Your life was of very little consequence to any one; even your parents, encumbered with a numerous family, had little time to indulge the softnesses of affection, or the solicitude of anxiety; and to every one else it was of no consequence at all. It is not possible for you, it would not even be right for you, in your present situation, to pay no more attention to your child than was paid to you. In these mimic experiments of education, there is always something which distinguishes them from reality; some weak part left unfortified, for the arrows of misfortune to find their way into. Achilles was a young nobleman, *dios Achilleus*, and therefore, though he had Chiron for his tutor, there was one foot left undipped. You may throw by Rousseau; your parents practised without having read it; you may read, but imperious circumstances forbid you the practice of it.

You are sensible of the advantages of simplicity of diet; and you make a point of restricting that of your child to the plainest food, for you are resolved that he shall not be nice. But this plain food is of the choicest quality, prepared by your own cook; his fruit is ripened from your walls; his cloth, his glasses, all the accompaniments of the table, are such as are only met with in families of opulence : the very servants who attend him are neat, well dressed, and have a certain air of fashion. You may call this simplicity; but I say he will be nice, — for it is a kind of simplicity which only wealth can attain to, and which will subject him to be disgusted at all common tables. Besides, he will from time to time partake of those delicacies which your table abounds with; you yourself will give him of them occasionally; you would be unkind if you did not : your servants, if good-natured, will do the same. Do you think you can keep the full stream of luxury running by his lips, and he not taste of it? Vain imagination !

I would not be understood to inveigh against wealth, or against the enjoyments of it; they are real enjoyments, and allied to many elegancies in manners and in taste; — I only wish to prevent unprofitable pains and inconsistent expectations.

You are sensible of the benefit of early rising; and

you may, if you please, make it a point that your
daughter shall retire with her governess, and your son
with his tutor, at the hour when you are preparing to
see company. But their sleep, in the first place, will
not be so sweet and undisturbed amidst the rattle of
carriages, and the glare of tapers glancing through the
rooms, as that of the village child in his quiet cottage,
protected by silence and darkness; and moreover,
you may depend upon it, that, as the coercive power
of education is laid aside, they will in a few months
slide into the habitudes of the rest of the family,
whose hours are determined by their company and
situation in life. You have, however, done good, as
far as it goes; it is something gained, to defer pernicious habits, if we cannot prevent them.

There is nothing which has so little share in education as direct precept. To be convinced of this, we
need only reflect that there is no one point we labor
more to establish with children, than that of their
speaking truth; and there is not any in which we
succeed worse. And why? Because children readily
see we have an interest in it. Their speaking truth is
used by us as an engine of government — "Tell me,
my dear child, when you have broken anything, and I
will not be angry with you." "Thank you for nothing,"
says the child; "if I prevent you from finding it out,
I am sure you will not be angry:" and nine times
out of ten he can prevent it. He knows that, in the
common intercourses of life, you tell a thousand false-
hoods. But these are necessary lies, on important
occasions.

Your child is the best judge how much occasion he
has to tell a lie: he may have as great occasion for it,
as you have to conceal a bad piece of news from a
sick friend, or to hide your vexation from an unwelcome visitor. That authority which extends its claims
over every action, and even every thought, which in-

sists upon an answer to every interrogation, however indiscreet or oppressive to the feelings, will, in young or old, produce falsehood ; or, if in some few instances the deeply imbibed fear of future and unknown punishment should restrain from direct falsehood, it will produce a habit of dissimulation, which is still worse. The child, the slave, or the subject, who, on proper occasions, may not say, " I do not choose to tell," will certainly, by the circumstances in which you place him, be driven to have recourse to deceit, even should he not be countenanced by your example.

I do not mean to assert that sentiments inculcated in education have no influence ; — they have much, though not the most : but it is the sentiments we let drop occasionally, the conversation they overhear when playing unnoticed in a corner of the room, which has an effect upon children ; and not what is addressed directly to them in the tone of exhortation. If you would know precisely the effect these set discourses have upon your child, be pleased to reflect upon that which a discourse from the pulpit, which you have reason to think merely professional, has upon you. Children have almost an intuitive discernment between the maxims you bring forward for their use, and those by which you direct your own conduct. Be as cunning as you will, they are always more cunning than you. Every child knows whom his father and mother love and see with pleasure, and whom they dislike ; for whom they think themselves obliged to set out their best plate and china ; whom they think it an honor to visit, and upon whom they confer honor by admitting them to their company. " Respect nothing so much as virtue," says Eugenio to his son ; " virtue and talents are the only grounds of distinction." The child presently has occasion to inquire why his father pulls off his hat to some people and not to others ; he is told, that outward respect must be proportioned to

different stations in life. This is a little difficult of
comprehension : however, by dint of explanation, he
gets over it tolerably well. But he sees his father's
house in the bustle and hurry of preparation; common business laid aside, everybody in movement, an
unusual anxiety to please and to shine. Nobody is at
leisure to receive his caresses or attend to his questions ; his lessons are interrupted, his hours deranged.
At length a guest arrives : it is my Lord ——, whom
he has heard you speak of twenty times as one of the
most worthless characters upon earth. Your child,
Eugenio, has received a lesson of education. Resume,
if you will, your systems of morality on the morrow,
you will in vain attempt to eradicate it. " You expect
company, mamma, must I be dressed to-day?" "No,
it is only good Mrs. Such-a-one." Your child has
received a lesson of education, one which he well understands, and will long remember. You have sent
your child to a public school; but to secure his
morals against the vice which you too justly apprehend
abounds there, you have given him a private tutor, a
man of strict morals and religion. He may help him
to prepare his tasks ; but do you imagine it will be in
his power to form his mind? His school-fellows, the
allowance you give him, the manners of the age and of
the place, will do that ; and not the lectures which he
is obliged to hear. If these are different from what
you yourself experienced, you must not be surprised to
see him gradually recede from the principles, civil and
religious, which you hold, and break off from your connections, and adopt manners different from your own.
This is remarkably exemplified amongst those of the
Dissenters who have risen to wealth and consequence.
I believe it would be difficult to find an instance of
families, who for three generations have kept their carriage and continued Dissenters.

Education, it is often observed, is an expensive

thing. It is so; but the paying for lessons is the smallest part of the cost. If you would go to the price of having your son a worthy man, you must be so yourself; your friends, your servants, your company must be all of that stamp. Suppose this to be the case, much is done: but there will remain circumstances, which perhaps you cannot alter, that will still have their effect. Do you wish him to love simplicity? Would you be content to lay down your coach, to drop your title? Where is the parent who would do this to educate his son? You carry him to the workshops of artisans, and show him different machines and fabrics, to awaken his ingenuity. The necessity of getting his bread would awaken it much more effectually. The single circumstance of having a fortune to get, or a fortune to spend, will probably operate more strongly upon his mind, not only than your precepts, but even than your example. You wish your child to be modest and unassuming; you are so, perhaps, yourself, — and you pay liberally a preceptor for giving him lessons of humility. You do not perceive, that the very circumstance of having a man of letters and accomplishments retained about his person, for his sole advantage, tends more forcibly to inspire him with an idea of self-consequence, than all the lessons he can give him to repress it. "Why do not you look sad, you rascal?" says the undertaker to his man, in the play of The Funeral; "I give you I know not how much money for looking sad, and the more I give you, the gladder I think you are." So will it be with the wealthy heir. The lectures that are given him on condescension and affability, only prove to him upon how much higher ground he stands than those about him; and the very pains that are taken with his moral character will make him proud, by showing him how much he is the object of attention. You cannot help these things. Your servants, out of respect to you, will bear with his petulance ; your company, out of respect to you, will forbear to check his impatience ; and you yourself, if he is clever, will repeat his observations.

In the exploded doctrine of sympathies, you are directed, if you have cut your finger, to let that alone, and put your plaster upon the knife. This is very bad doctrine, I must confess, in philosophy ; but very good in morals. Is a man luxurious, self-indulgent? do not apply your *physic of the soul* to him, but cure his fortune. Is he haughty? cure his rank, his title. Is he vulgar? cure his company. Is he diffident or mean-spirited? cure his poverty, give him consequence. But these prescriptions go far beyond the family recipes of education.

What then is the result? In the first place, that we should contract our ideas of education, and expect no more from it than it is able to perform. It can give instruction. There will always be an essential difference between a human being cultivated and uncultivated. Education can provide proper instructors in the various arts and sciences, and portion out to the best advantage those precious hours of youth which never will return. It can likewise give, in a great degree, personal habits ; and even if these should afterwards give way under the influence of contrary circumstances, your child will feel the good effects of them ; for the later and the less will he go into what is wrong. Let us also be assured, that the business of education, properly so called, is not transferable. You may engage masters to instruct your child in this or the other accomplishment, but you must educate him yourself. You not only ought to do it, but you must do it, whether you intend it or no. As education is a thing necessary for all, — for the poor and for the rich, for the illiterate as well as for the learned, — Providence has not made it dependent upon systems uncertain, operose, and difficult of investigation. It is not necessary, with

Rousseau or Madame de Genlis, to devote to the education of one child the talents and the time of a number of grown men; to surround him with an artificial
world; and to counteract, by maxims, the natural tendencies of the situation he is placed in, in society.
Every one has time to educate his child: the poor man
educates him while working in his cottage — the man
of business while employed in his counting-house.

Do we see a father who is diligent in his profession,
domestic in his habits, whose house is the resort of
well-informed, intelligent people — a mother whose
time is usefully filled, whose attention to her duties se-
cures esteem, and whose amiable manners attract affection? Do not be solicitous, respectable couple,
about the moral education of your offspring! do not be
uneasy because you cannot surround them with the
apparatus of books and systems; or fancy you must
retire from the world to devote yourselves to their improvement. In your world they are brought up much
better than they could be under any plan of factitious
education which you could provide for them : they will
imbibe affection from your caresses; taste from your
conversation; urbanity from the commerce of your society; and mutual love from your example. Do not
regret that you are not rich enough to provide tutors
and governors, to watch his steps with sedulous and
servile anxiety, and furnish him with maxims it is morally impossible he should act upon when grown up.
Do not you see how seldom this over-culture produces
its effect, and how many shining and excellent characters start up every day, from the bosom of obscurity,
with scarcely any care at all?

Are children then to be neglected? Surely not : but
having given them the instruction and accomplishments
which their situation in life requires, let us reject super-
fluous solicitude, and trust that their characters will form
themselves from the spontaneous influence of good ex-

amples, and circumstances which impel them to useful
action.

But the education of your house, important as it is,
is only a part of a more comprehensive system. Providence takes your child where you leave him. Providence continues his education upon a larger scale, and
by a process which includes means far more efficacious.
Has your son entered the world at eighteen, opinion-
ated, haughty, rash, inclined to dissipation? Do not
despair; he may yet be cured of these faults, if it
pleases Heaven. There are remedies which you could
not persuade yourself to use, if they were in your power,
and which are specific in cases of this kind. How often
do we see the presumptuous, giddy youth, changed
into the wise counsellor, the considerate, steady friend !
How often the thoughtless, gay girl, into the sober wife,
the affectionate mother ! Faded beauty, humbled self-
consequence, disappointed ambition, loss of fortune, —
this is the rough physic provided by Providence to
meliorate the temper, to correct the offensive petulan-
cies of youth, and bring out all the energies of the
finished character. Afflictions soften the proud; difficulties push forward the ingenious; successful industry
gives consequence and credit, and develops a thousand latent good qualities. There is no malady of the
mind so inveterate, which this education of events is
not calculated to cure, if life were long enough; and
shall we not hope, that He, in whose hand are all the
remedial processes of nature, will renew the discipline
in another state, and finish the imperfect man?

States are educated as individuals — by circumstances: the prophet may cry aloud, and spare not;
the philosopher may descant on morals; eloquence
may exhaust itself in invective against the vices of the
age : these vices will certainly follow certain states of
poverty or riches, ignorance or high civilization. But
what these gentle alteratives fail of doing, may be ac-

complished by an unsuccessful war, a loss of trade, or any of those great calamities by which it pleases Providence to speak to a nation in such language as *will* be heard. If, as a nation, we would be cured of pride, it must be by mortification; if of luxury, by a national bankruptcy, perhaps; if of injustice, or the spirit of domination, by a loss of national consequence. In comparison with these strong remedies, a fast, or a sermon, are prescriptions of very little efficacy.

ON PREJUDICE.

IT is to speculative people, fond of novel doctrines, and who, by accustoming themselves to make the most fundamental truths the subject of discussion, have divested their minds of that reverence which is generally felt for opinions and practices of long standing, that the world is ever to look for its improvement or reformation. But it is also these speculatists who introduce into it absurdities and errors, more gross than any which have been established by that common consent of numerous individuals which opinions long acted upon must have required for their basis. For systems of the latter class must at least possess one property, — that of being practicable : and there is likewise a presumption that they are, or at least originally were, useful; whereas the opinions of the speculatist may turn out to be utterly incongruous and eccentric. The speculatist may invent machines which it is impossible to put in action, or which, when put in action, may possess the tremendous power of tearing up society by the roots. Like the chemist, he is not sure in the moment of projection whether he shall blow up his own

dwelling and that of his neighbor, or whether he shall
be rewarded with a discovery which will secure the
health and prolong the existence of future generations.
It becomes us, therefore, to examine with peculiar care
those maxims which, under the appearance of following a closer train of reasoning, militate against the usual
practices or genuine feelings of mankind. No subject
has been more canvassed than education. With regard
to that important object there is a maxim avowed by
many sensible people, which seems to me to deserve
particular investigation. " Give your child," it is said,
" no *prejudices :* let reason be the only foundation of
his opinions ; where he cannot reason, let him suspend
his belief. Let your great care be, that as he grows up
he has nothing to unlearn ; and never make use of authority in matters of opinion, for authority is no test of
truth." The maxim sounds well, and flatters perhaps
the secret pride of man, in supposing him more the
creature of reason than he really is : but, I suspect, on
examination we shall find it exceedingly fallacious. We
must first consider what a *prejudice* is. A prejudice is
a sentiment in favor or disfavor of any person, practice,
or opinion, previous to and independent of examining
their merits by reason and investigation. Prejudice is
prejudging ; that is, judging previously to evidence. It
is therefore sufficiently apparent, that no *philosophical
belief* can be founded on mere prejudice ; because it is
the business of philosophy to go deep into the nature
and properties of things : nor can it be allowable for
those to indulge prejudice who aspire to lead the public opinion ; those to whom the high office is appointed
of sifting truth from error, of canvassing the claims of
different systems, of exploding old and introducing new
tenets. These must investigate, with a kind of auda-
cious boldness, every subject that comes before them ;
these, neither impressed with awe for all that mankind
have been taught to reverence, nor swayed by affection

for whatever the sympathies of our nature incline us to love, must hold the balance with a severe and steady hand, while they are weighing the doubtful scale of probabilities; and with a stoical apathy of mind, yield their assent to nothing but a preponderancy of evidence. But is this an office for a child? Is it an office for more than one or two men in a century? And is it desirable that a child should grow up without opinions to regulate his conduct, till he is able to form them fairly by the exercise of his own abilities Such an exercise requires at least the sober period of matured reason : reason not only sharpened by argumentative discussion, but informed by experience. The most sprightly child can only possess the former : for let it be remembered, that though the reasoning powers put forth pretty early in life, the faculty of using them to effect does not come till much later. The first efforts of a child in reasoning resemble those quick and desultory motions by which he gains the play of his limbs ; they show agility and grace, they are pleasing to look at, and necessary for the gradual acquirement of his bodily powers ; but his joints must be knit into more firmness, and his movements regulated with more precision, before he is capable of useful labor and manly exertion. A reasoning child is not yet a reasonable being. There is great propriety in the legal phraseology which expresses maturity, not by having arrived at the possession of reason, but of that power, the late result of information, thought, and experience — discretion, which alone teaches, with regard to reason, its powers, its limits, and its use. This the child of the most sprightly parts cannot have ; and therefore his attempts at reasoning, whatever acuteness they may show, and how much soever they may please a parent with the early promise of future excellence, are of no account whatever in the sober search after truth. Besides, taking it for granted (which however is utterly

impossible) that a youth could be brought up to the
age of fifteen or sixteen without prejudice in favor of
any opinions whatever, and that he is then set to examining for himself some important proposition, —
how is he to set about it? Who is to recommend books
to him? Who is to give him the previous information
necessary to comprehend the question? Who is to tell
him whether or no it is important? Whoever does
these, will infallibly lay a bias upon his mind, according
to the ideas he himself has received upon the subject.
Let us suppose the point in debate was the preference
between the Roman Catholic and Protestant modes of
religion. Can a youth in a Protestant country, born of
Protestant parents, with access, probably, to hardly a
single controversial book on the Roman Catholic side
of the question — can such a one study the subject
without prejudice? His knowledge of history, if he
has such knowledge, must, according to the books he
has read, have already given him a prejudice on the
one side or the other; so must the occasional conversation he has been witness to, the appellations he has
heard used, the tone of voice with which he has heard
the words monk or priest pronounced, and a thousand
other evanescent circumstances. It is likewise to be
observed, that every question of any weight and importance has numerous dependencies and points of
connection with other subjects, which make it impossible to enter upon the consideration of it without a great
variety of previous knowledge. There is no object of
investigation perfectly insulated ; — we must not conceive therefore, of a man's sitting down to it with a
mind perfectly new and untutored : he must have
passed more or less through a course of studies ; and,
according to the color of those studies, his mind will
have received a tincture, — that is, a prejudice. But
it is, in truth, the most absurd of all suppositions, that
a human being can be educated, or even nourished

and brought up, without imbibing numberless prejudices from every thing which passes around him.
A child cannot learn the signification of words without
receiving ideas along with them ; he cannot be impressed with affection to his parents and those about
him, without conceiving a predilection for their tastes,
opinions, and practices. He forms numberless associations of pain or pleasure, and every association
begets a prejudice ; he sees objects from a particular
spot, and his views of things are contracted or extended according to his position in society. As no two
individuals can have the same horizon, so neither can
any two have the same associations ; and different
associations will produce different opinions, as necessarily as, by the laws of perspective, different distances
will produce different appearances of visible objects.
Let us confess a truth, humiliating perhaps to human
pride ; — a very small part only of the opinions of the
coolest philosopher are the result of fair reasoning ;
the rest are formed by his education, his temperament,
by the age in which he lives, by trains of thought directed to a particular track through some accidental
association — in short, by *prejudice.* But why, after
all, should we wish to bring up children without prejudices ? A child has occasion to act, long before he
can reason. Shall we leave him destitute of all the
principles that should regulate his conduct, till he can
discover them by the strength of his own genius ? If it
were possible that one whole generation could be
brought up without prejudices, the world must return
to the infancy of knowledge, and all the beautiful
fabric which has been built up by successive generations, must be begun again from the very foundation.
Your child has a claim to the advantage of your experience, which it would be cruel and unjust to deprive
him of. Will any father say to his son, " My dear child,
you are entering upon a world full of intricate and per-

plexed paths, in which many miss their way, to their final misery and ruin. Amidst many false systems, and much vain science, there is also some true knowledge ; there is a right path : I believe I know it, for I have the advantage of years and experience, but I will instil no prejudices into your mind ; I shall therefore leave you to find it out as you can ; whether your abilities are great or small, you must take the chance of them. There are various systems in morals ; I have examined and found some of a good others of a bad tendency. There is such a thing as religion ; many people think it the most important concern of life : perhaps I am one of them : perhaps I have chosen from amidst the various systems of belief, — many of which are extremely absurd, and some even pernicious, — that which I cherish as the guide of my life, my comfort in all my sorrows, and the foundation of my dearest hopes : but far be it from me to influence you in any manner to receive it ; when you are grown up, you must read all the books upon these subjects which you can lay your hands on, for neither in the choice of these would I presume to prejudice your mind : converse with all who pretend to any opinions upon the subject ; and whatever happens to be the result, you must abide by it. In the mean time, concerning these important objects you must keep your mind in a perfect equilibrium. It is true you want these principles more now than you can do at any other period of your life ; but I had rather you never had them at all than that you should not come fairly by them." Should we commend the wisdom or the kindness of such a parent? The parent will perhaps plead in his behalf that it is by no means his intention to leave the mind of his child in the uncultivated state I have supposed. As soon as his understanding begins to open, he means to discuss with him those propositions on which he wishes him to form an opinion. He will make him read the best books on the subject, and by free conversation and explaining the arguments on both sides, he does not doubt but the youth will soon be enabled to judge satisfactorily for himself. I have no objection to make against this mode of proceeding : as a mode of *instruction*, it is certainly a very good one : but he must know little of human nature, who thinks that after this process the youth will be really in a capacity of judging for himself, or that he is less under the dominion of prejudice than if he had received the same truths from the mere authority of his parent ; for most assuredly the arguments on either side will not have · been set before him with equal strength or with equal warmth. The persuasive tone, the glowing language, the triumphant retort, will all be reserved for the side on which the parent has formed his own conclusions. It cannot be otherwise ; he cannot be convinced himself of what he thinks a truth, without wishing to convey that conviction, nor without thinking all that can be urged on the other side weak and futile. He cannot in a matter of importance neutralize his feelings : perfect impartiality can be the result only of indifference. He does not perhaps seem to dictate, but he wishes gently to guide his pupil ; and that wish is seldom disappointed. The child adopts the opinion of his parent, and seems to himself to have adopted it from the decisions of his own judgment ; but all these reasonings must be gone over again, and these opinions undergo a fiery ordeal, if ever he comes really to think and determine for himself.

The fact is, that no man, whatever his system may be, refrains from instilling prejudices into his child in any matter he has much at heart. Take a disciple of Rousseau, who contends that it would be very pernicious to give his son any ideas of a Deity till he is of an age to read Clarke or Leibnitz, and ask him if he waits so long to impress on his mind the sentiments of patriotism — the civic affection. Oh no ! you will find his little heart is early taught to beat at the very name of liberty, and that, long before he is capable of forming a single political idea, he has entered with warmth into all the party sentiments and connections of his parent. He learns to love and hate, to venerate or despise, by rote ; and he soon acquires decided opinions, of the real ground of which he can know absolutely nothing. Are not ideas of female honor and decorum impressed first as prejudices ; and would any parent wish they should be so much as canvassed till the most settled habits of propriety have rendered it safe to do it? In teaching first by prejudice that which is afterwards to be proved, we do but follow Nature. Instincts are prejudices she gives us : we follow them implicitly, and they lead us right ; but it is not till long afterwards that reason comes and justifies them. Why should we scruple to lead a child to right opinions in the same way by which Nature leads him to right practices !

Still it will be urged that man is a rational being, and therefore reason is the only true ground of belief, and authority is not reason. This point requires a little discussion. That he who receives a truth upon authority has not a reasonable belief, is in one sense true, since he has not drawn it from the result of his own inquiries ; but in another it is certainly false, since the authority itself may be to him the best of all reasons for believing it. There are few men who, from the exercise of the best powers of their minds, could derive so good a reason for believing a mathematical truth as the authority of Sir Isaac Newton. There are two principles deeply implanted in the mind of man, without which he could never attain knowledge, — curiosity, and credulity ; the former to lead him to make discoveries himself, the latter to dispose him to receive knowledge from others. The credulity of a child to those who cherish him, is in early life unbounded. This is one of the most useful instincts he has, and is in fact a precious advantage put into the hands of the parent for storing his mind with ideas of all kinds. Without this principle of assent he could never gain even the rudiments of knowledge. He receives it, it is true, in the shape of prejudice ; but the prejudice itself is founded upon sound reasoning, and conclusive though imperfect experiment. He finds himself weak, helpless, and ignorant ; he sees in his parent a being of knowledge and powers more than his utmost capacity can fathom ; almost a god to him. He has often done him good, therefore he believes he loves him ; he finds him capable of giving him information upon all the subjects he has applied to him about ; his knowledge seems unbounded, and his information has led him right whenever he has had occasion to try it by actual experiment : the child does not draw out his little reasonings into a logical form, but this is to him a ground of belief that his parent knows every thing, and is infallible. Though the proposition is not exactly true, it is sufficiently so for him to act upon : and when he believes in his parent with implicit faith, he believes upon grounds as truly rational as when, in after life, he follows the deductions of his own reason.

But you will say, I wish my son may have nothing to unlearn, and therefore I would have him wait to form an opinion till he is able to do it on solid grounds. And why do you suppose he will have less to unlearn if he follows his own reason, than if he followed yours? If he thinks, if he inquires, he will no doubt have a great deal to unlearn, whichever course you take with him ; but it is better to have some things to unlearn, than to have nothing learnt. Do you hold your own opinions so loosely, so hesitatingly, as not to think them safer to abide by than the first results of his stammering reason? Are there no truths to learn so indubitable as

to be without fear of their not approving themselves
to his mature and well-directed judgment? Are there
none you esteem so useful as to feel anxious that he
be put in possession of them? We are solicitous not
only to put our children in a capacity of acquiring
their daily bread, but to bequeath to them riches which
they may receive as an inheritance. Have you no
mental wealth you wish to transmit, no stock of ideas
he may begin with, instead of drawing them all from
the labor of his own brain? If, moreover, your son
should not adopt your prejudices, he will certainly adopt
those of other people ; or, if on subjects of high
interest he *could* be kept totally indifferent, the consequence would be, that he would conceive either that
such matters were not worth the trouble of inquiry, or
that nothing satisfactory was to be learnt about them :
for there are negative prejudices as well as positive.

Let parents, therefore, not scruple to use the power
God and Nature have put into their hands for the
advantage of their offspring. Let them not fear to
impress them with prejudices for whatever is fair and
honorable in action — whatever is useful and important
in systematic truth. Let such prejudices be wrought
into the very texture of the soul. Such truths let them
appear to know by intuition. Let the child never
remember the period when he did not know them.
Instead of sending him to that cold and hesitating
belief which is founded on the painful and uncertain
consequences of late investigation, let his conviction
of all the truths you deem important be mixed up with
every warm affection of his nature, and identified with
his most cherished recollections ; the time will come
soon enough when his confidence in you will have
received a check. The growth of his own reason and
the development of his powers will lead him with a
sudden impetus to examine every thing, to canvass
every thing, to suspect every thing. If he finds, as he

certainly will find, the results of his reasoning different in some respects from those you have given him, far from being now disposed to receive your assertions as proofs, he will rather feel disinclined to any opinion you profess, and struggle to free himself from the net you have woven about him.

The calm repose of his mind is broken, the placid lake is become turbid, and reflects distorted and broken images of things; but be not you alarmed at the new workings of his thoughts, — it is the angel of reason which descends and troubles the waters. To endeavor to influence by authority, would be as useless now as it was salutary before. Lie by in silence, and wait the result. Do not expect the mind of your son is to resemble yours, as your figure is reflected by the image in the glass; he was formed, like you, to use his own judgment, and he claims the high privilege of his nature. His reason is mature, his mind must now form itself. Happy must you esteem yourself, if amidst all lesser differences of opinion, and the wreck of many of your favorite ideas, he still preserves those radical and primary truths which are essential to his happiness, and which different trains of thought and opposite modes of investigation will very often equally lead to.

Let it be well remembered that we have only been recommending those prejudices which go before reason, not those which are contrary to it. To endeavor to make children, or others over whom we have influence, receive systems which we do not believe, merely because it is convenient to ourselves that they should believe them, though a very fashionable practice, makes no part of the discipline we plead for. These are not prejudices, but impositions. We may also grant that nothing should be received as a prejudice which can be easily made the subject of experiment. A child may be allowed to find out for himself that boiling water will scald his fingers, and mustard bite his tongue ; but he must be *prejudiced* against ratsbane, because the experiment would be too costly. In like manner it may do him good to have experienced that little instances of inattention or perverseness draw upon him the displeasure of his parent ; but that profligacy is attended with loss of character, is a truth one would rather wish him to take upon trust.

There is no occasion to inculcate by prejudices those truths which it is of no importance for us to know, till our powers are able to investigate them. Thus the metaphysical questions of space and time, necessity and free-will, and a thousand others, may safely be left for that age which delights in such discussions. They have no connection with conduct ; and none have any business with them at all, but those who are able by such studies to exercise and sharpen their mental powers ; but it is not so with those truths on which our wellbeing depends ; these must be taught to all, not only before they can reason upon them, but independently of the consideration whether they will ever be able to reason upon them as long as they live. What has hitherto been said, relates only to instilling prejudices into *others;* how far a man is to allow them in himself, or, as a celebrated writer expresses it, to *cherish* them, is a different question, on which perhaps I may some time offer my thoughts. In the mean time I cannot help concluding, that to reject the influence of prejudice in education is itself one of the most unreasonable of prejudices.

THE BABY-HOUSE.

DEAR Agatha, I give you joy,
And much admire your pretty toy, —
A mansion in itself complete,
And fitted to give guests a treat;
With couch and table, chest and chair,
The bed or supper to prepare.
We almost wish to change ourselves
To fairy forms of tripping elves,
To press the velvet couch, and eat
From tiny cups the sugared meat.
I much suspect that many a sprite
Inhabits it at dead of night;
That, as they dance, the listening ear
The pat of fairy feet might hear;
That, just as you have said your prayers,
They hurry-scurry down the stairs:
And you 'll do well to try to find
Tester or ring they 've left behind.

But think not, Agatha, you own
That toy, a Baby-house, alone;
For many a sumptuous one is found
To press an ampler space of ground.
The broad-based Pyramid that stands
Casting its shade in distant lands,
Which asked some mighty nation's toil
With mountain-weight to press the soil,
And there has raised its head sublime
Through eras of uncounted time. —
Its use if asked, 't is only said,
A Baby-house to lodge the dead.

Nor less beneath more genial skies
The domes of pomp and folly rise,
Whose sun through diamond windows streams,
While gems and gold reflect his beams ;
Where tapestry clothes the storied wall,
And fountains spout and waters fall.
The peasant faints beneath his load,
Nor tastes the grain his hands have sowed,
While scarce a nation's wealth avails
To raise thy Baby-house, Versailles.
And Baby-houses oft appear
On British ground, of prince or peer ;
Awhile their stately heads they raise,
The admiring traveller stops to gaze ;
He looks again — where are they now ?
Gone to the hammer or the plough :
Then trees, the pride of ages, fall,
And naked stands the pictured wall ;
And treasured coins from distant lands
Must feel the touch of sordid hands ;
And gems, of classic stores the boast,
Fall to the cry of — Who bids most ?
Then do not, Agatha, repine
That cheaper Baby-house is thine.

DIALOGUE IN THE SHADES.

Clio. — THERE is no help for it, — they must go.
The river Lethe is here at hand ; I shall tear them off
and throw them into the stream.

Mercury. — Illustrious daughter of Mnemosyne,
Clio ! the most respected of the Muses, — you seem
disturbed. What is it that brings us the honor of a
visit from you in these infernal regions ?

Clio. — You are a god of expedients, Mercury; I want to consult you. I am oppressed with the continually increasing demands upon me : I have had more business for these last twenty years than I have often had for two centuries; and if I had, as old Homer says, " a throat of brass and adamantine lungs " I could never get through it. And what did he want this throat of brass for? for a paltry list of ships, canoes rather, which would be laughed at in the Admiralty Office of London. But I must inform you, Mercury, that my roll is so full, and I have so many applications which cannot in decency be refused, that I see no other way than striking off some hundreds of names in order to make room; and I am come to inform the shades of my determination.

Mercury. — I believe, Clio, you will do right : and as one end of your roll is a little mouldy, no doubt you will begin with that; but the ghosts will raise a great clamor.

Clio. — I expect no less; but necessity has no law. All the parchment in Pergamus is used up, — my roll is long enough to reach from earth to heaven; it is grown quite cumbrous; it takes a life, as mortals reckon lives, to unroll it.

· *Mercury.* — Yet consider, Clio, how many of these have passed a restless life, and encountered all manner of dangers, and bled and died only to be placed upon your list, — and now to be struck off!

Clio. — And committed all manner of crimes, you might have added; — but go they must. Besides, they have been sufficiently recompensed. Have they not been praised, and sung, and admired for some thousands of years? Let them give place to others : What! Have they no conscience? no modesty? Would Xerxes, think you, have reason to complain, when his parading expeditions have already procured him above two thousand years of fame, though a Solyman or a Zingis Khan should fill up his place?

Mercury. — Surely you are not going to blot out Xerxes from your list of names?

Clio. — I do not say that I am : but that I keep him is more for the sake of his antagonists than his own. And yet their places might be well supplied by the Swiss heroes of Morgarten, or the brave though unsuccessful patriot, Aloys Reding. — But pray what noise is that at the gate?

Mercury. — A number of the shades who have received an intimation of your purpose, and are come to remonstrate against it.

Clio. — In the name of all the gods whom have we here? — Hercules, Theseus, Jason, Œdipus, Bacchus, Cadmus, with a bag of dragon's teeth, and a whole tribe of strange shadowy figures ! I shall expect to see the Centaurs and Lapithæ, or Perseus on his flying courser. Away with them ; they belong to my sisters, not to me ; Melpomene will receive them gladly.

Mercury. — You forget, Clio, that Bacchus conquered India.

Clio. — And had horns like Moses, as Vossius is pleased to say. No, Mercury, I will have nothing to do with these ; if ever I received them, it was when I was young and credulous. — As I have said, let my sisters take them ; or let them be celebrated in tales for children.

Mercury. — That will not do, Clio ; children in this age read none but wise books : stories of giants and dragons are all written for grown-up children now.

Clio. — Be that as it may, I shall clear my hands of them, and of a great many more, I do assure you.

Mercury. — I hope " the tale of Troy divine — ! "

Clio. — Divine let it be, but my share in it is very small ; I recollect furnishing the catalogue. — Mercury, I will tell you the truth. When I was young, my mother (as arrant a gossip as ever breathed) related to me a great number of stories : and as in those days people could not read or write, I had no better authority for what I recorded : but after letters were found out, and now since the noble invention of printing, — why, do you think, Mercury, any one would dare to tell lies in print ?

Mercury. — Sometimes, perhaps. I have seen a • splendid victory in the gazette of one country dwindle into an honorable retreat in that of another.

Clio. — In newspapers, very possibly : but with regard to myself, when I have time to consider and lay things together, I assure you, you may depend upon me. — Whom have we in that group which I see indistinctly in a sort of twilight ?

Mercury. — Very renowned personages ; Ninus, Sesostris, Semiramis, Cheops who built the largest pyramid.

Clio. — If Cheops built the largest pyramid, people -are welcome to inquire about him at the spot, — room must be made. As to Semiramis, tell her her place shall be filled up by an empress and a conqueror from the shores of the wintry Baltic.

Mercury. — The renowned Cyrus is approaching with a look of confidence, for he is introduced by a favorite of yours, the elegant Xenophon.

Clio. — Is that Cyrus ? Pray desire him to take off that dress which Xenophon has given him ; truly I took him for a Greek philosopher. I fancy queen Tomyris would scarcely recognize him.

Mercury. — Aspasia hopes, for the honor of her sex, that she shall continue to occupy a place among those you celebrate.

Clio. — Tell the mistress of Pericles we can spare her without inconvenience : many ladies are to be found in modern times who possess her eloquence and her talents, with the modesty of a vestal ; and should a more perfect likeness be required, modern times may furnish that also.

Mercury. — Here are two figures who approach you with a very dignified air.

Solon and Lycurgus. — We present ourselves, divine Clio, with confidence. We have no fear that you should strike from your roll the lawgivers of Athens and Sparta.

Clio. — Most assuredly not. Yet I must inform you that a name higher than either of yours, and a constitution more perfect, is to be found in a vast continent, of the very existence of which you had not the least suspicion.

Mercury. — I see approaching a person of a noble and spirited air, if he did not hold his head a little on one side as if his neck were awry.

Alexander. — Clio, I need not introduce myself: I am, as you well know, the son of Jupiter Ammon, and my arms have reached even to the remote shore of the Indus.

Clio. — Pray burn your genealogy; and for the rest, suffer me to inform you that the river Indus and the whole peninsula which you scarcely discovered, with sixty millions of inhabitants, is at this moment subject to the dominion of a few merchants in a remote island of the Northern Ocean, the very name of which never reached your ears.

Mercury. — Here is Empedocles, who threw himself into Ætna merely to be placed upon your roll; and Calanus, who mounted his funeral pile before Alexander, from the same motive.

Clio. — They have been remembered long enough in all reason : their places may be supplied by the two next madmen who shall throw themselves under the wheels of the chariot of Jaggernaut, — fanatics are the growth of every age.

Mercury. — Here is a ghost preparing to address

you with a very self-sufficient air: his robe is embroided with flower-de-luces.

Louis XIV. — I am persuaded, Clio, you will recognize *the immortal man.* I have always been a friend and patron of the Muses; my actions are well known; all Europe has resounded with my name, — the terror of other countries, the glory of my own: I am well assured you are not going to strike me off.

Clio. — To strike you off? certainly not; but to place you many degrees lower in the list; to reduce you from a sun, your favorite emblem, to a star in the galaxy. My sisters have certainly been partial to you: you bought their favor with — how many livres a year? not much more than a London bookseller will give for a quarto poem. But me you cannot bribe.

Louis. — But, Clio, you have yourself recorded my exploits; — the passage of the Rhine, Namur, Flanders, Franche Comté.

Clio. — O Louis, if you could but guess the extent of the present French empire; — but no, it could never enter into your imagination.

Louis. — I rejoice at what you say; I rejoice that my posterity have followed my steps, and improved upon my glory.

Clio. — Your posterity have had nothing to do with it.

Louis. — Remember too the urbanity of my character, how hospitably I received the unfortunate James of England, — England, the natural enemy of France.

Clio. — Your hospitality has been well returned. Your descendants, driven from their thrones, are at this moment supported by the bounty of the nation and king of England.

Louis. — O Clio, what is it that you tell me ! let me hide my diminished head in the deepest umbrage of the grove; let me seek out my dear Maintenon, and tell my beads with her till I forget that I have been either praised or feared.

Clio. — Comfort yourself, however; your name, like the red letter which marks the holiday, though insignificant in itself, shall still enjoy the honor of designating the age of taste and literature.

Mercury. — Here is a whole crowd coming, Clio; I can scarcely keep them off with my wand : they have all got notice of your intentions, and the infernal regions are quite in an uproar, — what is to be done?

Clio. — I cannot tell; the numbers distract me : to examine their pretensions one by one is impossible ; I must strike off half of them at a venture : the rest must make room, — they must crowd, they must fall into the background ; and where I used to write a name all in capitals with letters of gold illuminated, I must put it in *small pica.* I do assure you, Mercury, I cannot stand the fatigue I undergo, much longer. I am not provided, as you very well know, with either chariot or wings, and I am expected to be in all parts of the globe at once. In the good old times, my business lay almost entirely between the Hellespont and the Pillars of Hercules, with sometimes an excursion to the mouths (then seven) of the Nile, or the banks of the Euphrates. But now I am required to be in a hundred places at once ; I am called from Jena to Austerlitz, from Cape Trafalgar to Aboukir, and from the Thames to the Ganges and Burampooter ; besides a whole continent, a world by itself, fresh and vigorous, which I foresee will find me abundance of employment.

Mercury. — Truly I believe so ; I am afraid the old leaven is working in the new world.

Clio. — I am puzzled at this moment how to give the account, which always is expected of me, of the august sovereigns of Europe.

Mercury. — How so?

Clio. — I do not know where to find them ; they are most of them upon their *travels.*

Mercury. — You must have been very much employed in the French revolution.

Clio. — Continually; the actors in the scene succeeded one another with such rapidity, that the hero of to-day was forgotten on the morrow. Necker, Mirabeau, Dumourier, Lafayette, appeared successively, like the pictures in a magic lantern — shown for a moment and then withdrawn : and now the space is filled by one tremendous gigantic figure, that throws his broad shadow over half the globe.

Mercury. — The ambition of Napoleon has indeed procured you much employment.

Clio. — Employment! There is not a goddess so harassed as I am ; my sisters lead quite idle lives in comparison. Melpomene has in a manner slept through the last half-century, except when now and then she dictated to a certain favorite nymph. Urania, indeed, has employed herself with Herschel in counting the stars ; but her task is less than mine. Here am I expected to calculate how many hundred thousands of rational beings cut one another's throats at Austerlitz, and to take the tale of two hundred and thirteen thousand human bodies and ninety-five thousand horses, that lie stiff, frozen and unburied on the banks of the Berecina ; — and do you think, Mercury, this can be a pleasant employment?

Mercury. — I have had a great increase of employment myself lately, on account of the multitude of shades I have been obliged to convey ; and poor old Charon is almost laid up with the rheumatism : we used to have a holiday comparatively during the winter months ; but of late, winter and summer I have observed are much alike to heroes.

Clio. — I wish to Jupiter I could resign my office ! Son of Maia, I declare to you I am sick of the horrors I record ; I am sick of mankind. For above these three thousand years have I been warning them and reading lessons to them, and they will not mend : Robespierre was as cruel as Sylla, and Napoleon has no more moderation than Pyrrhus. The human frame, of curious texture, delicately formed, feeling, and irritable by the least annoyance, with face erect and animated with Promethean fire, they wound, they lacerate, they mutilate with most perverted ingenuity. I will go and record the actions of the tigers of Africa ; in them such fierceness is natural. Nay, the human race will be exterminated, if this work of destruction goes on much longer.

Mercury. — With regard to that matter, Clio, I can set your heart at rest. A great philosopher has lately discovered that the world is in imminent danger of be - ing over-peopled ; and that if twenty or forty thousand men could not be persuaded every now and then to stand and be shot at, we should be forced to eat one another. This discovery has had a wonderful effect in quieting tender consciences. The calculation is very simple, any schoolboy will explain it to you.

Clio. — O what a number of fertile plains and green savannahs, and tracts covered with trees of beautiful foliage, have never yet been pressed by human foot- steps ! My friend Swift's project of eating children was not so cruel as these bloody and lavish sacrifices to Mars, the most savage of all the gods.

Mercury. — You forget yourself, Clio ; Mars is not worshipped now in Christian Europe.

Clio. — By Jupiter, but he is ! Have I not seen the bloody and torn banners, with martial music and mili- tary procession, brought into the temple, — and whose temple, thinkest thou ? and to whom have thanks been given on both sides, amidst smoking towns and wasted fields, after the destruction of man and devastation of the fair face of nature ! — And Mercury, god of wealth and frauds, you have your temple too, though your name is not inscribed there.

Mercury. — I am afraid men will always love wealth.

Clio. — Oh, if I had to record only such pure names as a Washington or a Howard !

Mercury. — It would be very gratifying, certainly : but then, Clio, you would have very little to do, and might almost as well burn your roll.

KNOWLEDGE AND HER DAUGHTER.

A FABLE.

KNOWLEDGE, the daughter of Jupiter, descended from the skies to visit man. She found him naked and helpless, living on the spontaneous fruits of the earth, and little superior to the ox that grazed beside him. She clothed and fed him ; she built him palaces ; she showed him the hidden riches of the earth, and pointed with her finger the course of the stars as they rose and set in the horizon. Man became rich with her gifts, and accomplished from her conversation. In process of time Knowledge became acquainted with the schools of the philosophers ; and being much taken with their theories and their conversation, she married one of them. They had many beautiful and healthy children ; but among the rest was a daughter of a different complexion from all the rest, whose name was Doubt. She grew up under many disadvantages ; she had a great hesitation in her speech ; a cast in her eye, which, however, was keen and piercing ; and was subject to nervous tremblings. Her mother saw her with dislike : but her father, who was of the sect of the Pyrrhonists, cherished and taught her logic, in which she made a great progress. The Muse of History was much troubled with her intrusions : she would tear out whole leaves, and blot

4

over many pages of her favorite works. With the divines her depredations were still worse: she was forbidden to enter a church; notwithstanding which, she would slip in under the surplice, and spend her time in making mouths at the priest. If she got at a library, she destroyed or blotted over the most valuable manuscripts. A most undutiful child; she was never better pleased than when she could unexpectedly trip up her mother's heels, or expose a rent or an unseemly patch in her flowing and ample garment. With mathematicians she never meddled; but in all other systems of knowledge she intruded herself, and her breath diffused a mist over the page which often left it scarcely legible. Her mother at length said to her, " Thou art my child, and I know it is decreed that while I tread this earth thou must accompany my footsteps; but thou art mortal, I am immortal; and there will come a time when I shall be freed from thy intrusion, and shall pursue my glorious track from star to star, and from system to system, without impediment and without check."

WASHING-DAY.

.   .   .   and their voice,
Turning again towards childish treble, pipes
And whistles in its sound. ———

THE Muses are turned gossips; they have lost
The buskined step, and clear high-sounding phrase,
Language of gods. Come then, domestic Muse,
In slipshod measure loosely prattling on
Of farm or orchard, pleasant curds and cream,
Or drowning flies, or shoe lost in the mire
By little whimpering boy, with rueful face;
Come, Muse, and sing the dreaded Washing-Day.

Ye who beneath the yoke of wedlock bend,
With bowed soul, full well ye ken the day
Which week, smooth sliding after week, brings on
Too soon ; — for to that day nor peace belongs
Nor comfort ; — ere the first gray streak of dawn,
The red-armed washers come and chase repose.
Nor pleasant smile, nor quaint device of mirth,
E'er visited that day : the very cat,
From the wet kitchen scared, and reeking hearth,
Visits the parlor, — an unwonted guest.
The silent breakfast-meal is soon despatched ;
Uninterrupted, save by anxious looks
Cast at the lowering sky, if sky should lower.
From that last evil, O preserve us, héavens !
For should the skies pour down, adieu to all
Remains of quiet : then expect to hear
Of sad disasters, — dirt and gravel stains
Hard to efface, and loaded lines at once
Snapped short, — and linen-horse by dog thrown
    down,
And all the petty miseries of life.
Saints have been calm while stretched upon the
    rack,
And Guatimozin smiled on burning coals ;
But never yet did housewife notable
Greet with a smile a rainy washing-day.
— But grant the welkin fair, require not thou
Who call'st thyself perchance the master there,
Or study swept, or nicely dusted coat,
Or usual 'tendance ; — ask not, indiscreet,
Thy stockings mended, though the yawning rents
Gape wide as Erebus ; nor hope to find
Some snug recess impervious : shouldst thou try
The 'customed garden walks, thine eye shall rue
The budding fragrance of thy tender shrubs,
Myrtle or rose, all crushed beneath the weight,
Of coarse checked apron, — with impatient hand

Twitched off when showers impend : or crossing
    lines
Shall mar thy musings, as the wet cold sheet
Flaps in thy face abrupt. Woe to the friend
Whose evil stars have urged him forth to claim
On such a day the hospitable rites !
Looks, blank at best, and stinted courtesy,
Shall he receive. Vainly he feeds his hopes
With dinner of roast chickens, savory pie,
Or tart or pudding : — pudding he nor tart
That day shall eat ; nor, though the husband try,
Mending what can't be helped, to kindle mirth
From cheer deficient, shall his consort's brow
Clear up propitious : — the unlucky guest
In silence dines, and early slinks away.
I well remember, when a child, the awe
This day struck into me ; for then the maids,
I scarce knew why, looked cross, and drove me from
    them :
Nor soft caress could I obtain, nor hope
Usual indulgences, — jelly or creams,
Relic of costly suppers, and set by
For me their petted one ; or buttered toast,
When butter was forbid ; or thrilling tale
Of ghost or witch, or murder. So I went
And sheltered me beside the parlor fire :
There my dear grandmother, eldest of forms,
Tended the little ones, and watched from harm,
Anxiously fond, though oft her spectacles
With elfin cunning hid, and oft the pins
Drawn from her ravelled stockings, might have
    soured
One less indulgent.
At intervals my mother's voice was heard,
Urging despatch : briskly the work went on,
All hands employed to wash, to rinse, to wring,
To fold, and starch, and clap, and iron, and plait.

Then would I sit me down, and ponder much
Why washings were. Sometimes through hollow
    bowl
Of pipe amused we blew, and sent aloft
The floating bubbles ; little dreaming then
To see, Mongolfier, thy silken ball
Ride buoyant through the clouds — so near ap-
    proach
The sports of children and the toils of men.
Earth, air, and sky, and ocean, hath its bubbles,
And verse is one of them — this most of all.

TRUE MAGICIANS.

TO MISS C.

MY DEAR SARAH, — I have often reflected, since I
left you, on the wonderful powers of magic exhibited
by you and your sister. The dim obscurity of that
grotto hollowed out by your hands under the laurel
hedge, where you used to mix the ingredients of your
incantations, struck us with awe and terror ; and the
broom which you so often brandished in your hands
made you look very like witches indeed. I must confess, however, that some doubts have now and then
arisen in my mind, whether or no you were truly initi-
ated in the secrets of your art ; and these suspicions
gathered strength after you had suffered us and yourself to be so drenched as we all were on that rainy
Tuesday ; which, to say the least, was a very odd circumstance, considering you had the command of the
weather. As I was pondering these matters alone in
the chaise between Epsom and London, I fell asleep
and had the following dream.

I thought I had been travelling through an unknown country, and came at last to a thick wood cut out into several groves and avenues, the gloom of which inspired thoughtfulness, and a certain mysterious dread of unknown powers came upon me. I entered however one of the avenues, and found it terminated in a magnificent portal, through which I could discern confusedly among thick foliage, cloistered arches and Grecian porticos, and people walking and conversing amongst the trees. Over the portal was the following inscription : "*Here dwell the true magicians. Nature is our servant. Man is our pupil. We change, we conquer, we create.*"

As I was hesitating whether or no I should presume to enter, a pilgrim, who was sitting under the shade, offered to be my guide, assuring me that these magicians would do me no harm, and that so far from having any objection to be observed in their operations, they were pleased with any opportunity of exhibiting them to the curious. In therefore I went, and addressed the first of the magicians I met with, who asked me whether I liked panoramas. On replying that I thought them very entertaining, she took me to a little eminence and bade me look round. I did so, and beheld the representation of the beautiful vale of Dorking, with Norbury-park and Box-hill to the north, Reigate to the east, and Leith tower with the Surrey hills to the south. After I had admired for some time the beauty and accuracy of the painting, a vast curtain seemed to be drawn gradually up, and my view extended on all sides. On one hand I traced the windings of the Thames up to Oxford, and stretched my eye westward over Salisbury Plain, and across the Bristol Channel into the romantic country of South Wales; northward the view extended to Lincoln cathedral, and York minster towering over the rest of the churches. Across the Sussex downs I had a clear view of the

British Channel, and the opposite coast of France, with its ports blockaded by our fleets. As the horizon of the panorama still extended, I spied the towers of Notre Dame, and the Tuileries, and my eye wandered at large over "The vine-covered hills and gay regions of France," quite down to the source of the Loire. At the same time the great Atlantic ocean opened to my view; and on the other hand I saw the lake of Geneva, and the dark ridge of Mount Jura, and discovered the summits of the Alps covered with snow; and beyond, the orange groves of Italy, the majestic dome of St. Peter's, and the smoking crater of Vesuvius. As the curtain still rose, I stretched my view over the Mediterranean, the scene of ancient glory, the Archipelago studded with islands, the shores of the Bosphorus, and the gilded minarets and cypress groves of Constantinople. Throwing back a look to the less attractive north, I saw pictured the rugged, broken coast of Norway, the cheerless moors of Lapland, and the interminable desolation of the plains of Siberia. Turning my eye again southward, the landscape extended to the plains of Barbary, covered with date-trees; and I discerned the points of pyramids appearing above the horizon, and saw the Delta and the seven-mouthed Nile. In short, the curtain still rose, and the view extended further and further till the panorama took in the whole globe. I cannot express to you the pleasure I felt as I saw mountains, seas, and islands, spread out before me. Sometimes my eye wandered over the vast plains of Tartary, sometimes it expatiated in the savannahs of America. I saw men with dark skins, white cotton turbans wreathed about their heads, and long flowing robes of silk; others almost naked under a vertical sun. I saw whales sporting in the northern seas, and elephants trampling amidst fields of maize and forests of palm-trees. I seemed to have put a girdle about the earth, and was gratified with an infinite variety of objects which I thought I never could be weary of contemplating. At length, turning towards the magician who had entertained me with such an agreeable exhibition, and asking her name, she informed me it was *Geography*.

My attention was next arrested by a sorceress, who, I was told, possessed the power of calling up from the dead whomsoever she pleased, man or woman, in their proper habits and figures, and obliging them to converse and answer questions. She held a roll of parchment in her hand, and had an air of great dignity. I confess that I felt a little afraid; but having been somewhat encouraged by the former exhibition, I ventured to ask her to give me a specimen of her power, in case there was nothing unlawful in it. "Whom," said she, "do you wish to behold?" After considering some time, I desired to see Cicero, the Roman orator. She made some talismanic figures on the sand, and presently he rose to my view, his neck and head bare, the rest of his body in a flowing toga, which he gathered round him with one hand, and stretching out the other very gracefully, he recited to me one of his orations against Catiline. He also read to me — which was more than I could in reason have expected — several of his familiar letters to his most intimate friends. I next desired that Julius Cæsar might be called up: on which he appeared, his hair nicely arranged, and the fore part of his head, which was bald, covered with wreaths of laurel; and he very obligingly gave me a particular account of his expedition into Gaul. I wished to see the youth of Macedon, but was a little disappointed in his figure, for he was low in stature and held his head awry; but I saw him manage Bucephalus with admirable courage and address, and was afterwards introduced with him into the tent of Darius, where I was greatly pleased with the generosity and politeness of his be-havior. I afterwards expressed some curiosity to see a battle, if I might do it with safety, and was grat-ified with the sea-fight of Actium. I saw, after the first onset, the galleys of Cleopatra turning their prows and flying from the battle, and Antony, to his eternal shame, quitting the engagement and making sail after her. I then wished to call up all the kings of Eng-land, and they appeared in order, one after the other, with their crowns and the insignia of their dignity, and walked over the stage for my amusement, much like the descendants of Banquo in Macbeth. Their queens accompanied them, trailing their robes upon the ground, and the bishops with their mitres, and judges, and generals, and eminent persons of every class. I asked many questions as they passed, and received a great deal of information relative to the laws, manners, and transactions of past times. I did not, however, always meet with direct answers to my questions. For instance, when I called up Homer, and after some other conversation asked him where he was born, he only said, "Guess!" And when I asked Louis the Fourteenth who was the man in the iron mask, he frowned and would not tell me. I took a great deal of pleasure in calling up the shades of distinguished people in different ages and countries, making them stand close by one another, and comparing their man-ners and costume. Thus I measured Catharine of Russia against Semiramis, and Aristotle against Lord Bacon. I could have spent whole years in conversa-tion with so many celebrated persons, and promised myself that I would often frequent this obliging magi-cian. Her name, I found, was in heaven *Clio*, on earth *History*.

I saw another, who was making a charm for two friends, one of whom was going to the East Indies: they were bitterly lamenting that when they were

parted at so great a distance from each other they
could no longer communicate their thoûghts, but
must be cut off from each other's society.   Pre-
senting them with a talisman inscribed with four-and-
twenty black marks, "Take this," she said; "I have
breathed a voice upon it : by means of this talisman
you shall still converse, and hear one another as dis-
tinctly, when half the globe is between you, as if you
were talking together in the same room."   The two
friends thanked her for such an invaluable present,
and retired.   Her name was *Abracadabra.*

I was next invited to see a whispering-gallery, of a
most curious and uncommon structure.   To make
the experiment of its powers, a young poet of a very
modest appearance, who was stealing along in a retired walk, was desired to repeat a verse in it.   He
applied his lips to the wall, and whispered in a low
voice, "*Rura mihi et rigui placeant in vallibus am-
nes.*"   The sound ran along the walls for some time
in a kind of low whisper; but every minute it grew
louder and louder, till at length it was echoed and re-
echoed from every part of the gallery, and seemed
to be pronounced by a multitude of voices at once,
in different languages, till the whole dome was filled
with the sound.   There was a strong smell of incense.   The gallery was constructed by *Fame.*

The good pilgrim next conducted me to a cave
where several sorceresses, very black and grim, were
amusing themselves with making lightning, thunder,
and earthquakes.   I saw two vials of cold liquor
mixed together, and flames burst forth from them.
I saw some insignificant-looking black grains, which
would throw palaces and castles into the air.   I saw
— and it made my hair stand on end — a headless
man, who lifted up his arm and grasped a sword.   I
saw men flying through the air, without wings, over
the tops of towns and castles, and come down unhurt.

The cavern was very black, and the smoke and fires
and mephitic blasts and sulphureous vapors that is-
sued from it, gave the whole a very tremendous appearance. I did not stay long, but as I retired I saw
Chemistry written on the walls in letters of flame, with
several other names which I do not now remember.

My companion whispered me that some of these
were suspected of communication with the evil genii,
and that the demon of War had been seen to resort
to the cave. "But now," said the pilgrim, "I will
lead you to enchanters who deserve all your veneration, and are even more beneficent than those you
have already seen." He then led me to a cavern that
opened upon the sea shore : it blew a terrible storm,
the waves ran mountains high, the wind roared, and
vessels were driven against each other with a terrible
shock. A female figure advanced and threw a little
oil upon the waves; they immediately subsided, the
winds were still, the storm was laid, and the vessels
pursued their course in safety. " By what magic is
this performed?" exclaimed I. "The magician is
Meekness," replied my conductor; " she can smooth
the roughest sea, and allay the wildest storm."

My view was next directed to a poor wretch, who
lay groaning in a most piteous manner, and crushed
to the earth with a mountain on his breast; he uttered
piercing shrieks, and seemed totally unable to rise or
help himself. One of these good magicians, whose
name I found was *Patience*, advanced and struck the
mountain with a wand; on which, to my great surprise, it diminished to a size not more than the load
of an ordinary porter, which the man threw over
his shoulders, with something very like a smile, and
marched off with a firm step and very composed air.

I must not pass over a charmer of a very pleasing
appearance and lively aspect. She possessed the
power (a very useful one in a country so subject to

fogs and rains as this is) of gilding a landscape with sunshine whenever she breathed upon it. Her name was *Cheerfulness.* Indeed you may remember that your papa brought her down with him on that very rainy day when we could not go out at all, and he played on his flute to you and you all danced.

I was next struck, on ascending an eminence, with a most dreary landscape. All the flat country was one stagnant marsh. Amidst the rushy grass lay the fiend Ague, listless and shivering : on the bare and bleak hills sat Famine, with a few shells of acorns before her, of which she had eaten the fruit. The woods were tangled and pathless ; the howl of wolves was heard. A few smoky huts, or caves, not much better than the dens of wild beasts, were all the habitations of men that presented themselves. "Miserable country !" I exclaimed ; "step-child of nature !" "This," said my conductor, "is Britain as our ancestors possessed it." "And by what magic," I replied, "has it been converted into the pleasant land we now inhabit ?" "You shall see," said he. "It has been the work of one of our most powerful magicians. Her name is *Industry.*" At the word, she advanced and waved her wand over the scene. Gradually the waters ran off into separate channels, and left rich meadows covered with innumerable flocks and herds. The woods disappeared, except what waved gracefully on the tops of the hills, or filled up the unsightly hollows. Wherever she moved her wand, roads, bridges, and canals laid open and improved the face of the country. A numerous population, spread abroad in the fields, were gathering in the harvest. Smoke from warm cottages ascended through the trees, pleasant towns and villages marked the several points of distance. Last, the Thames was filled with forests of masts, and proud London appeared with all its display of wealth and grandeur.

I do not know whether it was the pleasure I received from this exhilarating scene, or the carriage having just got upon the pavement, which awakened me ; but I determined to write out my dream, and advise you to cultivate your acquaintance with all the *true Arts of Magic.*

A LECTURE ON THE USE OF WORDS.

My dear mamma, who worked you this scarf? it is excessively pretty.

I am sorry for it, my dear.

Sorry, mamma ! are you sorry it is pretty?

No, but I am sorry if it is *excessively* pretty.

Why so? — a thing cannot be too pretty, can it?

If so, it cannot be excessively pretty. Pray what do you mean by excessively pretty?

Why, excessively pretty means — it means very pretty.

What does the word excessively come from? What part of speech is it? You know your grammar?

It is an adverb : the words that end in *ly* are adverbs.

Adverbs are derived from adjectives by adding *ly*, you should have said ; — excessive, excessively. And what is the noun from which they are both derived?

Excess.

And what does excess mean?

It means too much of any thing.

You see then that it implies a fault, and therefore cannot be applied as a commendation. We say a man is excessively greedy, excessively liberal; a woman excessively fine : but not that a man is excessively wise, a woman excessively faithful to her hus-

band; because in these there is no excess: nor is
there in beauty, that being the true and just proportion
which gives pleasure.

But we say "excessively kind."

We do, because kindness has its limits. A person
may be too kind to us, who exposes himself to a great
and serious inconvenience to give us a slight pleasure :
we also may mean by it, exceeding that kindness which
we have a claim to expect. But when people use it,
as they often do, on the slightest occasion, it is certainly as wrong as "excessively pretty."

But, mamma, must we always consider so much the
exact meaning of words? Every body says "excessively pretty," and "excessively tall," and "infinitely
obliged to you." What harm can it do?

That every body does it, I deny ; that the generality
do it, is very true ; but it is likewise true, that the
generality are not to be taken as a pattern in any
thing. As to the harm it does, — in the first place it
hurts our sincerity.

Why, it is not telling a lie, sure?

Certainly I do not mean to say it is ; but it tends to
sap and undermine the foundations of our integrity,
by making us careless, if not in the facts we assert,
yet in the measure and degree in which we assert
them. If we do not pretend to love those we have
no affection for, or to admire those we despise, at least
we lead them to think we admire them more and love
them better than we really do ; and this prepares the
way for more serious deviations from truth. So much
for its concern with morality : — but it has likewise a
very bad effect on our taste. What, think you, is the
reason that young people, especially, run ·into these
vague and exaggerated expressions?

What is *vague*, mamma?

It means what has no precise, definite signification.
Young people run into these, sometimes indeed from

having more feeling than judgment, but more commonly from not knowing how to separate their ideas and tell what it is they are pleased with. They either do not know, or will not give themselves the trouble to mark, the qualities, or to describe the scenes which disgust or please them, and hope to cover their deficiency by these overwhelming expressions; as if your dress-maker, not knowing your shape, should make a large loose frock, that would cover you over were you twice as tall as you are. Now you would have shown your taste, if in commending my scarf you had said that the pattern was light, or it was rich, or that the work was neat and true; but by saying it was excessively pretty, you showed you had not considered what it was you admired in it. Did you never hear of the countryman who said, "There will be monstrous few apples this year, and those few will be huge little"? Poets run into this fault when they give unmeaning epithets instead of appropriate description; — young ladies, when in their letters they run into exaggerated expressions of friendship.

You have often admired, in this painting, the variety of tints shaded into one another. Well! what would you think of a painter who should spread one deep blue over all the sky, and one deep green over the grass and trees? would not you say he was a dauber? and made near objects and distant objects, and objects in the sun and objects in the shade, all alike? I think I have some of your early performances in which you have colored prints pretty much in this style; but you would not paint so now?

No, indeed.

Then do not talk so: do not paint so with words.

THE CATERPILLAR.

No, helpless thing, I cannot harm thee now;
Depart in peace, thy little life is safe.
For I have scanned thy form with curious eye,
Noted the silver line that streaks thy back,
The azure and the orange that divide
Thy velvet sides; thee, houseless wanderer,
My garment has enfolded, and my arm
Felt the light pressure of thy hairy feet;
Thou hast curled round my finger; from its tip,
Precipitous descent! with stretched out neck,
Bending thy head in airy vacancy,
This way and that, inquiring, thou hast seemed .
To ask protection; now, I cannot kill thee.
Yet I have sworn perdition to thy race,
And recent from the slaughter am I come
Of tribes and embryo nations: I have sought
With sharpened eye and persecuting zeal,
Where, folded in their silken webs they lay
Thriving and happy; swept them from the tree
And crushed whole families beneath my foot;
Or sudden, poured on their devoted heads
The vials of destruction. This I've done,
Nor felt the touch of pity: but when thou, —
A single wretch, escaped the general doom,
Making me feel and clearly recognize
Thine individual existence, life,
And fellowship of sense with all that breathes, —
Present'st thyself before me, I relent,
And cannot hurt thy weakness. So the storm

Of horrid war, o'erwhelming cities, fields,
And peaceful villages, rolls dreadful on :
The victor shouts triumphant ; he enjoys
The roar of cannon and the clang of arms,
And urges, by no soft relentings stopped,
The work of death and carnage.   Yet should one,
A single sufferer from the field escaped,
Panting and pale, and bleeding at his feet,
Lift his imploring eyes, — the hero weeps ;
He is grown human, and capricious Pity,
Which would not stir for thousands, melts for one
With sympathy spontaneous : — 'T is not Virtue,
Yet 't is the weakness of a virtuous mind.

EARTH.

ALL the different substances which we behold have
by the earliest philosophers been resolved into four elements, — Earth, Water, Air, and Fire.   These, combined with endless diversity, in their various dance,
under the direction of the great First Mover, form this
scene of things, — so complex, so beautiful, so infinitely
varied !

Earth is the element which on many accounts claims
our chief notice.   It forms the bulk of that vast body
of matter which composes our globe ; and, like the
bones to the human body, it gives firmness, shape, and
solidity to the various productions of Nature.   It is
ponderous, dull, unanimated, ever seeking the lowest
place ; and, except moved by some external impulse,
prone to rest in one sluggish mass. Yet when fermented
into life by the quickening power of vegetation, — in
how many forms of grace and beauty does it rise to
the admiring eye !   How gay, how vivid with colors !

how fragrant with smells ! how rich with tastes, — luscious, poignant, sapid, mild, pungent, or saccharine !
Into what delicate textures is it spread out in the thin
leaf of the rose, or the light film of the floating gossa-
mer ! How curious in the elegant ramifications of trees
and shrubs, or the light dust which the microscope discovers to contain the seed of future plants !

Nor has earth less of magnificence, in the various
appearances with which upon a larger scale its broad
surface is diversified ; whether we behold it stretched
out into immense plains and vast savannahs, whose
level green is bounded only by the horizon ; or moulded into those gentle risings and easy declivities whose
soft and undulating lines court the pencil of the land-
scape-painter ; or whether, swelled into bulk enormous,
it astonishes the eye with vast masses of solid rock and
long-continued bulwarks of stone.   Such are the Pyrenees, the Alps, the Andes, which stand the everlasting
boundaries of nations ; and, while kingdoms rise and
fall, and the lesser works of nature change their appearance all around them, immovable on their broad basis,
strike the mind with an idea of stability little short of
eternal duration.

If from the mountains which possess the middle of
Earth we bend our course to the green verge of her
dominions, the utmost limits of her shores, where land
and water, like two neighboring potentates, wage eternal war, — with what steady majesty does she repel the
encroachments of the ever-restless ocean, and dash the
turbulence of waves from her strong-ribbed sides !

Nor do thy praises end here.   With a kind of filial
veneration I hail thee, O universal mother of all the
elements, — to man the most mild, the most beneficent, the most congenial ! Man himself is formed from
thee : on thy maternal breast he reposes when weary ;
thy teeming lap supplies him with never-failing plenty ;
and when for a few years he has moved about upon thy

surface, he is gathered again to thy peaceful bosom, at once his nurse, his cradle, and his grave.

Who can reckon up the benefits supplied to us by this parent Earth, — ever serviceable, ever indulgent! with how many productions does she reward the labor of the cultivator! how many more does she pour out spontaneously! How faithfully does she keep, with what large interest does she restore, the seed committed to her by the husbandman! What an abundance does she yield, of food for the poor, of delicacies for the rich! Her wealth is inexhaustible; and all that is called riches among men consists in possessing a small portion of her surface.

How patiently does she support the various burdens laid upon her! We tear her with ploughs and harrows, we crush her with castles and palaces; nay, we penetrate her very bowels, and bring to light the veined marble, the pointed crystal, the ponderous ores and sparkling gems, deep hid in darkness, the more to excite the industry of man. Yet, torn and harassed as she might seem to be, our mother Earth is still fresh and young, as if she but now came out of the hands of her Creator. Her harvests are as abundant, her horn of plenty as overflowing, her robe as green, her unshorn tresses (the waving foliage of brown forests) as luxuriant; and all her charms as blooming and full of vigor. Such she remains, and such we trust she will remain, till in some fated hour the more devouring element of fire, having broke the bonds of harmonious union, shall seize upon its destined prey, and all nature sink beneath the mighty ruin.

ON THE USES OF HISTORY.

LETTER I.

MY DEAR LYDIA, — I was told the other day that you
have not forgotten a promise of mine to correspond
with you upon some subject which might be worth dis-
cussing, and relative to your pursuits. I have often
recollected it also ; and, as promises ought not only to
be recollected but fulfilled, I will without further preface throw together some thoughts on *History*, — a
study that I know you value as it deserves ; and I trust
it will not be disagreeable to you, if you should find
some observations which your own mind may have sug-
gested, or which you may recollect to have heard from
me in some of those hours which we spent together
with mutual pleasure.

Much has been said of the uses of history. They
are no doubt many, yet do not apply equally to all :
but it is quite sufficient to make it a study worth our
pains and time, that it satisfies the desire which naturally arises in every intelligent mind to know the transactions of the country, of the globe in which he lives.
Facts, as facts, interest our curiosity and engage our
attention.

Suppose a person placed in a part of the country
where he was a total stranger ; he would naturally ask,
who are the chief people of the place, what family they
are of, whether any of their ancestors have been famous,
and for what. If he see a ruined abbey, he will inquire
what the building was used for ; and if he be told it

is a place where people got up at midnight to sing psalms, and scourged themselves in the day, he will ask how there came to be such people, or why there are none now. If he observes a dilapidated castle which appears to have been battered by violence, he will ask in what quarrel it suffered, and why they built formerly structures so different from any we see now. If any part of the inhabitants should speak a different language from the rest, or have some singular customs among them, he would suppose they came originally from some remote part of the country, and would inform himself, if he could, of the cause of their peculiarities.

If he were of a curious temper, he would not rest till he had informed himself whom every estate in the parish belonged to, what hands they had gone through, how one man got this field by marrying an heiress, and the other lost that meadow by a ruinous lawsuit. As a man of spirit, he would feel delighted on hearing the relation of the opposition made by an honest yeoman to an overbearing rich man, on the subject of an accustomed pathway or right of common. If he should find the town or village divided into parties he would take some pains to trace the original cause of their dissension, and to find out, if possible, who had the right on his side. Circumstances would often occur to excite his attention. If he saw a bridge, he would ask when and by whom it was built. If in digging in his garden he should find utensils of a singular form and construction, or a pot of money with a stamp and legend quite different from the common coin, he would be led to inquire when they were in use, and to whom they had belonged. His curiosity would extend itself by degrees. If a brook ran through the meadows, he would be pleased to trace it till it swelled into a river, and the river till it lost itself in the sea. He would be asking whose seat he saw upon the edge of a distant forest,

and what sort of country lay behind the range of hills
that bounded his utmost view. If any strangers came
to visit or reside in the place where he lived, he would
be questioning them about the country they came from,
their connections and alliances, and the remarkable
transactions that had taken place within their memory
or that of their parents. The answers to these questions would insensibly grow up into history, which, as
you see, does not originate in abstruse speculations, but
grows naturally out of our situation and relative connections. It gratifies a curiosity which all feel in some
degree, but which spreads and enlarges itself with the
cultivation of our powers, till at length it embraces the
whole globe which we inhabit. To know is as natural
to the mind as to see is to the eye, and knowledge is
itself an ultimate end. But though this may be esteemed an ultimate and sufficient end, the study of
history is important to various purposes. Few pursuits
tend more to enlarge the mind. It gives us, and it
only can give us, an extended knowledge of human
nature ; — not human nature as it exists in one age or
climate or particular spot of earth, but human nature
under all the various circumstances by which it can be
affected. It shows us what is radical and what is
adventitious ; it shows us that man is still man in Tur-
key and in Lapland, as a vassal in Russia or a member
of a wandering tribe in India, in ancient Athens or
modern Rome ; yet that his character is susceptible of
violent changes, and becomes moulded into infinite
diversities by the influence of government, climate,
civilization, wealth, and poverty. By showing us how
man has acted, it shows us to a certain degree how he
will ever act in given circumstances ; and general rules
and maxims are drawn from it for the service of the
lawgiver and the statesman.

Here I must observe however, with regard to *events*,
that a knowledge of history does not seem to give us

any great advantage in foreseeing and preparing for them. The deepest politician, with all his knowledge of the revolutions of past ages, could probably no more have predicted the course and termination of the late French Revolution, than a common man. The state of our own national debt has baffled calculation; the course of ages has presented nothing like it. Who could have pronounced that the struggle of the Americans would be successful—that of the Poles unsuccessful? Human characters indeed act always alike : but events depend upon circumstances as well as characters; and circumstances are infinitely various and changed by the slightest causes. A battle won or lost may decide the fate of an empire : but a battle may be won or lost by a shower of snow being blown to the east or the west; by a horse (the general's) losing his shoe; by a bullet or an arrow taking a direction a tenth part of an inch one way or the other. The whole course of the French affairs might have been changed if the king had not stopped to breakfast, or if the postmaster of Varennes had not happened to know him. These are particulars which no man can foresee; and therefore no man can with precision foresee events.

The rising up of certain characters at particular periods ranks among those unforeseen circumstances that powerfully influence events. Often does a single man, as Epaminondas, illustrate his country, and leave a long track of light after him to future ages. And who can tell how much even America owed to the *accident* of being served by such a man as Washington? There are always many probable events. All that history enables the politician to do, is to predict that one or other of them will take place. If so and so, it will be this; if so and so, it will be that : but which, we cannot tell. There are always combinations of circumstances which have never met before from the creation of the world, and which mock all power of calculation. But let the circumstances be known and the characters upon the stage, and history will tell him what to expect from them. It will tell him with certainty, for instance, that a treaty extorted by force from distress, will be broken when opportunity offers ; that if the church and the monarch are united they will oppress, if at variance they will divide, the people ; that a powerful nation will make its advantage of the divisions of a weaker which applies for its assistance.

It is another advantage of history, that it stores the mind with facts that apply to most subjects which occur in conversation among enlightened people. Whether morals, commerce, languages, polite literature be the object of discussion, it is history that must supply her large storehouse of proofs and illustrations. A man or a woman may decline without blame many subjects of literature, but to be ignorant of history is not permitted to any of a cultivated mind. It may be reckoned among its advantages, that this study naturally increases the love of every man to his country. We can only love what we know ; it is by becoming acquainted with the long line of patriots, heroes, and distinguished men, that we learn to love the country which has produced them.

But I must conclude this letter, already perhaps too long, though I have not got to the end of my subject : it will give me soon another opportunity of subscribing myself

Your ever affectionate friend.

LETTER II.

I LEFT off, my dear Lydia, with mentioning, among the advantages of an acquaintance with history, that it fosters the sentiments of patriotism.

What is a man's country? To the unlettered peasant who has never left his native village, that village is his country, and consequently all of it he can love. The man who mixes in the world, and has a large acquaintance with the characters existing along with himself upon the stage of it, has a wider range. His idea of a country extends to its civil polity, its military triumphs, the eloquence of its courts, and the splendor of its capital. All the great and good characters he is acquainted with swell his idea of its importance, and endear to him the society of which he is a member. But how wonderfully does this idea expand, and how majestic a form does it put on, when history conducts our retrospective view through past ages! How much more has the man to love, how much to interest him in his country, in whom her image is identified with the virtues of an Alfred, with the exploits of the Henrys and Edwards, with the fame and fortunes of the Sidneys and Hampdens, the Lockes and Miltons, who have illustrated her annals! Like a man of noble birth who walks up and down in a long gallery of portraits, and is able to say, "This, my progenitor, was admiral in such a fight; that, my great-uncle, was general in such an engagement; he on the right hand held the seals in such a reign; that lady in so singular a costume was a celebrated beauty two hundred years ago; this little man in the black cap and peaked beard was one of the luminaries of his age, and suffered for his religion;" — he learns to value himself upon his ancestry, and to feel interested for the honor and prosperity of the whole line of de-

scendants.   Could a Swiss, think you, be so good a
patriot who had never heard of the name of William
Tell? or the Hollander, who should be unacquainted
with the glorious struggles which freed his nation from
the tyranny of the Duke of Alva?

The Englishman conversant in history has been
long acquainted with his country.   He knew her in
the infancy of her greatness; has seen her, perhaps,
in the wattled huts and slender canoes in which Cæsar
discovered her: he has watched her rising fortunes,
has trembled at her dangers, rejoiced at her deliver-
ances, and shared with honest pride triumphs that
were celebrated ages before he was born.   He has
traced her gradual improvement through many a dark
and turbulent period, many a storm of civil warfare, to
the fair reign of her liberty and law, to the fulness
of her prosperity and the amplitude of her fame.

Or, should our patriot have his lot cast in some age
and country which has declined from this high station of pre-eminence; should he observe the gathering glooms of superstition and ignorance ready to
close again over the bright horizon; should Liberty
lie prostrate at the feet of a despot, and the golden
stream of commerce, diverted into other channels,
leave nothing but beggary and wretchedness around
him; — even then, in these ebbing fortunes of his country, history, like a faithful meter, would tell him how
high the tide had once risen; he would not tread un-
consciously the ground where the Muses and the Arts
had once resided, like the goat that stupidly browses
upon the fane of Minerva.   Even the name of his
country will be dear and venerable to him.   He will
muse over her fallen greatness, sit down under the
shade of her never-dying laurels, build his little cottage amidst the ruins of her towers and temples, and
contemplate with tenderness and respect the decaying
age of his once illustrious parent.

But if an acquaintance with history thus increases a rational love of our country, it also tends to check those low, illiberal, vulgar prejudices which adhere to the uninformed of every nation. Travelling will also cure them : but to travel is not within the power of every one. There is no use, but a great deal of harm in fostering a contempt for other nations ; in an arrogant assumption of superiority, and the clownish sneer of ignorance at every thing in laws, government, or manners which is not fashioned after our partial ideas and familiar usages. A well-informed person will not be apt to exclaim at every event out of the common way, that nothing like it has ever happened since the creation of the world, that such atrocities are totally unheard-of in any age or nation, — sentiments we have all of us so often heard of late on the subject of the French Revolution,—when in fact we can scarcely open a page of their history without being struck with similar and equal enormities. Indeed, party spirit is very much cooled and checked by an acquaintance with the events of past times.

When we see the mixed and imperfect virtue of the most distinguished characters ; the variety of motives, some pure and some impure, which influence political conduct; the partial success of the wisest schemes, and the frequent failure of the fairest hopes ; — we shall find it more difficult to choose a side, and to keep up an interest towards it in our minds, than to restrain our feelings and language within the bounds of good sense and moderation. This, by the way, makes it particularly proper that *ladies* who interest themselves in the events of public life should have their minds cultivated by an acquaintance with history, without which they are apt to let the whole warmth of their natures flow out, upon party matters, in an ardor more honest than wise, more zealous than candid.

With regard to the moral uses of history, what has just been mentioned may stand for one. It serves also by exercise to strengthen the moral feelings. The traits of generosity, heroism, disinterestedness, magnanimity, are scattered over it like sparkling gems, and arrest the attention of the most common reader. It is wonderfully interesting to follow the revolutions of a great state, particularly when they lead to the successful termination of some glorious contest. Is it true? — a child asks, when you tell him a wonderful story that strikes his imagination. The writer of fiction has the unlimited command of events and of characters ; yet that single circumstance of truth, — that the events related really came to pass, that the heroes brought upon the stage really existed, — counterbalances, with respect to interest, all the privileges of the former, and in a mind a little accustomed to exertion will throw the advantage on the side of the historian.

The more history approaches to biography the more interest it excites. Where the materials are meagre and scanty, the antiquarian and chronologer may dwell upon the page ; but it will seldom excite the glow of admiration or draw the delicious tear of sensibility. I must acknowledge, however, in order to be candid, that the emotions excited by the actions of our species are not always of so pleasing or so edifying a nature. The miseries and the vices of man form a large part of the picture of human society : the pure mind is disgusted by depravity, the existence of which it could not have imagined to itself; and the feeling heart is cruelly lacerated by the sad repetition of wrongs and oppression, chains and slaughter, sack and massacre, which assail it in every page : till the mind has gained some strength, so frightful a picture should hardly be presented to it. Chosen periods of history may be selected for youth, as the society of chosen characters precedes in well-regulated educa-

tion a more indiscriminate acquaintance with the
world. In favor of a more extended view, I can
only say that truth is truth, — man must be shown as
the being he really is, or no real knowledge is gained.
If a young person were to read only the *Beauties of
History*, or, according to Madame Genlis's scheme,
stories and characters in which all that was vicious
should be left out, he might as well, for any real acquaintance with life he would gain, have been reading
all the while Sir Charles Grandison or the Princess of
Cleves.

One consoling idea will present itself with no small
degree of probability on comparing the annals of past
and present times, — that of a tendency to ameliora-
tion ; at least it is evidently found in those countries
with which we are most connected. But the only
balm that can be poured with full effect into the feeling mind which bleeds for the folly and wickedness of
man, is the belief that all events are directed and con-
trolled by supreme wisdom and goodness. Without
this persuasion, the world becomes a desert, and its
devastators the wolves and tigers that prowl over it.

It is needless to insist on the uses of history to those
whose situation in life gives them room to expect
that their actions may one day become the objects of
it. Besides the immediate necessity to them of the
knowledge it supplies, it affords the strongest motives
for their conduct, of hope and fear. The solemn
award, the incorruptible tribunal, and the severe soul-
searching inquisition of posterity is calculated to strike
an awe into their souls. They cannot take refuge
in oblivion : it is not permitted them to die : — they
may be the objects of gratitude or detestation as long
as the world stands. They may flatter themselves
that they have silenced the voice of truth ; they may
forbid newspapers and pamphlets and conversation ; —
an unseen hand is all the while tracing out their his-

tory, and often their minutest actions, in indelible characters ; and it will soon be held up for the judgment of the world at large.

Lastly, this permanency of human characters tends to cherish in the mind the hope and belief of an existence after death. If we had no notices from the page of history of those races of men that have lived before us, they would seem to be completely swept away ; and we should no more think of inquiring what human beings filled our place upon the earth a thousand harvests ago, than we should think about the generations of cattle which at that time grazed the marshes of the Tiber, or the venerable ancestors of the goats that are browsing upon Mount Hymettus ; — no vestige would remain of one any more than of the other, and we might more pardonably fall into the opinion that they both had shared a similar fate. But when we see illustrious characters continuing to live on in the eye of posterity, their memories still fresh, and their noble actions shining with all the vivid coloring of truth and reality, ages after the very dust of their tombs is scattered, high conceptions kindle within us ; and feeling one immortality we are lead to hope for another. We find it hard to persuade ourselves that the man, who like Antoninus or Socrates, fills the world with the sweet perfume of his virtue, the martyr or the patriot to whom posterity is doing the justice which was denied him by his contemporaries, should all the while himself be blotted out of existence ; that he should be benefiting mankind and doing good so long after he is capable of receiving any ; that we should be so well acquainted with him, and that he should never know any thing of us. That one who is an active agent in the world, instructing, informing it, inspiring friendship, making disciples, should be nothing — this does not seem probable ; the records of time suggest to us eternity. — Farewell.

LETTER III.

MY DEAR LYDIA, — We have considered the uses of History ; I would now direct your attention to those collateral branches of science which are necessary for the profitable understanding of it. It is impossible to understand one thing well without understanding to a certain degree many other things ; there is a mutual dependence between all parts of knowledge. This is the reason that a child never fully comprehends what he is taught : he receives an idea, but not the full idea, perhaps not the principal of what you want to teach him. But as his mind opens, this idea enlarges and receives accessory ideas, till slowly and by degrees he is master of the whole. This is particularly the case in history. You may recollect probably that the mere *adventure* was all you entered into, in those portions of it which were presented to you at a very early age. You could understand nothing of the springs of action, nothing of the connection of events with the intrigues of cabinets, with religion, with commerce ; nothing of the state of the world at different periods of society and improvement : and as little could you grasp the meas- ured distances of time and space which are set between them. This you could not do, not because the history was not related with clearness, but because you were destitute of other knowledge.

The first studies which present themselves as acces- sories in this light are Geography and Chronology, which have been called the two eyes of History. When was it done ? Where was it done ? are the two first questions you would ask concerning any fact that was related to you. Without these two particulars there can be no precision or clearness.

Geography is best learned along with history ; for if the first explains history, the latter gives interest to geography, which without it is but a dry list of names. For this reason, if a young person begin with ancient history, I should think it advisable, after a slight general acquaintance with the globe, to confine his geography to the period and country of which he is reading ; and it would be a desirable thing to have maps adapted to each remarkable period in the great empires of the world. These should not contain any towns or be divided into any provinces which were not known at that period. A map of Egypt for instance, calculated for its ancient monarchy, should have Memphis marked in it, but not Alexandria, because the two capitals did not exist together. A map of Judea for the time of Solomon, or any period of its monarchy, should not exhibit the name of Samaria, nor the villages of Bethany and Nazareth : but each country should have the towns and divisions, as far as they are known, calculated for the period the map was meant to illustrate. Thus geography, civil geography, would be seen to grow out of history ; and the mere view of the map would suggest the political state of the world at any period.

It would be a pleasing speculation to see how the arbitrary divisions of kingdoms and provinces vary and become obsolete, and large towns flourish and fall again into ruins : while the great natural features, the mountains, rivers, and seas remain unchanged, by whatever names we please to call them, whatever empire encloses them within its temporary boundaries. We have, it is true, ancient and modern maps ; but the one set includes every period from the Flood to the provinciating the Roman empire under Trajan, and the other takes in all the rest. About half a dozen sets for the ancient states and empires, and as many for the modern, would be sufficient to exhibit the most important changes, and would be as many as we should be able to give with any clearness. The young student should make it an invariable rule never to read history without a map before him ; to which should be added plans of towns, harbors, &c. These should be conveniently placed under the eye, separate if possible from the book he is reading, that by frequent glancing upon them the image of the country may be indelibly impressed on his imagination.

Besides the necessity of maps for understanding history, the memory is wonderfully assisted by the local association which they supply. The battles of Issus and the Granicus will not be confounded by those who have taken the pains to trace the rivers on whose banks they were fought : the exploits of Hannibal are connected with a view of the Alps, and the idea of Leonidas is inseparable from the straits of Thermopylæ. The greater accuracy of maps, and still more the facility, from the arts of printing and engraving, of procuring them, is an advantage the moderns have over the ancients. They have been perfected by slow degrees. The Egyptians and Chaldeans studied the science of mensuration ; and the first map — rude enough no doubt — is said to have been made by order of Sesostris when he became master of Egypt. Commerce and war have been the two parents of this science. Pharaoh Necho ordered the Phœnicians whom he sent round Africa, to make a survey of the coast. This they finished in three years. Darius caused the Ethiopic Sea and the mouth of the Indus to be surveyed. That maps were known in Greece you no doubt recollect from the pretty story of Socrates and Alcibiades. Anaximander, a disciple of Thales, is said to have made the first sphere, and first delineated what was then known of the countries of the earth. He flourished 547 years before Christ. Herodotus mentions a map of brass or copper which was presented by Aristagoras, tyrant of Miletus, to Cleomenes, king of Sparta, in which he had described the known world with its seas and rivers. Alexander the Great, in his expedition into

Asia, took two geographers with him; and from their itineraries many things have been copied by succeeding writers.

From Greece the science of geography passed to Rome. The enlightened policy of the Romans culti- vated it as a powerful means of extending and secur- ing their dominion. One of the first things they did was to make roads, for which it was necessary to have the country measured. They had a custom when they had conquered a country, to have a painted map of it always carried aloft in their triumphs. The great historian Polybius reconnoitred under a commission from Scipio Emilianus the coasts of Africa, Spain, and France, and measured the distances of Hannibal's march over the Alps and Pyrenees. Julius Cæsar em- ployed men of science to survey and measure the globe; and his own Commentaries show his attention to this part of knowledge. Strabo, a great geographer whose works are extant, flourished under Augustus; Pomponius Mela, in the first century.

Many of the Roman itineraries which are still extant show the systematic care which they bestowed on a science so necessary for the orderly distribution and government of their large dominions. But still it was late before geography was settled upon its true basis, — astronomical observations. The greater part of the early maps were laid down in a very loose, inaccurate manner; and where particular parts were done with the greatest care, yet if the longitude and latitude were wanting, their relative situation to the rest of the earth could not be known. Some attempts had indeed been made by Hipparchus and Posidonius, Greek philoso- phers, to settle the parallels of latitude by the length of the days; but the foundation they had laid was neg- lected till the time of Ptolemy, who flourished at Alexandria about 150 years after Christ, under Adrian and Antoninus Pius. This is he from whom the Ptolemaic system took its name. He diligently compared and revised the ancient maps and charts, correcting their errors and supplying their defects by the reports of travellers and navigators, the measured or reputed distances of maps and itineraries, and astronomical calculations, all digested together ; he reduced geography to a regular system, and laid down the situation of places according to minutes and degrees of longitude and latitude as we now have them. His maps were in general use till the last three or four centuries, in which time the progress of the moderns in the knowledge of the globe we inhabit has thrown at a great distance all the ancient geographers.

We are now, some few breaks and chasms excepted, pretty well acquainted with the outline of the globe, and with those parts of it with which we are connected by our commercial or political relations ; but we are still profoundly ignorant of the interior of Africa, and imperfectly acquainted with that of South America, and the western part of North America. We know little of Thibet and the central parts of Asia, and have as yet only touched upon the great continent of New Holland.

The best ancient maps are those of D'Anville. It has required great learning and proportionate skill to bring together the scattered notices which are found in various authors, and to fix the position of places which have been long ago destroyed ; very often the geographer has no other guide than the relation of the historian, that such a place is within six or eight days' journey from another place. In some instances the maps of Ptolemy are lately come into repute again, — as in his delineation of the course of the Niger, which is thought to be favored by modern discoveries. Major Rennel has done much to improve the geography of India.

There are many valuable maps scattered in voyages

and travels, and many of the atlases contain a collection sufficient for all common purposes ; but a complete collection of the best maps and charts, with plans
of harbors, towns, &c. becomes an object of even
princely expense. The French took the lead in this,
as in some other branches of science. The late empress of Russia caused a geographical survey to be
taken of her dominions, which has much improved our
knowledge of the north-eastern regions of Europe and
Asia. We have now, however, both single maps and
atlases which yield to none in accuracy or elegance.

Yours affectionately.

LETTER IV.

DEAR LYDIA, — Geography addresses itself to the eye,
and is easily comprehended : to give a clear idea of
chronology is somewhat more difficult. It is easy to
define it by saying it gives an answer to the question,
When was it done? but the meaning of the *when* is
not quite so obvious. A date is a very artificial thing,
and the world had existed for a long course of centuries before men were aware of its use and necessity.
When is a relative term ; the most natural application
of it is, How long ago, reckoning backwards from the
present moment. Thus, if you were to ask an Indian
when such an event happened he would probably say
— So many harvests ago, when I could but just reach
the boughs of yonder tree ;— in the time of my father,
grandfather, great-grandfather ; still making the time
then present to him the date from which he sets out.
Even where a different method is well understood, we
use in more familiar life this natural kind of chronology,
— The year before I was married, — When Henry, who

is now five years old, was born,—The winter of the
hard frost. These are the epochs which mark the annals of domestic life more readily and with greater
clearness, so far as the real idea of time is concerned,
than the year of our Lord, as long as these are all within the circle of our personal recollection. But when
events are recorded, the relater may be forgotten, and
when again occurs : "When did the historian live? I
understand the relative chronology of his narration ; I
know how the events of it follow one another ; but what
is their relation to general chronology, to time as it relates to me and to other events?"

To know the transactions of a particular reign, that
of Cyrus for instance, in the regular order in which
they happened in that reign, but not to know where
to place them with respect to the history of other
times and nations, is as if we had a very accurate map
of a small island existing somewhere in the boundless
ocean, and could lay down all the bearings and distances of its several towns and villages, but for want of
its longitude and latitude were ignorant of the relative
position of the island itself. Chronology supplies this
longitude and latitude, and fixes every event to its precise point in the chart of universal time. It supplies
a common measure by which I may compare the relater of an event with myself, and his *now* or *ten years
ago* with the present *now* or *ten years*, reckoning from
the time in which I live.

In order to find such a common measure, men have
been led by degrees to fix upon some one known event,
and to make that the centre from which, by regular
distances, the different periods of time are reckoned,
instead of making the present time, which is always
varying, and every man's own existence, the centre.

The first approach to such a mode of computing
time is to date by the reigns of kings ; which, being
public objects of great notoriety, seem to offer them-

selves with great advantage for such a purpose. The
Scripture history, which is the earliest of histories, has
no other than this kind of successive dates: "Now it
came to pass in the fifth year of the king Hezekiah."
"And the time that Solomon reigned in Jerusalem over
all Israel was forty years : and Solomon slept with his
fathers ; and Rehoboam his son reigned in his stead."
From this method a regular chronology might certainly
be deduced, if we had the whole unbroken series ; but
unfortunately there are many gaps and chasms in history ; and you easily see that if any links of the chain
are wanting, the whole computation is rendered imperfect.   Besides, it requires a tedious calculation to bring
it into comparison with other histories and events.   To
say that an event happened in the tenth year of the
reign of King Solomon, gives you only an idea of the
time relative to the histories of that king, but leaves you
quite in the dark as to its relation with the time you
live in, or with the events of the Roman history.

We want therefore an universal date, like a lofty
obelisk, seen by all the country round, from and to
which every distance should be measured.   The most
obvious that offers itself for this purpose is the creation of the world, an event equally interesting to all ;
to us the beginning of time, and from which therefore
time would flow regularly down in an unbroken stream
from the earliest to the latest generations of the human
race.   This would probably therefore have been made
use of, if the date of the creation itself could be ascertained with any exactness ; but as chronologers differ
by more than a thousand years as to the time of that
event, it is necessary previously to mention what system is made use of ; which renders this era obscure
and inconvenient.   It has therefore been found more
convenient, in fact, to take some known event within
the limit of well authenticated history, and to reckon
from that fixed point backwards and forwards.   As we

cannot find the head of the river, and know not its termination, we must raise a pillar upon its banks, and measure our distances from that, both up and down the stream. This event ought to be important, conspicuous, and as interesting as possible, that it may be generally received; for it would spare a great deal of trouble in computation if all the world would make use of the same date. This however has never been the case, chance and national vanity having had their full share in settling them.

The Greeks reckoned by olympiads, but not till more than sixty years after the death of Alexander the Great. The Olympic games were the most brilliant assembly in Greece, the Greeks were very fond of them, they began 776 years before Christ, and each olympiad includes four years. Some of the earlier Greek historians digested their histories by ages, or by the succession of the priestesses of Juno at Argos; others by the archons of Athens or the kings of Lacedæmon. Thucydides uses simply the beginning of the Peloponnesian war, the subject of his history; for, writing to his contemporaries, it seems not to have occurred to him that another date would ever be necessary. The Arundelian marbles, composed sixty years after the death of Alexander the Great, reckon backwards from the then present time.

The Roman era was the building of their city, the eternal city, as they loved to call it.

The Mahometans date from the Hegira, or flight of Mahomet from Mecca, his birth-place, to Medina, A. D. 622; and they have this advantage, that they began almost immediately to use it.

The era used all over the Christian world is the birth of Christ. This was adopted as a date about A. D. 360; and though there is an uncertainty of a few years, which are in dispute, the accuracy is sufficient for any present purpose.

The reign of Nabonassar, the first king of Babylon, of Yesdigerd, the last king of Persia, — who was conquered by the Saracens, — and of the Seleucidæ of Syria, have likewise furnished eras.

Julius Scaliger[1] formed an era which he called the *Julian Period*, being a cycle of 7980 years, produced by multiplying several cycles into one another, so as to carry us back to a period 764 years before the creation of the world. This era, standing out of all history, like the fulcrum which Archimedes wished for, and independent of variation or possibility of mistake, was a very grand idea ; and in measuring everything by itself, measured it by the eternal truth of the laws of the heavenly bodies. But it is not greatly employed, the common era serving all ordinary purposes. In modern histories the olympiads, Roman eras, and others, are reduced, in the margin, to the year of our Lord, or of the creation.

Such is the nature of eras now in such common use that we can with difficulty conceive the confusion in which, for the want of them, all the early part of history is involved, and the strenuous labors of the most learned men which have been employed in arranging them and reducing history to the order in which we now have it.

The earliest history which we possess, as we have before observed, is that of the Jewish scriptures ; these carry us from the creation to about the time of Herodotus : having no date, we are obliged to compute from generations, and to take the reigns of kings where they are given. But a great schism occurs at the very outset. The Septuagint translation of the Mosaic history into Greek, which was made by order of Ptolemy Philadelphus, differs from the Hebrew text by 1400 years from the creation to the birth of Abraham.

[1] Joseph Justus Scaliger, the son of Julius, was the inventor of the Julian period.

The chronology of the Assyrian and Babylonish monarchies is involved in inextricable difficulties; nor are we successful in harmonizing the Greek with the oriental writers of history. The Persian historians make no mention of the defeat of Xerxes by the Greeks, or that of Darius by Alexander. All nations have had the vanity to make their origin mount as high as possible; and they have often invented series of kings, or have reckoned the contemporary individuals of different dynasties as following each other in regular succession, as if one should take the kings of the Heptarchy singly instead of together.

You will perhaps ask, if we have no eras, what have we to reckon by? We have generations and successions of kings. Sir Isaac Newton, who joined wonderful sagacity to profound learning and astronomical skill, made very great reforms in the ancient chronology. He pointed out the difference between generations and successions of kings. A generation is not the life of man; it is the time that elapses before a man sees his successor; and this, reckoning to the birth of the eldest son, is estimated at about thirty years. The succession of kings would seem at first sight to be the same, and so it had been reckoned; but Newton corrected it, on the principle that kings are often cut off prematurely in turbulent times, or are succeeded either by their brothers, or by their uncles, or others older than themselves. The lines of kings of France, England, and other countries within the range of exact chronology, confirmed this principle. He therefore rectified all the ancient chronology according to it; and with the assistance of astronomical observations he found reason to allow, as the average length of a reign, about eighteen or twenty years.

But after all, great part of the chronology of ancient history is founded upon conjecture and clouded with uncertainty.

Although I recommend to you a constant attention
to chronology, I do not think it desirable to load your
memory with a great number of specific dates, both
because it would be too great a burden on the reten-
tive powers, and because it is, after all, not the best
way of attaining clear ideas on the subjects of history.
In order to do this, it is necessary to have in your
mind the relative situation of other countries at the
time of any event recorded in one of them. For
instance, if you have got by heart the dates of the
accession of the kings of Europe, and want to know
whether John lived at the time of the crusades, and in
what state the Greek empire was, you cannot tell without an arithmetical process, which perhaps you may
not be quick enough to make. You cannot tell
whether Constantinople had been taken by the Turks
when the Sicilian Vespers happened; for each fact is
insulated in your mind; and indeed your dates give
you only the dry catalogue of accessions. Nay, you
may read separate histories, and yet not bring them
together if the countries be remote. Each exists in
your mind separately, and you have at no time the
state of the world. But you ought to have an idea at
once of the whole world, as far as history will give it.
You do not see truly what the Greeks were, except you
know that the British Isles were then barbarous.

A few dates therefore, perfectly learned, may suffice,
and will serve as landmarks to prevent your going far
astray in the rest : but it will be highly useful to connect the histories you read in such a manner in your
own mind, that you may be able to refer from one to
the other, and to form them all into a whole. For this
purpose, it is very desirable to observe and retain in
your memory certain coincidences, which may link, as it
were, two nations together. Thus you may remember
that Haroun al Raschid sent to Charlemagne the first
clock that was seen in Europe. If you are reading the

history of Greece when it flourished most, and want to know what the Romans were doing at the same time, you may recollect that they sent to Greece for instruction when they wanted to draw up the laws of the Twelve Tables. Solon and Crœsus connect the history of Lesser Asia with that of Greece. Egbert was brought up in the court of Charlemagne; Philip Augustus of France and Richard I. of England fought in the same crusade against Saladin. Queen Elizabeth received the French ambassador in deep mourning after the massacre of St. Bartholomew.

It may be desirable to keep one kingdom as a meter for the rest. Take for this purpose first the Jews, then the Greeks, the Romans, and, because it is so, our own country: then harmonize and connect all the other dates with these.

That the literary history of a nation may be connected with the political, study also biography, and endeavor to link men of science and literature and artists with political characters. Thus Hippocrates was sent for to the plague of Athens; Leonardo da Vinci died in the arms of Francis I. Often an anecdote, a smart saying, will indissolubly fix a date.

Sometimes you may take a long reign, as that of Elizabeth or Louis XIV., and making that the centre, mark all the contemporary sovereigns, and also the men of letters. Another way is, to make a line of life, composed of distinguished characters who touch each other. It will be of great service to you in this view to study Dr. Priestley's biographical chart; and of still greater, to make one for yourself, and fill it by degrees, as your acquaintance with history extends. Marriages connect the history of different kingdoms; as those of Mary Queen of Scots and Francis II., Philip II. and Mary of England.

These are the kind of dates which make everything lie in the mind in its proper order; they also take fast hold of it. If you forget the exact date by years, you have nothing left; but of circumstances you never lose all idea. As we come nearer to our own times, dates must be more exact. A few years more or less signify little in the destruction of Troy, if we knew it exactly; but the conclusion of the American war should be accurately known, or it will throw other events near it into confusion.

In so extensive a study no auxiliary is to be neglected. Poetry impresses both geography and history in a most agreeable manner upon those who are fond of it. Thus,

"... fair Austria spreads her mournful charms,
The queen, the beauty, sets the world in arms."

A short, lively character in verse is never forgotten :

" From Macedonia's madman to the Swede."

Historic plays deeply impress, but should be read with caution. We take our ideas from Shakespeare more than history : he, indeed, copied pretty exactly from the chroniclers, but other dramatic writers have taken great liberties both with characters and events.

Painting is a good auxiliary; and though in this country history is generally read before we see pictures, they mutually illustrate one another : painting also shows the costume. In France, where pictures are more accessible, there is more knowledge generally diffused of common history. Many have learned Scripture history from the rude figures on Dutch tiles.

I will conclude with the remark, that though the beginner in history may and ought to study dates and epochs for his guidance, chronology can never be fully possessed till after history has been long studied and carefully digested.

Farewell ; and believe me
Yours affectionately.

FASHION.

A VISION.

YOUNG as you are, my dear Flora, you cannot but
have noticed the eagerness with which questions relative to civil liberty have been discussed in every
society. To break the shackles of oppression, and
assert the native rights of man, is esteemed by many
among the noblest efforts of heroic virtue; but vain
is the possession of political liberty if there exists a
tyrant of our own creation, who, without law or reason, or even external force, exercises over us the most
despotic authority; whose jurisdiction is extended
over every part of private and domestic life; controls
our pleasures, fashions our garb, cramps our motions,
fills our lives with vain cares and restless anxiety.
The worst slavery is that which we voluntarily impose
upon ourselves; and no chains are so cumbrous and
galling as those which we are pleased to wear by way
of grace and ornament. Musing upon this idea gave
rise to the following dream or vision:

Methought I was in a country of the strangest and
most singular appearance I had ever beheld: the rivers were forced into jet-d'eaus, and wasted in artificial
water-works; the lakes were fashioned by the hand
of art; the roads were sanded with spar and gold-
dust; the trees all bore the marks of the shears, they
were bent and twisted into the most whimsical forms,
and connected together by festoons of ribbon and silk
fringe; the wild flowers were transplanted into vases
of fine china, and painted with artificial white and red.

The disposition of the ground was full of fancy,
but grotesque and unnatural in the highest degree; it

was all highly cultivated, and bore the marks of wonderful industry; but among its various productions I could hardly discern one that was of any use.

My attention, however, was soon called off from the scenes of inanimate life, by the view of the inhabitants, whose form and appearance were so very preposterous, and, indeed, so unlike anything human, that I fancied myself transported to the country of

> " The Anthropophagi, and men whose heads
> Do grow beneath their shoulders : "

for the heads of many of these people were swelled to an astonishing size, and seemed to be placed in the middle of their bodies. Of some, the ears were distended till they hung upon the shoulders; and of others, the shoulders were raised till they met the ears : there was not one free from some deformity, or monstrous swelling, in one part or other; either it was before, or behind, or about the hips, or the arms were puffed up to an unusual thickness, or the throat was increased to the same size with the poor objects once exhibited under the name of the monstrous Craws : some had no necks; others had necks that reached almost to their waists; the bodies of some were bloated up to such a size, that they could scarcely enter a pair of folding doors ; and others had suddenly sprouted up to such a disproportionate height, that they could not sit upright in their loftiest carriages.

Many shocked me with the appearance of being nearly cut in two, like a wasp ; and I was alarmed at the sight of a few, in whose faces, otherwise very fair and healthy, I discovered an eruption of black spots, which I feared was the fatal sign of some pestilential disorder.

The sight of these various and uncouth deformities inspired me with much pity; which however was soon changed into disgust, when I perceived, with great surprise, that every one of these unfortunate men and women was exceeding proud of his own peculiar deformity, and endeavored to attract my notice to it as much as possible. A lady, in particular, who had a swelling under her throat, larger than any *goître* in the Valais, and which, I am sure, by its enormous projection, prevented her from seeing the path she walked in, brushed by me with an air of the greatest self-complacency, and asked me if she was not a charming creature.

But by this time I found myself surrounded by an immense crowd, who were all pressing along in one direction; and I perceived that I was drawn along with them by an irresistible impulse, which grew stronger every moment. I asked whither we were hurrying with such eager steps; and was told that we were going to the court of Queen Fashion, the great Diana whom all the world worshippeth. I would have retired, but felt myself impelled to go on, though without being sensible of any outward force.

When I came to the royal presence, I was astonished at the magnificence I saw around me. The queen was sitting on a throne, elegantly fashioned in the form of a shell, and inlaid with gems and mother-of-pearl. It was supported by a chameleon, formed of a single emerald. She was dressed in a light robe of changeable silk, which fluttered about her in a profusion of fantastic folds, that imitated the form of clouds, and like them were continually changing their appearance. In one hand she held a rouge-box, and in the other one of those optical glasses which distort figures in length or in breadth, according to the position in which they are held. At the foot of the throne was displayed a profusion of the richest productions of every quarter of the globe, tributes from land and sea, from every animal and plant; perfumes, sparkling stones, drops of pearl, chains of gold, webs of the finest linen; wreaths of flowers, the produce of art, which vied

with the most delicate productions of nature ; forests
of feathers waving their brilliant colors in the air and
canopying the throne ; glossy silks, network of lace,
silvery ermine, soft folds of vegetable wool, rustling
paper, and shining spangles ; — the whole intermixed
with pendants and streamers of the gayest tinctured
ribbon.

All these together made so brilliant an appearance
that my eyes were at first dazzled, and it was some
time before I recovered myself enough to observe the
ceremonial of the court.   Near the throne, and its
chief supports, stood the queen's two prime ministers,
Caprice on one side, and Vanity on the other.   Two
officers seemed chiefly busy among the attendants.
One of them was a man with a pair of shears in his
hand and a goose by his side, — a mysterious emblem, of which I could not fathom the meaning : he
sat cross-legged, like the great lama of the Tartars.
He was busily employed in cutting out coats and garments ; not, however, like Dorcas, for the poor, — nor,
indeed, did they seem intended for any mortal whatever, so ill were they adapted to the shape of the human body.   Some of the garments were extravagantly
large, others as preposterously small : of others, it was
difficult to guess to what part of the person they were
meant to be applied.   Here were coverings which did
not cover ; ornaments which disfigured ; and defences
against the weather, more slight and delicate than
what they were meant to defend ; but all were eagerly
caught up, without distinction, by the crowd of votaries
who were waiting to receive them.

The other officer was dressed in a white succinct
linen garment, like a priest of the lower order.   He
moved in a cloud of incense more highly scented than
the breezes of Arabia ; he carried a tuft of the whitest
down of the swan in one hand, and in the other a small
iron instrument heated red-hot, which he brandished

in the air. It was with infinite concern I beheld the Graces, bound at the foot of the throne, and obliged to officiate as handmaids under the direction of these two officers.

I now began to inquire by what laws this queen governed her subjects, but soon found her administration was that of the most arbitrary tyrant ever known. Her laws are exactly the reverse of those of the Medes and Persians; for they are changed every day, and every hour: and what makes the matter still more perplexing, they are in no written code, nor even made public by proclamation: they are promulgated only by whispers, an obscure sign, or turn of the eye, which those only who have the happiness to stand near the queen can catch with any degree of precision: yet the smallest transgression of the laws is severely punished; not indeed by fines or imprisonment, but by a sort of interdict similar to that which in superstitious times was laid by the Pope on disobedient princes, and which operated in such a manner that no one would eat, drink, or associate with the forlorn culprit, and he was almost deprived of the use of fire and water.

This difficulty of discovering the will of the goddess occasioned so much crowding to be near the throne, such jostling and elbowing of one another, that I was glad to retire and observe what I could among the scattered crowd: and the first thing I took notice of was various instruments of torture which everywhere met my eyes. Torture has in most other governments of Europe been abolished by the mild spirit of the times; but it reigns here in full force and terror. I saw officers of this cruel court employed in boring holes with red-hot wires, in the ears, nose, and various parts of the body, and then distending them with the weight of metal chains, or stones cut into a variety of shapes: some had invented a contrivance for cramp-

ing the feet in such a manner that many are lamed by
it for their whole lives. Others I saw, slender and
delicate in their form and naturally nimble as the
young antelope, who were obliged to carry constantly
about with them a cumbrous unwieldy machine, of a
pyramidal form, several ells in circumference.

But the most common and one of the worst instruments of torture was a small machine armed with fish-
bone and ribs of steel, wide at top but extremely small
at bottom. In this detestable invention the queen orders the bodies of her female subjects to be inclosed :
it is then, by means of silk cords, drawn closer and
closer at intervals, till the unhappy victim can scarcely
breathe ; and they have found the exact point that
can be borne without fainting, which, however, not un-
frequently happens. The flesh is often excoriated, and
the very ribs bent, by this cruel process. Yet what astonished me more than all the rest, these sufferings are
borne with a degree of fortitude which, in a better cause,
would immortalize a hero or canonize a saint. The
Spartan who suffered the fox to eat into his vitals, did
not bear pain with greater resolution : and as the Spartan mothers brought their children to be scourged at
the altar of Diana, so do the mothers here bring their
children,—and chiefly those whose tender sex one would
suppose excused them from such exertions,— and early
inure them to this cruel discipline. But neither Spartan, nor Dervise, nor Bonze, nor Carthusian monk, ever
exercised more unrelenting severities over their bodies,
than these young zealots : indeed the first lesson they are
taught, is a surrender of their own inclinations and an
implicit obedience to the commands of the goddess.

But they have, besides, a more solemn kind of ded-
ication, something similar to the rite of confirmation.
When a young woman approaches the marriageable
age, she is led to the altar : her hair, which before
fell loosely about her shoulders, is tied up in a tress,

sweet oils drawn from roses and spices are poured
upon it; she is involved in a cloud of scented dust,
and invested with ornaments under which she can
scarcely move. After this solemn ceremony, which is
generally concluded by a dance round the altar, the
damsel is obliged to a still stricter conformity than before to the laws and customs of the court, and any de-
viation from them is severely punished.

The courtiers of Alexander, it is said, flattered him
by carrying their heads on one side, because he had
the misfortune to have a wry neck; but all adulation
is poor, compared to what is practised in this court.
Sometimes the queen will lisp and stammer, — and
then none of her attendants can speak plain; sometimes she chooses to totter as she walks, — and then
they are seized with sudden lameness: according as
she appears half undressed, or veiled from head to
foot, her subjects become a procession of nuns, or a
troop of Bacchanalian nymphs. I could not help ob-
serving, however, that those who stood at the greatest
distance from the throne were the most extravagant in
their imitation.

I was by this time thoroughly disgusted with the
character of a sovereign at once so light and so cruel,
so fickle and so arbitrary, when one who stood next
me bade me attend to still greater contradictions in her
character, and such as might serve to soften the indignation I had conceived. He took me to the back of
the throne, and made me take notice of a number of
industrious poor, to whom the queen was secretly dis-
tributing bread. I saw the Genius of Commerce doing her homage, and discovered the British cross woven
into the insignia of her dignity.

While I was musing on these things, a murmur arose
among the crowd, and I was told that a young votary
was approaching. I turned my head, and saw a light
figure, the folds of whose garment showed the elegant

turn of the limbs they covered, tripping along with
the step of a nymph.   I soon knew it to be yourself :
— I saw you led up to the altar, — I saw your beautiful
hair tied in artificial tresses, and its bright gloss stained
with colored dust, — I even fancied I beheld produced
the dreadful instruments of torture ; — my emotions increased : — I cried out, " Oh, spare her ! spare my
Flora !" with so much vehemence that I awaked.

DESCRIPTION OF TWO SISTERS.

DEAR COUSIN, — Our conversation last night upon
beauties put me in mind of two charming sisters, with
whom I think you must be acquainted as well as I,
though they were not in your list of belles.   Their
charms are very different however ; the youngest is
generally thought the handsomest, and yet other beauties shine more in her company than in her sister's ;
whether it be that her gay looks diffuse a lustre on all
around, while her sister's beauty has an air of majesty
which strikes with awe, or that the younger sets every
one she is with in the fairest light, and discovers perfections which were before concealed, whilst the elder
seems only solicitous to set off her own person and
throw a shade upon every one else.   Yet, what you will
think strange, it is she who is generally preferred for a
confidant ; for her sister, with all her amiable qualities,
cannot keep a secret.

Oh, what an eye the younger has, as if she could
look a person through ; yet modest is her countenance,
even and composed her pace, and she treads so softly,
— " smooth sliding without step," as Milton says
She seldom meets you without blushing, — her sister
cannot blush, — she dresses very gayly, sometimes in

clouded silks, which indeed she first brought into fashion, but blue is her most becoming color, and she generally appears in it. Now and then, she wears a very
rich scarf, or sash, braided with all manner of colors.

The elder, like the Spanish ladies, dresses in black
in order to set off her jewels, of which she has a greater
quantity than Lady ——, and, if I might judge, much
finer. I cannot pretend to give you a catalogue of
them ; they are of all sizes, and set in all figures : her
enemies say she does well to adorn her dusky brow
with brilliants, and that without them she would be but
little taken notice of; but certain it is, she has inspired
more serious and enthusiastic passions than her sister,
whose admirers are often fops more in love with themselves than with her. A learned clergyman some time
ago fell deeply in love with her, and wrote a fine copy
of verses on her ; and what was worst, her sister could
not go into company without hearing them.

One thing they quite agree in, — not to go out of
their way or alter their pace for anybody. Once or
twice indeed I have heard that the younger . . . but it
was a great while ago, and she was not so old then,
and was more complaisant. She is generally waked
with a fine concert of music, the other prefers a good
solo.

But see, the younger beauty looks pale and sick, —
she faints, — she is certainly dying, — a slight blush
still upon her cheek, — it fades, fast, fast. — She is
gone, yet a sweet smile overspreads her countenance.
Will she revive? Shall I ever see her again? Who can
tell me?

PIC-NIC.

PRAY, mamma, what is the meaning of *pic-nic?* I have heard lately once or twice of a *pic-nic supper,* and I cannot think what it means ; I looked for the word in Johnson's Dictionary and could not find it.

I should wonder if you had ; the word was not coined in Johnson's time ; and if it had been, I believe he would have disdained to insert it among the legitimate words of the language. I cannot tell you the derivation of the phrase. I believe pic-nic is originally a cant word, and was first applied to a supper or other meal in which the entertainment is not provided by any one person, but each of the guests furnishes his dish. In a pic-nic supper one supplies the fowls, another the fish, another the wine and fruit, &c. ; and they all sit down together and enjoy it.

A very sociable way of making an entertainment.

Yes, and I would have you observe, that the principle of it may be extended to many other things. No one has a right to be entertained gratis in society ; he must expend, if he wishes to enjoy. Conversation, particularly, is a pic-nic feast, where every one is to contribute something, according to his genius and ability. Different talents and acquirements compose the different dishes of the entertainment, and the greater variety, the better ; but every one must bring something, for society will not tolerate any one long who lives wholly at the expense of his neighbors. Did not you observe how agreeably we were entertained at Lady Isabella's party last night?

Yes : one of the young ladies sung, and another exhibited her drawings, and a gentleman told some very
good stories.

True : another lady who is very much in the fashionable world gave us a great deal of anecdote ; Dr. R.,
who is just returned from the continent, gave us an
interesting account of the state of Germany ; and in
another part of the room a cluster was gathered round
an Edinburgh student and a young Oxonian, who were
holding a lively debate on the power of galvanism.
But Lady Isabella herself was the charm of the party.

I think she talked very little ; and I do not recollect
anything she said which was particularly striking.

That is true. But it was owing to her address and
attention to her company that others talked and were
heard by turns ; that the modest were encouraged and
drawn out, and those inclined to be noisy restrained
and kept in order. She blended and harmonized the
talents of each ; brought those together who were
likely to be agreeable to each other, and gave us no
more of herself than was necessary to set off others. I
noticed particularly her good offices to an accomplished
but very bashful lady and a reserved man of science,
who wished much to be known to one another, but
who would never have been so without her introduction. As soon as she had fairly engaged them in an
interesting conversation, she left them, regardless of
her own entertainment, and seated herself by poor Mr.
——, purely because he was sitting in a corner and no
one attended to him. You know that in chemical
preparations two substances often require a third, to
enable them to mix and unite together. Lady Isabella
possesses this amalgamating power : — this is what she
brings to the pic-nic. I should add, that two or three
times I observed she dexterously changed topics, and
suppressed stories which were likely to bear hard on
the profession or connections of some of the company.

In short, the party which was so agreeable under her
harmonizing influence, would have had quite a different aspect without her.   These merits, however, might
easily escape a young observer. But I dare say you did
not fail to notice Sir Henry B——'s lady, who was de-
claiming with so much enthusiasm, in the midst of a
circle of gentlemen which she had drawn around her,
upon the *beau ideal.*

No indeed, mamma; I never heard so much fire
and feeling : — and what a flow of elegant language ! I
do not wonder her eloquence was so much admired.

She has a great deal of eloquence and taste : she
has travelled, and is acquainted with the best works of
art.   I am not sure, however, whether the gentlemen
were admiring most her declamation or the fine turn
of her hands and arms.   She has a different attitude
for every sentiment. Some observations which she
made upon the beauty of statues seemed to me to go
to the verge of what a modest female will allow herself
to say upon such subjects, — but she has travelled.
She was sensible that she could not fail to gain by
the conversation while beauty of form was the subject
of it.

Pray what did ——, the great poet, bring to the
pic-nic? — for I think he hardly opened his mouth.

He brought his fame. Many would be gratified
with merely seeing him who had entertained them in
their closets ; and he who had so entertained them had
a right to be himself entertained in that way which he
had no talent for joining in.   Let every one, I repeat,
bring to the entertainment something of the best he
possesses, and the pic-nic table will seldom fail to afford a plentiful banquet.

WRITTEN ON A MARBLE.

THE world's something bigger,
But just of this figure,
And speckled with mountains and seas ;
Your heroes are overgrown schoolboys
Who scuffle for empires and toys,
And kick the poor ball as they please.
Now Cæsar, now Pompey, gives law ;
And Pharsalia's plain,
Though heaped with the slain,
Was only a game at *taw*.

LETTER FROM GRIMALKIN TO SELIMA.

MY DEAR SELIMA, — As you are now going to quit
the fostering cares of a mother, to enter, young as you
are, into the wide world, and conduct yourself by your
own prudence, I cannot forbear giving you some part-
ing advice in this important era of your life.

Your extreme youth, and permit me to add, the
giddiness incident to that period, make me particularly
anxious for your welfare. In the first place, then, let
me beg you to remember that life is not to be spent in
running after your own tail. Remember you were sent
into the world to catch rats and mice. It is for this
you are furnished with sharp claws, whiskers to improve
your scent, and with such an elasticity and spring in
your limbs. Never lose sight of this great end of your
existence. When you and your sister are jumping over

my back, and kicking and scratching one another's
noses, you are indulging the propensities of your nature,
and perfecting yourselves in agility and dexterity. But
remember that these frolics are only preparatory to the
grand scene of action. Life is long, but youth is short.
The gayety of the kitten will most assuredly go off.
In a few months, nay even weeks, those spirits and that
playfulness, which now exhilarate all who behold you,
will subside ; and I beg you to reflect how contemptible
you will be, if you should have the gravity of an old cat
without that usefulness which alone can ensure respect
and protection for your maturer years.

In the first place, my dear child, obtain a command
over your appetites, and take care that no tempting
opportunity ever induces you to make free with the
pantry or larder of your mistress. You may possibly
slip in and out without observation ; you may lap a
little cream, or run away with a chop without its being
missed : but depend upon it, such practices sooner or
later will be found out ; and if in a single instance
you are discovered, everything which is missing will be
charged upon you. If Mrs. Betty or Mrs. Susan chooses
to regale herself with a cold breast of chicken which was
set by for supper, — you will have clawed it ; or a rasp-
berry cream, — you will have lapped it. Nor is this all.
If you have once thrown down a single cup in your
eagerness to get out of the storeroom, every china plate
and dish that is ever broken in the house, you will have
broken it ; and though your back promises to be pretty
broad, it will not be broad enough for all the mischief
that will be laid upon it. Honesty you will find is the
best policy.

Remember that the true pleasures of life consist in
the exertion of our own powers. If you were to feast
every day upon roasted partridges from off Dresden
china, and dip your whiskers in syllabubs and creams,
it could never give you such true enjoyment as the

commonest food procured by the labor of your own paws. When you have once tasted the exquisite pleasure of catching and playing with a mouse, you will despise the gratification of artificial dainties.

I do not, with some moralists, call cleanliness a half virtue only. Remember, it is one of the most essential to your sex and station ; and if ever you should fail in it, I sincerely hope Mrs. Susan will bestow upon you a good whipping.

Pray do not spit at strangers who do you the honor to take notice of you. It is very uncivil behavior, and I have often wondered that kittens of any breeding should be guilty of it.

Avoid thrusting your nose into every closet and cupboard, — unless indeed you smell mice ; in which case it is very becoming.

Should you live, as I hope you will, to see the children of your patroness, you must prepare yourself to exercise that branch of fortitude which consists in patient endurance : for you must expect to be lugged about, pinched and pulled by the tail, and played a thousand tricks with ; all which you must bear without putting out a claw : for you may depend upon it, if you attempt the least retaliation you will forever lose the favor of your mistress.

Should there be favorites in the house, such as tame birds, dormice, or a squirrel, great will be your temptations. In such a circumstance, if the cage hangs low and the door happens to be left open, — to govern your appetite I know will be a difficult task. But remember that nothing is impossible to the governing mind ; and that there are instances upon record of cats who, in the exercise of self-government, have overcome the strongest propensities of their nature.

If you would make yourself agreeable to your mistress, you must observe times and seasons. You must not startle her by jumping upon her in a rude manner :

and above all, be sure to sheathe your claws when you lay your paw upon her lap.

You have, like myself, been brought up in the coun-try, and I fear you may regret the amusements it af-fords; such as catching butterflies, climbing trees, and watching birds from the windows, which I have done with great delight for a whole morning together. But these pleasures are not essential. A town life has also its gratifications. You may make many pleasant ac-quaintances in the neighboring courts and alleys. A concert upon the tiles in a fine moonlight summer's evening may at once gratify your ear and your social feelings. Rats and mice are to be met with every-where: and at any rate you have reason to be thank-ful that so creditable a situation has been found for you; without which you must have followed the fate of your poor brothers, and with a stone about your neck have been drowned in the next pond.

It is only when you have kittens yourself that you will be able to appreciate the cares of a mother. How unruly have you been when I wanted to wash your face! how undutiful in galloping about the room in-stead of coming immediately when I called you! But nothing can subdue the affections of a parent. Being grave and thoughtful in my nature, and having the ad-vantage of residing in a literary family, I have mused deeply on the subject of education; I have pored by moonlight over Locke, and Edgeworth, and Mrs. Ham-ilton, and the laws of association: but after much cogi-tation I am only convinced of this, that kittens will be kittens, and old cats old cats. May you, my dear child, be an honor to all your relations and to the whole feline race. May you see your descendants of the fiftieth generation. And when you depart this life, may the lamentations of your kindred exceed in pathos the melody of an Irish howl.

Signed by the paw of your affectionate mother,

GRIMALKIN.

ALLEGORY ON SLEEP.

My dear Miss D., — The affection I bear you, and
the sincere regard I have for your welfare, will, I hope,
excuse the liberty I am going to take in remonstrating
against the indulgence of a too partial affection which
I see with sorrow is growing upon you every day.

You start at the imputation : but hear me with patience ; and if your own heart, your own reason, does
not bear witness to what I say, then blame my suspicions and my freedom.

But need I say much to convince you of the power
this favored lover, whose name I will not mention,
has over you, when at this very moment he absorbs
all your faculties, and engrosses every power of your
mind to such a degree as leaves it doubtful whether
this friendly admonition will reach your ear, lost as
you are in the soft enchantment? Is it not evident
that in his presence you are dead to everything
around you? The voice of your nearest friends, your
most sprightly and once-loved amusements, cannot
draw your attention ; you breathe, you exist, only for
him. And when at length he has left you, do not I
behold you languid, pale, bearing in your eyes and
your whole carriage the marks of his power over you?
When we parted last night, did not I see you impatient to sink into his arms? Have you never been
caught reclined on his bosom, on a soft carpet of
flowers, on the banks of a purling stream, where the
murmuring of the waters, the whispering of the trees,
the silence and solitude of the place, and the luxuri-

ous softness of everything around you, favored his approach and disposed you to listen to his addresses? Nay, in that sacred temple which ought to be dedicated to higher affections, has he never stolen insensibly on your mind, and sealed your ears against the voice of the preacher, though never so persuasive? Has not his influence over you greatly increased within these few weeks? Does he not every day demand, do you not every day sacrifice to him, a larger portion of your time?

Not content with devoting to him those hours

" When business, noise, and day are fled,"

does he not encroach upon the morning watches, break in upon your studies, and detain your mind from the pursuit of knowledge and the pursuit of pleasure, — of all pleasure but the enervating indulgence of your passion?

Diana, who still wishes to number you in her train, invites you to join in her lively sports; for you Aurora bathes the new-born rose in dew, and streaks the clouds with gold and crimson; and Youth and Health offer a thousand innocent pleasures to your acceptance.

And, let me ask you, what can you find in the company of him with whom you are thus enamored, to make you amends for all that you give up for his sake? Does he entertain you with anything but the most incoherent rhapsodies, the most romantic and visionary tales? To believe the strange, improbable, and contradictory things he tells you, requires a credulity beyond that of an infant. If he has ever spoken truth, it is mixed with so much falsehood and obscurity, that it is esteemed the certain sign of a weak mind to be much affected with what he says.

As I wish to draw a true portrait, I will by no means disguise his good qualities; and shall therefore allow that he is a friend to the unhappy and the friendless, that his breast is the only pillow for misfortune to repose on, and that his approaches are so gentle and insinuating as in some moments to be almost irresistible. If he is at all disposed to partiality, it is in favor of the poor and mean, with whom he is generally thought to associate more readily than with the rich. Yet he dispenses favors to all: and those who are most disposed to rebel against his power and treat him with contempt, could never render themselves quite independent of him.

He is of a very ancient family, and came in long before the Conquest. He has a half-brother, somewhat younger than himself, who has made his name very famous in the world: he is a tall meagre figure, with a ghastly air and a most forbidding countenance ; he delights in slaughter, and has destroyed more men than Cæsar or Alexander.

He who is the subject of my letter is fond of peace, sleek and corpulent, with a mild heavy eye and a physiognomy perfectly placid ; yet with all this opposition of feature and character, there is such a resemblance between them (as often happens in family likenesses), that in some lights and attitudes you can scarce distinguish the one from the other.

To finish the description of your lover, — he is generally crowned with flowers, but of the most languid kind, such as poppies and cowslips ; and he is attended by a number of servants, thin and light-footed, to whom he does not give the same livery ; for some are dressed in the gayest, others in the most gloomy habits imaginable, but all fantastic.-

He is subject to many strange antipathies, and as strange likings. The warbling of the lark, to others so agreeable, is to him the harshest discord, and Peter could not start more at the crowing of a cock. The slightest accident, the cry of an infant, a mouse behind the wainscot, will oftentimes totally disconcert and put him to flight, and at other times he will not regard the loudest thunder. His favorite animal is the dormouse, and his music the dropping of water, the low tinkling of a distant bell, the humming of bees, and the hollow sound of the wind rustling through the trees.

But I have now said enough to let you into the true character of this powerful enchanter. You will answer, I know, to all this, that he begins by enslaving every faculty that might resist him, and that his power must be already broken before Reason can exert herself. You will perhaps likewise tell me (and I must acknowledge the justice of the retort) that I myself, though my situation affords a thousand reasons to resist him which do not take place with you, have been but too sensible of his attractions.

With blushes I confess the charge. At this moment, however, the charm is broken, and Reason has her full empire over me. Let me exhort you therefore. . . . But why exhort you to what is already done? for if this letter has made its way to your ear, if your eye is now perusing its contents, the spell is dissolved, and you are no longer sunk in the embraces of *Sleep*.

A HYMN.

LIFT up thyself, O mourning soul! lift up thyself, raise thine eyes that are wet with tears!

Why are thine eyes wet with tears? why are they bent continually upon the earth? and why dost thou go mourning as one forsaken of thy God?

O thou that toilest ever and restest not; thou that wishest ever and art not satisfied; thou that carest ever and art not 'stablished;

Why dost thou toil and wish? why is thine heart withered with care, and thine eyes sunk with watching?

Rest quietly on thy couch, steep thine eyelids in sleep, wrap thyself in sleep as in a garment; for he careth for thee :

He is with thee, he is about thee, he compasseth thee, he compasseth thee on every side.

The voice of thy Shepherd among the rocks! he calleth thee, he beareth thee tenderly in his arms; he suffereth thee not to stray.

Thy soul is precious in his sight, O child of many hopes!

For he careth for thee in the things which perish, and he hath provided yet better things than those.

Raise thyself, O beloved soul! turn thine eyes from care, and sin, and pain; turn them to the brightness of the heavens, and contemplate thine inheritance; for thy birthright is in the skies, and thine inheritance amongst the stars of light.

The herds of the pasture sicken and die, they lie down among the clods of the valley, the foot passeth over them; they are no more. But it is not so with thee.

For the Almighty is the father of thy spirit, and he hath given thee a portion of his own immortality.

Look around thee and behold the earth, for it is the gift of thy Father to thee and to thy sons, that they should possess it.

Out of the ground cometh forth food; the hills are covered with fresh shade; and the animals, thy subjects, sport among the trees.

Delight thyself in them, for they are good; and all that thou seest is thine.

But nothing that thou seest is like unto thyself; thou art not of them, nor shalt thou return to them.

Thou hast a mighty void which they cannot fill; thou hast an immortal hunger which they cannot sat-

8

isfy : they cannot nourish, they cannot support, they are not worthy that they should occupy thee.

As the fire which while it resteth on the earth yet sendeth forth sparks continually towards heaven ; so do thou from amidst the world send up fervent thoughts to God.

As the lark, though her nest is on the low ground, as soon as she becometh fledged, poiseth her wings, and finding them strong to bear her through the light air, springeth up aloft, singing as she soars ;

So let thy desires mount swiftly upwards, and thou shalt see the world beneath thy feet.

And be not overwhelmed with many thoughts. Heaven is thine, and God is thine : thou shalt be blessed with everlasting salvation and peace upon thy head forever more.

ON FRIENDSHIP.

FRIENDSHIP is that warm, tender, lively attachment, which takes place between persons in whom a similarity of tastes and manners, joined to frequent intercourse, has produced an habitual fondness for each other. It is not among our duties, for it does not flow from any of the necessary relations of society ; but it has its duties when voluntarily entered into. In its highest perfection it can only, I believe, subsist between two ; for that unlimited confidence and perfect conformity of inclinations which it requires, cannot well be found in a larger number : besides, one such friendship fills the heart, and leaves no want or desire after another.

Friendship, where it is quite sincere and affectionate, free from affectation or interested views, is one of the greatest blessings of life. It doubles our joys, and it lessens our sorrows, when we are able to pour both into the bosom of one who takes the tenderest part in all our interests, who is to us as another self. We love to communicate all our feelings ; and it is in the highest degree grateful where we can do it to one who will enter into them all ; who takes an interest in everything that befalls us ; before whom we can freely indulge even our little weaknesses and foibles, and show our minds as it were undressed ; who will take part in all our schemes, advise us in any emergency ; who rejoices in our company, and who, we are sure, thinks of us in our absence.

With regard to the choice of friends, there is little to say : for a friend was never chosen. A secret sympathy, the attraction of a thousand nameless qualities ; a charm in the expression of the countenance, even in the voice, or the manner, a similarity of circumstances, — these are the things that begin attachment, which is fostered by being in a situation which gives occasion for frequent intercourse ; and this depends upon chance. Reason and prudence have, however, much to do in restraining our choice of improper or dangerous friends. They are improper, if our line of life and pursuits are so totally different as to make it improbable we shall long keep up an intimacy, at least without sacrificing to it connections of duty ; they are dangerous, if they are in any respect vicious.

It has been made a question whether friendship can subsist among the vicious. If by vicious be meant those who are void of the social, generous, and affectionate feelings, it is most certain it cannot ; because these make the very essence of it. But it is very possible for persons to possess fine feelings, without that steady principle which alone constitutes virtue ; and it does not appear why such may not feel a real friendship. It will not indeed be so likely to be lasting, and is often succeeded by bitter enmities.

The duties of friendship are, first, sincere and disinterested affection.   This seems self-evident : and yet there are many who pretend to love their friends, when at the same time they only take delight in them, as we delight in a fine voice or a good picture.   If you love your friend, you will love him when his powers of pleasing and entertaining you have given way to malady or depression of spirits ; you will study *his* interest and satisfaction, you will be ready to resign his company, to promote his advantageous settlement at a distant residence, to favor his connection with other friends ; — these are the tests of true affection : without such a disposition, you may enjoy your friend, but you do not love him.

Next, friendship requires pure sincerity and the most unreserved confidence.   Sincerity every man has a right to expect from us, but every man has not a right to our confidence : this is the sacred and peculiar privilege of friendship ; and so essential is it to the very idea of this connection, that even to serve a friend without giving him our confidence, is but going half way ; — it may command gratitude, but will not produce love.   Above all things, the general tenor of our thoughts and feelings must be shown to our friends exactly as they are ; without any of those glosses, colorings, and disguises which we do, and partly must, put on in our commerce with the world.

Another duty resulting from this confidence is inviolable secrecy in what has been entrusted to us.   To every one indeed we owe secrecy in what we are formally entrusted with ; but with regard to a friend, this extends to the concealing everything which in the fulness of his heart and in the freedom of unguarded conversation he has let drop, if you have the least idea it may in any manner injure or offend him.   In short, you are to consider yourself as always, to him, under an implied promise of secrecy ; and should even the friendship dissolve, it would be in the highest degree ungenerous to consider this obligation as dissolved with it.

In the next place, a friend has a right to our best advice on every emergency ; and this even though we run the risk of offending him by our frankness. Friends should consider themselves as the sacred guardians of each other's virtue ; and the noblest testimony they can give of their affection is the correction of the faults of those they love. But this generous solicitude must be distinguished from a teasing, captious, or too officious notice of all the little defects and frailties which their close intercourse with each other brings continually into view : these must be overlooked or borne with ; for as we are not perfect ourselves, we have no right to expect our friends should be so.

Friends are most easily acquired in youth, but they are likewise most easily lost : the petulance and impetuosity of that age, the eager competitions and rivalships of an active life, and more especially the various changes in rank and fortune, connections, party, opinions, or local situation, burst asunder or silently untwist the far greater part of those friendships which, in the warmth of youthful attachment, we had fondly promised ourselves should be indissoluble.

Happy is he to whom, in the maturer season of life, there remains one tried and constant friend : their affection, mellowed by the hand of time, endeared by the recollection of enjoyments, toils, and even sufferings shared together, becomes the balm, the consolation, and the treasure of life. Such a friendship is inestimable, and should be preserved with the utmost care ; for it is utterly impossible for any art ever to transfer to another the effect of all those accumulated associations which endear to us the friend of our early years.

These considerations should likewise induce us to

show a tender indulgence to our friends, even for those faults which most sensibly wound the feeling heart, — a growing coldness and indifference. These may be brought on by many circumstances, which do not imply a bad heart; and provided we do not by bitter complaints and an open rupture preclude the possibility of a return, in a more favorable conjuncture the friendships of our youth may knit again, and be cultivated with more genuine tenderness than ever.

I must here take occasion to observe, that there is nothing young people ought to guard against with more care than a parade of feeling, and a profusion of exaggerated protestations. These may sometimes proceed from the amiable warmth of a youthful heart; but they much oftener flow from the affectation of sentiment, which is both contemptible and morally wrong.

All that has been said of the duties or of the pleasures of friendship in its most exalted sense, is applicable in a proportionate degree to every connection in which there exists any portion of this generous affection : so far as it does exist in the various relations of life, so far it renders them interesting and valuable ; and were the capacity for it taken away from the human heart, it would find a dreary void, and starve amidst all the means of enjoyment the world could pour out before it.

CONFIDENCE AND MODESTY.

A FABLE.

WHEN the gods, knowing it to be for the benefit of mortals that the few should lead and that the many should follow, sent down into this lower world Ignorance and Wisdom, they decreed to each of them an attendant and guide, to conduct their steps and facilitate their introduction. To Wisdom they gave Confidence, and Ignorance they placed under the guidance of Modesty. Thus paired, the parties travelled about the world for some time with mutual satisfaction.

Wisdom, whose eye was clear and piercing, and commanded a long reach of country, followed her conductor with pleasure and alacrity. She saw the windings of the road at a great distance; her foot was firm, her ardor was unbroken, and she ascended the hill or traversed the plain with speed and safety.

Ignorance, on the other hand, was short-sighted and timid. When she came to a spot where the road branched out in different directions, or was obliged to pick her way through the obscurity of the tangled thicket, she was frequently at a loss, and was accustomed to stop till some one appeared, to give her the necessary information, which the interesting countenance of her companion seldom failed to procure her.

Wisdom in the mean time, led by a natural instinct, advanced toward the temple of Science and Eternal Truth. For some time the way lay plain before her, and she followed her guide with unhesitating steps: but she had not proceeded far before the paths grew intricate and entangled; the meeting branches of the trees spread darkness over her head, and steep mountains barred her way, whose summits, lost in clouds, ascended beyond the reach of mortal vision. At every new turn of the road her guide urged her to proceed; but after advancing a little way, she was often obliged to measure back her steps, and often found herself involved in the mazes of a labyrinth which, after exercising her patience and her strength, ended but where it began.

In the mean time Ignorance, who was naturally impatient, could but ill bear the continual doubts and hesitation of her companion. She hated deliberation, and could not submit to delay. At length it so happened that she found herself on a spot where three ways met, and no indication was to be found which might direct her to the right road. Modesty advised her to wait; and she had waited till her patience was exhausted. At that moment Confidence, who was in disgrace with Wisdom for some false steps he had led her into, and who had just been discarded from her presence, came up, and offered himself to be her guide. He was accepted. Under his auspices Ignorance, naturally swift of foot, and who could at any time have outrun Wisdom, boldly pressed forward, pleased and satisfied with her new companion. He knocked at every door, visited castle and convent, and introduced his charge to many a society whence Wisdom found herself excluded.

Modesty, in the mean time, finding she could be of no further use to her charge, offered her services to Wisdom. They were mutually pleased with each other, and soon agreed never to separate. And ever since that time Ignorance has been led by Confidence, and Modesty has been found in the society of Wisdom.

ON EXPENSE.

A DIALOGUE.

You seem to be in a reverie, Harriet; or are you tired with your long bustling walk through the streets of London?

Not at all, papa; but I was wondering at something.

A grown person even cannot even walk through such a metropolis without meeting with many things to wonder at. But let us hear the particular subject of your admiration; was it the height and circumference of St. Paul's, or the automatons, or the magical effect of the Panorama that has most struck you?

No, papa; but I was wondering how you who have always so much money in your pockets can go through the streets of London, all full of fine shops, and not buy things: I am sure if I had money I could not help spending it all.

As you never have a great deal of money, and it is given you only to please your fancy with, there is no harm in your spending it in any thing you have a mind to; but it is very well for you and me too that the money does not *burn* in my pocket as it does in yours.

No, to be sure you would not spend all your money in those shops, because you must buy bread and meat, but you might spend a good deal. But you walk past just as if you did not see them: you never stop to give one look. Now tell me really, papa, can you help *wishing* for all those pretty things that stand in the shop windows?

For all! Would you have me wish for all of them? But I will answer you seriously. I do walk by these tempting shops without wishing for· any thing, and indeed in general without seeing them.

Well, that is because you are a man, and you do not care for what I admire so very much.

No, there you are mistaken; for though I may not admire them so very much as you say you do, there are a vast number of things sold in London which it would give me great pleasure to have in my possession. I should greatly like one of Dollond's best reflecting telescopes. I could lay out a great deal of money, if I had it to spare, in books of botany and natural history. Nay, I assure you I should by no means be indifferent to the fine fruit exposed at the fruit-shops; the plums with the blue upon them as if they were just taken from the tree, the luscious hot-house grapes, and the melons and pine-apples. Believe me, I could eat these things with as good a relish as you could.

Then how can you help buying them, when you have money; and especially, papa, how can you help thinking about them and wishing for them?

London is the best place in the world to cure a person of extravagance, and even of extravagant wishes. I see so many costly things here which I know I could not buy, even if I were to lay out all the money I have in the world, that I never think of buying any thing which I do not really want. Our furniture, you know, is old and plain. Perhaps if there were only a little better furniture to be had, I might be tempted to change it; but when I see houses where a whole fortune is laid out in decorating a set of apartments, I am content with chairs whose only use is to sit down upon, and tables that were in fashion half a century ago. In short, I have formed the habit of *self-government*, one of the most useful powers a man can be possessed of. Self-government belongs only to civilized man, — a savage has no idea of it. A North-American Indian is temperate when he has no liquor; but as soon as liquor is within his reach, he invariably drinks till he is first furious and then insensible. He possesses no power over himself, and he literally can no more help it than iron can help being drawn by the loadstone.

But he seldom gets liquor, so he has not a habit of drinking.

You are right; he has not the habit of drinking, but he wants the habit of self-control: this can only be gained by being often in the midst of temptations, and resisting them. This is the wholesome discipline of the mind. The first time a man denies himself any thing he likes and which it is in his power to procure, there is a great struggle within him, and uneasy wishes will disturb for some time the tranquillity of his mind. He has gained the victory, but the enemy dies hard. The next time, he does not wish so much, but he still thinks about it. After a while he does not think of it; he does not even see it. A person of moderate fortune, like myself, who lives in a gay and splendid metropolis, is accustomed to see every day a hundred things which it would be madness to think of buying.

Yes; but if you were very rich, papa, — if you were a lord?

No man is so rich as to buy every thing his unrestrained fancy might prompt him to desire. Hounds and horses, pictures and statues and buildings, will exhaust any fortune. There is hardly any one taste so simple or innocent, but what a man might spend his whole estate in it, if he were resolved to gratify it to the utmost. A nobleman may just as easily ruin himself by extravagance as a private man, and indeed many do so.

But if you were a king?

If I were a king, the mischief would be much greater; for I should ruin not only myself, but my subjects.

A king could not hurt his subjects, however, with buying toys or things to eat.

Indeed but he might.   What is a diamond but a mere toy? but a large diamond is an object of princely expense.   That called the Pitt diamond was valued at £1,000,000.   It was offered to George the Second, but he wisely thought it too dear.   The dress of the late queen of France was thought by the prudent Necker a serious object of expense in the revenues of that large kingdom; and her extravagance and that of the king's brothers had a great share in bringing on the calamities of the kingdom.   As to eating, you could gratify yourself with laying out a shilling or two at the pastry-cook's: but Prince Potemkin, who had the revenues of the mighty empire of Russia at command, could not please his appetite without a dish of sterlet soup, which cost every time it was made above thirty pounds; and he would send one of his aides-de-camp an errand from Yassy to Petersburg, a distance of nearly 700 miles, to fetch him a tureen of it.   He once bought all the cherries of a tree in a green-house at about half-a-crown apiece.   The Roman empire was far richer than the Russian, and in the time of the Emperors was all under the power of one man.   Yet when they had such gluttons as Vitellius and Heliogabalus, the revenue of whole provinces was hardly sufficient to give them a dinner: they had tongues of nightingales, and such kind of dishes, the value of which was merely in the expense.

I think the throat of the poor little nightingales might have given them much more pleasure than the tongue.

True: but the proverb says, The belly has no ears. In modern Rome, Pope Adrian, a frugal Dutchman, complained of the expense his predecessor Leo X. was at in peacock sausages. The expenses of Louis XIV. were of a more elegant kind ;— he was fond of fine tapestry, mirrors, gardens, statues, magnificent palaces. These tastes were becoming in a great king, and would have been serviceable to his kingdom if kept within proper limits : but he could not deny himself any thing, however extravagant, that it came into his mind to wish for ; and indeed would have imagined it beneath him to think at all about the expense : and therefore while he was throwing up water fifty feet high at his palaces of Versailles and Marli, and spouting it out of the mouths of dolphins and tritons, thousands of his people in the distant provinces were wanting bread.

I am sure I would not have done so to please my fancy.

Nor he neither perhaps, if he had seen them ; but these poor men and their families were a great way off, and all the people about him looked pleased and happy, and said he was the most generous prince the world had ever seen.

Well, but if I had Aladdin's lamp I might have every thing I wished for.

I am glad at least I have driven you to fairyland. You might no doubt with the lamp of Aladdin, or Fortunatus's purse, have every thing you wished for ; but do you know what the consequences would be?

Very pleasant, I should think.

On the contrary, you would become whimsical and capricious, and would soon grow tired of every thing. We do not receive pleasure long from any thing that is not bought with our own labor : this is one of those permanent laws of nature which man cannot change ; and therefore pleasure and exertion will never be separated even in imagination in a well-regulated mind. I could tell you of a couple who received more true enjoyment of their fortune than Aladdin himself.

Pray do.

The couple I am thinking of lived about a century ago in one of our rich trading towns, which was then just beginning to rise by manufacturing tapes and inkle. They had married because they loved one another; they had very little to begin with, but they were not afraid, because they were industrious. When the husband had come to be the richest merchant in the place, he took great pleasure in talking over his small beginnings; but he used always to add, that poor as he was when he married, he would not have taken a thousand pounds for the table his dame and he ate their dinner from.

What! had he so costly a table before he was grown rich?

On the contrary, he had no table at all; and his wife and he used to sit close together, and place their dish of pottage upon their knees;—their knees were the table. They soon got forward in the world, as industrious people generally do, and were enabled to purchase one thing after another: first perhaps a deal table; after a while a mahogany one; then a sumptuous sideboard. At first they sat on wooden benches; then they had two or three rush-bottom chairs; and when they were rich enough to have an arm-chair for the husband, and another for a friend, to smoke their pipes in, how magnificent they would think themselves! At first they would treat a neighbor with a slice of bread and cheese and a draught of beer; by degrees, with a good joint and a pudding; and at length, with all the delicacies of a fashionable entertainment: and all along they would be able to say, "The blessing of God upon our own industry has procured us these things." By this means they would relish every gradation and increase of their enjoyments: whereas the man born to a fortune swallows his pleasures *whole*, he does not *taste* them. Another inconvenience that attends the man who is born rich, is, that he has not early learned to deny himself. If I were a nobleman, though I could not buy every thing I might fancy for myself, yet play-things for you would not easily ruin me, and you would probably have a great deal of pocket-money ; and you would grow up with a confirmed habit of expense, and no ingenuity ; for you would never try to make any thing, or find out some substitute if you could not get just the thing you wanted. That is a very fine cabinet of shells which the young heiress showed you the other day : it is perfectly arranged and mounted with the utmost elegance, and yet I am sure she has not half the pleasure in it, which you have had with those little drawers of shells of your own collecting, aided by the occasional contributions of friends, which you have arranged for yourself and display with such triumph. And now, to show you that I do sometimes think of the pleasures of my dear girl, here is a plaything for you which I bought while you were chatting at the door of a shop with one of your young friends.

A magic-lantern !—how delightful ! Oh, thank you, papa ! Edward, come and look at my charming magic-lantern.

THE WASP AND BEE.

A FABLE.

A WASP met a Bee, and said to him, Pray, can you tell me what is the reason that men are so ill-natured to me, while they are so fond of you? We are both very much alike, only that the broad golden rings about my body make me much handsomer than you are : we are both winged insects, we both love honey, and we both sting people when we are angry ; yet men always hate me and try to kill me, though I am much more familiar with them than you are, and pay them visits in their houses, and at their tea-table, and at all their meals ; while you are very shy, and hardly ever come near them : yet they build you curious houses, thatched with straw, and take care of and feed you in the winter very often : — I wonder what is the reason.

The Bee said, Because you never do them any good, but, on the contrary, are very troublesome and mischievous ; therefore they do not like to see you ; but they know that I am busy all day long in making them honey. You had better pay them fewer visits, and try to be useful.

THE YOUNG MOUSE.

A FABLE.

A YOUNG Mouse lived in a cupboard where sweet-meats were kept : she dined every day upon biscuit, marmalade, or fine sugar. Never had any little Mouse lived so well. She had often ventured to peep at the family while they sat at supper ; nay, she had sometimes stole down on the carpet, and picked up the crumbs, and nobody had ever hurt her. She would have been quite happy, but that she was sometimes frightened by the cat, and then she ran trembling to her hole behind the wainscot. One day she came running to her mother in great joy ! Mother ! said she, the good people of this family have built me a house to live in ; it is in the cupboard : I am sure it is for me, for it is just big enough : the bottom is of wood, and it is covered all over with wires ; and I dare say they have made it on purpose to screen me from that terrible cat, which ran after me so often : there is an entrance just

big enough for me, but puss cannot follow : and they
have been so good as to put in some toasted cheese,
which smells so deliciously, that I should have run in
directly and taken possession of my new house, but I
thought I would tell you first, that we might go in together and both lodge there to-night, for it will hold us
both.

My dear child, said the old Mouse, it is most happy
you did not go in, for this house is called a trap, and
you would never have come out again, except to have
been devoured, or put to death in some way or other.
Though man has not so fierce a look as a cat, he is as
much our enemy, and has still more cunning.

ALFRED.

A DRAMA.

Persons of the Drama.

ALFRED,	King of England.
GUBBA,	a Farmer.
GANDELIN,	his Wife.
ELLA,	an Officer of Alfred.

SCENE, the Isle of Athelney.

Alf. — How retired and quiet is every thing in this
little spot ! The river winds its silent waters round
this retreat ; and the tangled bushes of the thicket
fence it in from the attack of an enemy. The bloody
Danes have not yet pierced into this wild solitude. I
believe I am safe from their pursuit. But I hope I
shall find some inhabitants here, otherwise I shall die
of hunger. Ha ! here is a narrow path through the
wood ; and I think I see the smoke of a cottage rising
between the trees. I will bend my steps thither.

9

SCENE : *Before the Cottage.*

GUBBA *coming forward.* GANDELIN *within.*

Alf. — Good even to you, good man.   Are you disposed to show hospitality to a poor traveller?

Gub. — Why truly, there are so many poor travellers
now-a-days, that if we entertain them all, we shall have
nothing left for ourselves.   However, come along to
my wife, and we will see what can be done for you.
Wife, I am very weary ; I have been chopping wood
all day.

Gan. — You are always ready for your supper, but
it is not ready for you, I assure you : the cakes will
take an hour to bake, and the sun is yet high ; it has
not yet dipped behind the old barn.   But who have
you with you, I trow?

Alf. — Good mother, I am a stranger ; and entreat
you to afford me food and shelter.

Gan. — Good mother, quotha !   Good wife, if you
please, and welcome.   But I do not love strangers ;
and the land has no reason to love them.   It has never
been a merry day for Old England since strangers
came into it.

Alf. — I am not a stranger in England, though I am
a stranger here.   I am a true born Englishman.

Gub. — And do you hate those wicked Danes, that
eat us up, and burn our houses, and drive away our
cattle?

Alf. — I do hate them.

Gan. — Heartily?   He does not speak heartily, husband.

Alf. — Heartily I hate them ; most heartily.

Gub. — Give me thy hand then ; thou art an honest
fellow.

Alf. — I was with King Alfred in the last battle he
fought.

Gan. — With King Alfred? heaven bless him.

Gub. — What is become of our good king?

Alf. — Did you love him, then?

Gub. — Yes, as much as a poor man may love a king; and kneeled down and prayed for him every night, that he might conquer those Danish wolves; but it was not to be so.

Alf. — You could not love Alfred better than I did.

Gub. — But what is become of him?

Alf. — He is thought to be dead.

Gub. — Well, these are sad times; heaven help us! Come, you shall be welcome to share the brown loaf with us; I suppose you are too sharp-set to be nice.

Gan. — Ay, come with us; you shall be as welcome as a prince! But hark ye, husband; though I am very willing to be charitable to this stranger (it would be a sin to be otherwise), yet there is no reason he should not do something to maintain himself: he looks strong and capable.

Gub. — Why, that's true. What can you do, friend?

Alf. — I am very willing to help you in any thing you choose to set me about. It will please me best to earn my bread before I eat it.

Gub. — Let me see. Can you tie up fagots neatly?

Alf. — I have not been used to it. I am afraid I should be awkward.

Gub. — Can you thatch? There is a piece blown off the cow-house.

Alf. — Alas, I cannot thatch.

Gan. — Ask him if he can weave rushes: we want some new baskets.

Alf. — I have never learned.

Gub. — Can you stack hay?

Alf. — No.

Gub. — Why, here's a fellow! and yet he hath as many pair of hands as his neighbors. Dame, can you employ him in the house? He might lay wood on the fire, and rub the tables.

Gan. — Let him watch these cakes, then : I must go and milk the kine.

Gub. — And I 'll go and stack the wood, since supper is not ready.

Gan. — But pray observe, friend! do not let the cakes burn : turn them often on the hearth.

Alf. — I shall observe your directions.

ALFRED *alone.*

Alf. — For myself, I could bear it; but England, my bleeding country, for thee my heart is wrung with bitter anguish! From the Humber to the Thames the rivers are stained with blood! My brave soldiers cut to pieces! My poor people — some massacred, others driven from their warm homes, stripped, abused, insulted : — and I, whom heaven appointed their shepherd, unable to rescue my defenceless flock from the ravenous jaws of these devourers! Gracious heaven! if I am not worthy to save this land from the Danish sword, raise up some other hero to fight with more success than I have done, and let me spend my life in this obscure cottage, in these servile offices : I shall be content, if England is happy.

Oh, here come my blunt host and hostess.

Enter GUBBA *and* GANDELIN.,

Gan. — Help me down with the pail, husband. This new milk, with the cakes, will make an excellent supper : but, mercy on us, how they are burnt! black as my shoe ; they have not once been turned : you oaf, you lubbard, you lazy loon —

Alf. — Indeed, dame, I am sorry for it; but my mind was full of sad thoughts.

Gub. — Come, wife, you must forgive him ; perhaps he is in love. I remember when I was in love with thee —

Gan. — You remember?

Gub. — Yes, dame, I do remember it, though it was many a long year since ; my mother was making a kettle of furmenty —

Gan. — Prithee, hold thy tongue, and let us eat our suppers.

Alf. — How refreshing is this sweet new milk, and this wholesome bread !

Gub. — Eat heartily, friend. Where shall we lodge him, Gandelin?

Gan. — We have but one bed, you know ; but there is fresh straw in the barn.

Alf. (*aside*) — If I shall not lodge like a king, at least I shall lodge like a soldier. Alas, how many of my poor soldiers are stretched on the bare ground !

Gan. — What noise do I hear? It is the trampling of horses. Good husband, go and see what is the matter.

Alf. — Heaven forbid my misfortunes should bring destruction on this simple family. I had rather have perished in the wood.

GUBBA *returns followed by* ELLA *with his sword drawn.*

Gan. — Mercy defend us, a sword !

Gub. — The Danes ! the Danes ! O do not kill us !

Ella. (*kneeling*) — My liege, my lord, my sovereign ; have I found you !

Alf. (*embracing him*) — My brave Ella !

Ella. — I bring you good news, my sovereign ! Your troops that were shut up in Kinwith Castle made a desperate sally — the Danes were slaughtered. The fierce Hubba lies gasping on the plain.

Alf. — Is it possible ! Am I yet a king?

Ella. — Their famous standard, the Danish raven, is taken ; their troops are panic struck ; the English soldiers call aloud for Alfred. Here is a letter which will inform you of more particulars. (*Gives a letter.*)

Gub. (*aside*) — What will become of us ! Ah, dame, that tongue of thine has undone us !

Gan. — Oh, my poor, dear husband ! we shall all be hanged, that 's certain. But who could have thought it was the king?

Gub. — Why, Gandelin, do you see, we might have guessed he was born to be a king, or some such great man, because, you know, he was fit for nothing else.

Alf. (*coming forward*) — God be praised for these tidings ! Hope is sprung up out of the depths of despair. Oh, my friend ! shall I again shine in arms — again fight at the head of my brave Englishmen — lead them on to victory ! Our friends shall now lift their heads again.

Ella. — Yes, you have many friends, who have long been obliged, like their master, to skulk in deserts and caves, and wander from cottage to cottage. When they hear you are alive, and in arms again, they will leave their fastnesses, and flock to your standard.

Alf. — I am impatient to meet them : my people shall be revenged.

Gub. and *Gan.* (*throwing themselves at the feet of* ALFRED) — Oh, my lord ——

Gan. — We hope your majesty will put us to a merciful death. Indeed, we did not know your majesty's grace.

Gub. — If your majesty could but pardon my wife's tongue ; she means no harm, poor woman !

Alf. — Pardon you, good people ! I not only pardon you, but thank you. You have afforded me protection in my distress ; and if ever I am seated again on the throne of England, my first care shall be to reward your hospitality. I am now going to protect *you.* Come, my faithful Ella, to arms ! to arms ! My bosom burns to face once more the haughty Dane ; and here I vow to heaven, that I will never sheathe the sword against these robbers, till either I lose my life in this just cause, or

> Till dove-like Peace return to England's shore,
> And war and slaughter vex the land no more.

CANUTE'S REPROOF TO HIS COURTIERS.

Persons.

CANUTE. . . . . King of England.
OSWALD, OFFA . . . Courtiers.

SCENE, the Sea-Side, near Southampton — the tide coming in.

Can. — Is it true, my friends, what you have so often told me, that I am the greatest of monarchs?

Offa. — It is true, my liege ; you are the most powerful of all kings.

Osw. — We are all your slaves : we kiss the dust of your feet.

Offa. — Not only we, but even the elements, are your slaves. The land obeys you from shore to shore ; and the sea obeys you.

Can. — Does the sea, with its loud boisterous waves, obey me? Will that terrible element be still at my bidding?

Offa. — Yes, the sea is yours ; it was made to bear your ships upon its bosom, and to pour the treasures of the world at your royal feet. It is boisterous to your enemies, but it knows you to be its sovereign.

Can. — Is not the tide coming up?

Osw. — Yes, my liege; you may perceive the swell already.

Can. — Bring me a chair then; set it here upon the sands.

Offa. — Where the tide is coming up, my gracious lord?

Can. — Yes, set it just here.

Osw. (*aside*) — I wonder what he is going to do.

Offa. (*aside*) — Surely he is not such a fool as to believe us.

Can. — O mighty Ocean! thou art my subject; my courtiers tell me so; and it is thy bounden duty to obey me. Thus, then, I stretch my sceptre over thee, and command thee to retire. Roll back thy swelling waves, nor let them presume to wet the feet of me, thy royal master.

Osw. (*aside*) — I believe the sea will pay very little regard to his royal commands.

Offa. — See how fast the tide rises!

Osw. — The next wave will come up to the chair. It is a folly to stay; we shall be covered with salt water.

Can. — Well, does the sea obey my commands? If it be my subject, it is a very rebellious subject. See how it swells, and dashes the angry foam and salt spray over my sacred person. Vile sycophants! did you think I was the dupe of your base lies? that I believed your abject flatteries? Know, there is only one Being whom the sea will obey. He is Sovereign of heaven and earth, King of kings, and Lord of lords. It is only he who can say to the ocean, " Thus far shalt thou go, but no farther, and here shall thy proud waves be stayed." A king is but a man; and a man is but a worm. Shall a worm assume the power of the great God, and think the elements will obey him? Take away this crown, I will never wear it more. May kings learn to be humble from my example, and courtiers learn truth from your disgrace!

THE MASQUE OF NATURE.

WHO is this beautiful virgin that approaches, clothed in a robe of light green? She has a garland of flowers on her head, and flowers spring up wherever she sets her foot. The snow which covered the fields, and the ice which was in the rivers, melt away when she breathes upon them. The young lambs frisk about her, and the birds warble in their little throats to welcome her coming; and when they see her, they begin to choose their mates, and to build their nests. Youths and maidens, have ye seen this beautiful virgin? If ye have, tell me who is she, and what is her name.

WHO is this that cometh from the south, thinly clad in a light transparent garment? Her breath is hot and sultry; she seeks the refreshment of the cool shade; she seeks the clear streams, the crystal brooks, to bathe her languid limbs. The brooks and rivulets fly from her, and are dried up at her approach. She cools her parched lips with berries, and the grateful acid of all fruits; the seedy melon, the sharp apple, and the red pulp of the juicy cherry, which are poured out plentifully around her. The tanned haymakers welcome her coming; and the sheep-shearer, who clips the fleeces off his flock with his sounding shears. When she cometh, let me lie under the thick shade of a spreading beech tree; let me walk with her in the early morning, when the dew is yet upon the grass;

let me wander with her in the soft twilight, when the shepherd shuts his fold, and the star of evening appears. Who is she that cometh from the south? Youths and maidens, tell me, if you know, who is she, and what is her name.

———

Who is he that cometh with sober pace, stealing upon us unawares? His garments are red with the blood of the grape, and his temples are bound with a sheaf of ripe wheat. His hair is thin and begins to fall, and the auburn is mixed with mournful gray. He shakes the brown nuts from the tree. He winds the horn, and calls the hunters to their sport. The gun sounds. The trembling partridge and the beautiful pheasant flutter bleeding in the air, and fall dead at the sportsman's feet. Who is he that is crowned with the wheat-sheaf? Youths and maidens, tell me, if ye know, who is he and what is his name.

———

Who is he that cometh from the north, clothed in furs and warm wool? He wraps his cloak close about him. His head is bald : his beard is made of sharp icicles. He loves the blazing fire high piled upon the hearth, and the wine sparkling in the glass. He binds skates to his feet, and skims over the frozen lakes. His breath is piercing and cold, and no little flower dares to peep above the surface of the ground when he is by. Whatever he touches turns to ice.

If he were to stroke you with his cold hand, you would be quite stiff and dead like a piece of marble. Youths and maidens, do you see him? He is coming fast upon us, and soon he will be here. Tell me, if you know, who he is, and what is his name.

THINGS BY THEIR RIGHT NAMES.

Charles. — PAPA, you grow very lazy. Last winter you used to tell us stories, and now you never tell us any ; and we are all got round the fire quite ready to hear you. Pray, dear papa, let us have a very pretty one.

Father. — With all my heart ; what shall it be ?

C. — A bloody murder, papa !

F. — A bloody murder ! Well then, — Once upon a time, some men, dressed all alike —

C. — With black crapes over their faces ?

F. — No ; they had steel caps on : — having crossed a dark heath, wound cautiously along the skirts of a deep forest —

C. — They were ill-looking fellows, I dare say.

F. — I cannot say so ; on the contrary, they were tall, personable men as most one shall see : — leaving on their right hand an old ruined tower on the hill —

C. — At midnight, just as the clock struck twelve ; was it not, papa ?

F. — No, really ; it was on a fine balmy summer's morning : — and moved forwards, one behind another —

C. — As still as death, creeping along under the hedges.

F. — On the contrary, they walked remarkably upright ; and so far from endeavoring to be hushed and still, they made a loud noise as they came along, with several sorts of instruments.

C. — But, papa, they would be found out immediately.

F. — They did not seem to wish to conceal themselves : on the contrary, they gloried in what they
were about. They moved forwards, I say, to a large
plain, where stood a neat pretty village, which they
set on fire —

C. — Set a village on fire? wicked wretches !

F. — And while it was burning, they murdered —
twenty thousand men.

C. — Oh fie, papa ! You don't intend I should believe this ; I thought all along you were making up a
tale, as you often do ; but you shall not catch me this
time. What ! they lay still, I suppose, and let these
fellows cut their throats !

F. — No, truly ; they resisted as long as they could.

C. — How should these men kill twenty thousand
people, pray?

F. — Why not? the *murderers* were thirty thousand.

C. — O, now I have found you out ! You mean a
BATTLE.

F. — Indeed I do. I do not know of any *murders*
half so bloody.

THE GOOSE AND HORSE.

A FABLE.

A *Goose*, who was plucking grass upon a common,
thought herself affronted by a *Horse* who fed near
her, and in hissing accents thus addressed him : " I
am certainly a more noble and perfect animal than
you ; for the whole range and extent of your faculties
are confined to one element. I can walk upon the
ground as well as you ; I have besides wings, with

which I can raise myself in the air; and when I please, I can sport in ponds and lakes, and refresh myself in the cool waters; I enjoy the different powers of a bird, a fish, and a quadruped."

The *Horse*, snorting somewhat disdainfully, replied, " It is true you inhabit three elements, but you make no very distinguished figure in any one of them. You fly indeed; but your flight is so heavy and clumsy, that you have no right to put yourself on a level with the lark or the swallow. You can swim on the surface of the waters, but you cannot live in them as fishes do; you cannot find your food in that element, nor glide smoothly along the bottom of the waves. And when you walk, or rather waddle, upon the ground, with your broad feet and your long neck stretched out, hissing at every one who passes by, you bring upon yourself the derision of all beholders. I confess that I am only formed to move upon the ground; but how graceful is my make! how well turned my limbs! how highly finished my whole body! how great my strength! how astonishing my speed! I had rather be confined to one element, and be admired in that, than be a *Goose* in all."

ON MANUFACTURES.

Father — Henry.

Hen. — MY dear father, you observed the other day that we had a great many *manufactures* in England. Pray, what is a manufacture?

Fa. — A manufacture is something made by the hand of man. It is derived from two Latin words, *manus*, the hand, and *facere*, to make. Manufactures are therefore opposed to *productions*, which latter are what the bounty of nature spontaneously affords us; as fruits, corn, marble.

Hen. — But there is a great deal of trouble with corn; you have often made me take notice how much pains it costs the farmer to plough his ground, and put the seed in the earth, and keep it clear from weeds.

Fa. — Very true; but the farmer does not *make* the corn; he only prepares for it a proper soil and situation, and removes every hindrance arising from the hardness of the ground, or the neighborhood of other plants, which might obstruct the secret and wonderful process of vegetation; but with the vegetation itself he has nothing to do. It is not *his* hand that draws out the slender fibres of the root, pushes up the green stalk, and by degrees the spiky ear; swells the grain, and embrowns it with that rich tinge of tawny russet, which informs the husbandman it is time to put in his sickle: all this operation is performed without his care or even knowledge.

Hen. — Now then I understand; corn is a *production*, and bread a *manufacture*.

Fa. — Bread is certainly, in strictness of speech, a manufacture; but we do not in general apply the term to any thing in which the original material is so little changed. If we wanted to speak of bread philosophically, we should say, it is a *preparation* of corn.

Hen. — Is sugar a manufacture.

Fa. — No, for the same reason. Besides which, I do not recollect the term being applied to any article of food, — I suppose from an idea that food is of too perishable a nature, and generally obtained by a process too simple to deserve the name. We say, therefore, sugar-works, oil-mills, chocolate-works; we do not say a beer-manufactory, but a brewery; but this is only a nicety of language, for properly all those are manufactories, if there is much of art and curiosity in the process.

Hen. — Do we say a manufactory of *pictures ?*

Fa. — No ; but for a different reason. A picture, especially if it belong to any of the higher kinds of painting, is an effort of genius. A picture cannot be produced by any given combinations of canvas and color. It is the hand, indeed, that executes, but the head that works. Sir Joshua Reynolds could not have gone, when he was engaged to paint a picture, and hired workmen, the one to draw the eyes, another the nose, a third the mouth ; the whole must be the painter's own, that particular painter's, and no other ; and no one who has not his ideas can do his work. His work is therefore nobler, of a higher species.

Hen. — Pray give me an instance of a manufacture.

Fa. — The making of watches is a manufacture : the silver, iron, gold, or whatever else is used in it, are productions, the material of the work ; but it is by the wonderful art of man that they are wrought into the numberless wheels and springs of which this complicated machine is composed.

Hen. — Then is there not so much art in making a watch as a picture? Does not the head work?

Fa. — Certainly, in the original invention of watches, as much or more, than in painting ; but when once invented, the art of watchmaking is capable of being reduced to a mere mechanical labor, which may be exercised by any man of common capacity, according to certain precise rules, when made familiar to him by practice. This, painting is not.

Hen. — But, my dear father, making of books surely requires a great deal of thinking and study ; and yet I remember the other day at dinner a gentleman said that Mr. Pica had *manufactured* a large volume in less than a fortnight.

Fa. — It was meant to convey a satirical remark on

his book, because it was compiled from other authors, from whom he had taken a page in one place, and a page in another : so that it was not produced by the labor of his brain, but of his hands. Thus you heard your mother complain that the London cream was *manufactured;* which was a pointed and concise way of saying that the cream was not what it ought to be, nor what it pretended to be ; for cream, when genuine, is a pure production ; but when mixed up and adulterated with flour and isinglass, and I know not what, it becomes a manufacture. It was as much as to say, art has been here, where it has no business ; where it is not beneficial, but hurtful. A great deal of the delicacy of language depends upon an accurate knowledge of the specific meaning of single terms, and a nice attention to their relative propriety.

Hen. — Have all nations manufactures?

Fa. — All that are in any degree cultivated ; but it very often happens that countries naturally the poorest have manufactures of the greatest extent and variety.

Hen. — Why so?

Fa. — For the same reason, I apprehend, that individuals, who are rich without any labor of their own, are seldom so industrious and active as those who depend upon their own exertions : thus the Spaniards, who possess the richest gold and silver mines in the world, are in want of many conveniences of life, which are enjoyed in London and Amsterdam.

Hen. — I can comprehend that ; I believe if my uncle Ledger were to find a gold mine under his warehouse, he would soon shut up shop.

Fa. — I believe so. It is not, however, easy to establish manufactures in a *very poor* nation ; they require science and genius for their invention ; art and contrivance for their execution ; order, peace, and union, for their flourishing ; they require a number of men to combine together in an undertaking, and to prosecute

it with the most patient industry; they require, therefore, laws and government for their protection. If you
see extensive manufactures in any nation, you may be
sure it is a civilized nation; you may be sure property
is accurately ascertained, and protected. They require
great expenses for their first establishment, costly machines for shortening manual labor, and money and
credit for purchasing materials from distant countries.
There is not a single manufacture of Great Britain
which does not require, in some part or other of its
process, productions from the different parts of the
globe; oils, drugs, varnish, quicksilver, and the like;
it requires therefore, *ships* and a friendly intercourse
with foreign nations to transport commodities, and
exchange productions. We could not be a manufacturing, unless we were also a commercial nation.
They require time to take root in any place, and their
excellence often depends upon some nice and delicate
circumstance; a peculiar quality, for instance, in the
air or water, or some other local circumstance not
easily ascertained. Thus, I have heard, that the Irish
women spin better than the English, because the
moister temperature of their climate makes their skin
more soft and their fingers more flexible: thus, again,
we cannot dye so beautiful a scarlet as the French can,
though with the same drugs, perhaps on account of the
superior purity of their air. But though so much is
necessary for the perfection of the more curious and
complicated manufactures, all nations possess those
which are subservient to the common conveniences of
life; the loom and the forge, particularly, are of the
highest antiquity.

Hen. — Yes, I remember Hector bids Andromache
return to her apartment, and employ herself in weaving
with her maids; and I remember the shield of Achilles.

Fa. — True; and you likewise remember, in an
earlier period, the fine linen of Egypt; and, to go

still higher, the working in brass and iron is recorded of Tubal Cain before the flood.

Hen.—Which is the most important, manufactures or agriculture?

Fa.—Agriculture is the most *necessary*, because it is first of all necessary that man should live; but almost all the enjoyments and comforts of life are produced by manufactures.

Hen.—Why are we obliged to take so much pains to make ourselves comfortable?

Fa.—To exercise our industry. Nature provides the materials for man. She pours out at his feet a profusion of gems, metals, dyes, plants, ores, barks, stones, gums, wax, marbles, woods, roots, skins, earths, and minerals of all kinds! She has likewise given him tools.

Hen.—I did not know that Nature gave us tools.

Fa.—No! what are those two instruments you carry always about with you, so strong and yet so flexible, so nicely jointed, and branched out into five long, taper, unequal divisions, any of which may be contracted or stretched out at pleasure: the extremities of which have a feeling so wonderfully delicate, and which are strengthened and defended by horn?

Hen.—The hands.

Fa.—Yes. Man is as much superior to the brutes in his outward form, by means of the hand, as he is in his mind by the gift of reason. The trunk of the elephant comes perhaps the nearest to it in its exquisite feeling and flexibility (it is, indeed, called his hand in Latin), and accordingly that animal has always been reckoned the wisest of brutes. When Nature gave man the hand, she said to him, "Exercise your ingenuity, and work." As soon as ever man rises above the state of a savage, he begins to contrive and to make things, in order to improve his forlorn condition; thus you may remember Thomson represents Industry coming to the poor shivering wretch, and teaching him the arts of life.

> " Taught him to chip the wood, and hew the stone,
> Till by degrees the finish'd fabric rose :
> Tore from his limbs the blood-polluted fur,
> And wrapt them in the woolly vestment warm,
> Or bright in glossy silk and flowing lawn."

Hen. — It must require a great deal of knowledge, I suppose, for so many curious works; what kind of knowledge is most necessary !

Fa. — There is not any which may not be occasionally employed ; but the two sciences which most assist the manufacturer are *mechanics* and *chemistry.* The one for building mills, working of mines, and in general for constructing wheels, wedges, pulleys, &c. either to shorten the labor of man, by performing it in less time, or to perform what the strength of man alone could not accomplish : — the other in fusing and working ores, in dyeing and bleaching, and extracting the virtues of various substances for particular uses : making of soap, for instance, is a chemical operation ; and by chemistry an ingenious gentleman has lately found out a way of bleaching a piece of cloth in eight and forty hours, which by the common process would have taken up a great many weeks. You have heard of Sir Richard Arkwright who died lately —

Hen. — Yes, I have heard he was at first only a barber, and shaved people for a penny apiece.

Fa. — He did so ; but having a strong turn for mechanics, he invented, or at least perfected, a machine, by which one pair of hands may do the work of twenty or thirty ; and, as in this country every one is free to rise by merit, he acquired the largest fortune in the county, had a great many hundreds of workmen under his orders, and had leave given him by the king to put *Sir* before his name.

Hen. — Did that do him any good?

Fa. — It pleased him, I suppose, or he would not have accepted of it; and you will allow, I imagine, that if titles are used, it does honor to those who bestow them, that they are given to such as have made themselves noticed for something useful. — Arkwright used to say, that if he had time to perfect his inventions, he would put a fleece of wool into a box, and it should come out broadcloth.

Hen. — What did he mean by that; was there any fairy in the box to turn it into broadcloth with her wand?

Fa. — He was assisted by the only fairies that ever had the power of transformation, — Art and Industry: he meant that he would contrive so many machines, wheel within wheel, that the combing, carding, and other various operations, should be performed by mechanism, almost without the hand of man.

Hen. — I think, if I had not been told, I should never have been able to guess that my coat came off the back of a sheep.

Fa. — You hardly would; but there are manufactures in which the material is much more changed than in woollen cloth. What can be meaner in appearance than sand and ashes? Would you imagine that any thing beautiful could be made out of such a mixture? Yet the furnace transforms this into that transparent crystal we call *glass*, than which nothing is more sparkling, more brilliant, more full of lustre. It throws about the rays of light as if it had life and motion.

Hen. — There is a glass-shop in London, which always puts me in mind of Aladdin's palace.

Fa. — It is certain that if a person ignorant of the manufacture were to see one of our capital shops, he would think all the treasures of Golconda were centred there, and that every drop of cut glass was worth a prince's ransom. Again, who would suppose, on seeing the green stalks of a plant, that it could be formed into a texture so smooth, so snowy-white, so firm, and yet so flexible, as to wrap round the limbs and adapt itself to every movement of the body? Who would guess this fibrous stalk could be made to float in such light undulating folds as in our lawns and cambrics? not less fine, we presume, than that transparent drapery which the Romans called *ventus textilis, woven wind.*

Hen. — I wonder how anybody can spin such fine thread.

Fa. — Their fingers must have the touch of a spider, that, as Pope says,

> Feels at each thread, and lives along the line.

And indeed you recollect that Arachne *was* a spinster. Lace is a still finer production from flax, and is one of those in which the original material is most improved. How many times the price of a pound of flax do you think that flax will be worth when made into lace?

Hen. — A great many times, I suppose.

Fa. — Flax at the best hand is bought at fourteen pence a pound. They make lace at Valenciennes, in French Flanders, of ten guineas a yard, I believe indeed higher, but we will say ten guineas; this yard of lace will weigh probably not more than half an ounce: what is the value of half an ounce of flax? Reckon it.

Hen. — It comes to one farthing and three quarters of a farthing.

Fa. — Right; now tell me how many times the original value the lace is worth.

Hen. — Prodigious! it is worth 5760 times as much as the flax it is made of.

Fa. — Yet there is another material that is still more improvable than flax.

Hen. — What can that be?

Fa. — Iron. The price of pig-iron is ten shillings a hundred weight; this is not quite one farthing for two ounces; now you have seen some of the beautiful cut steel that looks like diamonds?

Hen. — Yes, I have seen buckles, and pins, and watch-chains.

Fa. — Then you can form an idea of it; but you have seen only the most common sorts. There was a chain made at Woodstock, in Oxfordshire, and sent to France, which weighed only two ounces, and cost 170*l.* Calculate how many times *that* has increased its value.

Hen. — Amazing! It was worth 163,600 times the value of the iron it was made of.

Fa. — That is what manufacturers can do; here man is a kind of creator, and, like the great Creator, he may please himself with his work, and say it is good. In the last mentioned manufacture, too, that of steel, the English have the honor of excelling all the world.

Hen. — What are the chief manufactures of England?

Fa. — We have at present a greater variety than I can pretend to enumerate, but our staple manufacture is woollen cloth. England abounds in fine pastures and extensive downs, which feed great numbers of sheep; hence our wool has always been a valuable article of trade; but we did not always know how to work it. We used to sell it to the Flemish or Lombards, who wrought it into cloth; till, in the year 1326, Edward the Third invited some Flemish weavers over to teach us the art; but there was not much made in England till the reign of Henry the Seventh. Manchester and Birmingham are towns which have arisen to great consequence from small beginnings, almost within the memory of old men now living; the first for cotton and muslin goods, the second for cutlery and hardware, in which we at this moment excel all Europe. Of late years, too, carpets, beautiful as fine tapestry, have been fabricated in this country. Our clocks and watches are greatly esteemed. The earthen-ware plates and dishes, which we all use in common, and the elegant set for the tea-table, ornamented with musical instruments, which we admired in our visit yesterday, belong to a very extensive manufactory, the seat of which is at Burslem in Staffordshire. The principal potteries there belong to one person, an excellent chemist, and a man of great taste ; he, in conjunction with another man of taste who is since dead, has made our clay more valuable than the finest porcelain of China. He has moulded it into all the forms of grace and beauty that are to be met with in the precious remains of the Greek and Etruscan artists. In the more common articles he has pencilled it with the most elegant designs, shaped it into shelves and leaves, twisted it into wicker-work, and trailed the ductile foliage round the light basket. He has filled our cabinets and chimney-pieces with urns, lamps, and vases, on which are lightly traced, with the purest simplicity, the fine forms and floating draperies of Herculaneum. In short, he has given to our houses a classic air, and has made every saloon and every dining-room schools of taste. I should add that there is a great demand abroad for this elegant manufacture. The Empress of Russia has had some magnificent services of it ; and the other day one was sent to the King of Spain, intended as a present from him to the Archbishop of Toledo, which cost a thousand pounds. Some morning you shall go through the rooms in the London warehouse.

Hen. — I should like very much to see manufactures, now you have told me such curious things about them.

Fa. — You will do well ! There is much more entertainment to a cultivated mind in seeing a pin made, than in many a fashionable diversion which young people half ruin themselves to attend. In the mean time I will give you some account of one of the most elegant of them, which is *paper.*

Hen. — Pray do, my dear father.

Fa. — It shall be left for another evening, however, for it is now late.   Good night.

THE FLYING FISH.

THE Flying Fish, says the fable, had originally no wings, but being of an ambitious and discontented temper, she repined at being always confined to the waters, and wished to soar in the air. "If I could fly like the birds," said she, " I should not only see more of the beauties of nature, but I should be able to escape from those fish which are continually pursuing me, and which render my life miserable." She therefore petitioned Jupiter for a pair of wings : and immediately she perceived her fins to expand. They suddenly grew to the length of her whole body, and became at the same time so strong as to do the office of a pinion. She was at first much pleased with her new powers, and looked with an air of disdain on all her former companions ; but she soon perceived herself exposed to new dangers. When flying in the air, she was incessantly pursued by the Tropic bird and the Albatross ; and when for safety she dropped into the water, she was so fatigued with her flight, that she was less able than ever to escape from her old enemies, the fish.   Finding herself more unhappy than before, she now begged of Jupiter to recall his present ; but Jupiter said to her, " When I gave you your wings, I well knew they would prove a curse ; but your proud and restless disposition deserved this disappointment.   Now, therefore, what you begged as a favor keep as a punishment."

A LESSON IN THE ART OF DISTINGUISHING.

F. — COME hither, Charles ; what is that you see grazing in the meadow before you?

C. — It is a horse.

F. — Whose horse is it?

C. — I do not know ; I never saw it before.

F. — How do you know it is a horse, if you never saw it before?

C. — Because it is like other horses.

F. — Are all horses alike then?

C. — Yes.

F. — If they are all alike, how do you know one horse from another?

C. — They are not quite alike.

F. — But they are so much alike that you can easily distinguish a horse from a cow?

C. — Yes, indeed.

F. — Or from a cabbage?

C. — A horse from a cabbage ! yes, surely I can.

F. — Very well ; then let us see if you can tell how a horse differs from a cabbage.

C. — Very easily ; a horse is alive.

F. — True ; and how is every thing called which is alive?

C. — I believe all things that are alive are called *animals*.

F. — Right ; but can you tell me what a horse and a cabbage are alike in?

C. — Nothing, I believe.

F. — Yes, there is one thing in which the slenderest moss that grows upon the wall is like the greatest man or the highest angel.

C. — Because God made them?

F. — Yes; and how do you call every thing that is made?

C. — A creature.

F. — A horse then is a creature, but a living creature; that is to say, an animal.

C. — And a cabbage is a dead creature; that is the difference.

F. — Not so, neither; nothing is dead that has never been alive.

C. — What must I call it then, if it is neither dead nor alive?

F. — An inanimate creature; there is the animate and inanimate creation. Plants, stones, metals, are of the latter class; horses belong to the former.

C. — But the gardener told me some of my cabbages *were* dead, and some were alive.

F. — Very true. Plants have a *vegetative* life, a principle of growth and decay; this is common to them with all organized bodies; but they have not sensation, at least we do not know they have; they have not *life*, therefore, in the sense in which animals enjoy it.

C. — A horse is called an animal, then.

F. — Yes; but a salmon is an animal, and so is a sparrow; how will you distinguish a horse from these?

C. — A salmon lives in the water, and swims; a sparrow flies, and lives in the air.

F. — I think a salmon could not walk upon the ground, even if it could live out of the water.

C. — No, indeed; it has no legs.

F. — And a bird would not gallop like a horse.

C. — No; it would hop away upon its two slender legs.

F. — How many legs has a horse?

C. — Four.

F. — And an ox?

C. — Four likewise.

F. — And a camel?

C. — Four still.

F. — Do you know any animals which live upon the earth that have not four legs?

C. — I think not; they have all four legs; except worms and insects, and such things.

F. — You remember, I suppose, what an animal is called that has four legs; you have it in your little books.

C. — A quadruped.

F. — A horse then is a *quadruped:* by this we distinguish him from the birds, fishes, and insects.

C. — And from men.

F. — True; but if you had been talking about birds, you would not have found it so easy to distinguish them.

C. — How so! a man is not at all like a bird.

F. — Yet an ancient philosopher could find no way to distinguish them, but by calling man *a two-legged animal without feathers.*

C. — I think he was very silly; they are not at all alike, though they have both two legs.

F. — Another ancient philosopher, called Diogenes, was of your opinion. He stripped a cock of his feathers, and turned him into the school where Plato — that was his name — was teaching, and said, Here is Plato's man for you.

C. — I wish I had been there, I should have laughed very much.

F. — Probably. Before we laugh at others, however, let us see what we can do ourselves. We have not yet found any thing which will distinguish a horse from an elephant, or from a Norway rat.

C. — Oh, that is easy enough. An elephant is very large, and a rat is very small; a horse is neither large nor small.

F. — Before we go any further, look, what is settled on the skirt of your coat?

C. — It is a butterfly; what a prodigious large one! I never saw such a one before.

F. — Is it larger than a rat, think you?

C. — No, that it is not.

F. — Yet you called the butterfly large, and you called the rat small.

C. — It is very large for a butterfly.

F. — It is so. You see, therefore, that large and small are *relative terms.*

C. — I do not well understand that phrase.

F. — It means that they have no precise and determinate signification in themselves, but are applied differently, according to the other ideas which you join with them, and the different positions in which you view them. This butterfly, therefore, is *large*, compared with those of its own species, and *small*, compared with many other species of animals. Besides, there is no circumstance which varies more than the size of individuals. If you were to give an idea of a horse from its size, you would certainly say it was much bigger than a dog; yet if you take the smallest Shetland horse, and the largest Irish greyhound, you will find them very much upon a par : size, therefore, is not a circumstance by which you can accurately distinguish one animal from another ; nor yet his color.

C. — No ; there are black horses, and bay, and white, and pied.

F. — But you have not seen that variety of colors in a hare, for instance.

C. — No, a hare is always brown.

F. — Yet if you were to depend upon that circumstance, you would not convey the idea of a hare to a mountaineer, or an inhabitant of Siberia; for he sees them white as snow. We must, therefore, find out some circumstances that do not change like size and color, and, I may add, shape; though they are not so obvious, nor perhaps so striking. Look at the feet of quadrupeds; are they all alike?

C. — No; some have long taper claws, and some have thick clumsy feet without claws.

F. — The thick feet are horny, are they not?

C. — Yes, I recollect they are called hoofs.

F. — And the feet that are not covered with horn, and are divided into claws, are called *digitated*, from *digitus*, a finger; because they are parted like fingers. Here, then, we have one grand division of quadrupeds into *hoofed* and *digitated*. Of which division is the horse?

C. — He is hoofed.

F. — There are a great many different kinds of horses; did you ever know one that was not hoofed?

C. — No, never.

F. — Do you think we run any hazard of a stranger telling us, Sir, horses are hoofed indeed in your country, but in mine, which is in a different climate, and where we feed them differently, they have claws?

C. — No, I dare say not.

F. — Then we have got something to our purpose; a circumstance easily marked, which always belongs to the animal, under every variation of situation or treatment. But an ox is hoofed, and so is a sheep; we must distinguish still farther. You have often stood by, I suppose, while the smith was shoeing a horse. What kind of a hoof has he?

C. — It is round and all in one piece.

F. — And is that of an ox so?

C. — No, it is divided.

F. — A horse, then, is not only hoofed, but *whole hoofed*. Now how many quadrupeds do you think there are in the world that are whole hoofed?

C. — Indeed I do not know.

F. — There are, among all animals that we are acquainted with, either in this country or in any other, only the horse, the ass, and the zebra, which is a species of wild ass. Now, therefore, you see we have nearly accomplished our purpose ; we have only to distinguish him from the ass.

C. — That is easily done, I believe ; I should be sorry if anybody could mistake my little horse for an ass.

F. — It is not so easy, however, as you imagine ; the eye readily distinguishes them by the air and general appearance, but naturalists have been rather puzzled to fix upon any specific difference, which may serve the purpose of a definition. Some have, therefore, fixed upon the ears, others on the mane and tail. What kind of ears has an ass?

C. — O, very long clumsy ears. Asses' ears are always laughed at.

F. — And the horse?

C. — The horse has small ears, nicely turned, and upright.

F. — And the mane, is there no difference there?

C. — The horse has a fine, long, flowing mane ; the ass has hardly any.

F. — And the tail ; is it not fuller of hair in the horse than in the ass?

C. — Yes ; the ass has only a few long hairs at the end of his tail ; but the horse has a long bushy tail, when it is not cut.

F. — Which, by the way, it is pity it ever should. Now, then, observe what particulars we have got. *A horse is an animal of the quadruped kind, whole-hoofed, with short erect ears, a flowing mane, and a tail covered in every part with long hairs.* Now is there any other animal, think you, in the world, that answers these particulars?

C. — I do not know; 'this does not tell us a great deal about him.

F. — And yet it tells us enough to distinguish him from all the different tribes of the creation which we are acquainted with in any part of the earth. Do you know now what we have been making?

C. — What?

F. — A Definition. It is the business of a definition to distinguish precisely the thing defined from every other thing, and to do it in as few terms as possible. Its object is to separate the subject of definition, first, from those with which it has only a general resemblance; then, from those which agree with it in a greater variety of particulars; and so on, till by constantly throwing out all which have not the qualities we have taken notice of, we come at length to the individual or the species we wish to ascertain. It is a kind of chase, and resembles the manner of hunting in some countries, where they first enclose a very large circle with their dogs, nets, and horses; and then, by degrees, draw their toils closer and closer, driving their game before them till it is at length brought into so narrow a compass, that the sportsmen have nothing to do but to knock down their prey.

C. — Just as we have been hunting this horse, till at last we held him fast by his ears and his tail.

F. — I should observe to you, that in the definition naturalists give of a horse, it is generally mentioned that he has six cutting teeth in each jaw; because this circumstance of the teeth has been found a very convenient one for characterizing large classes: but as it is not absolutely necessary here, I have omitted it; a definition being the more perfect the fewer particulars you make use of, provided you can say with certainty from those particulars, The object so characterized must be this, and no other whatever.

C. — But, papa, if I had never seen a horse, I

should not know what kind of animal it was by this definition.

F. — Let us hear, then, how you would give me an idea of a horse.

C. — I would say it was a fine large prancing creature, with slender legs and an arched neck, and a sleek smooth skin, and a tail that sweeps the ground, and that he snorts and neighs very loud, and tosses his head, and runs as swift as the wind.

F. — I think you learned some verses upon the horse in your last lesson: repeat them.

> *C.* — The wanton courser thus with reins unbound
> Breaks from his stall, and beats the trembling ground;
> Pampered and proud, he seeks the wonted tides,
> And laves, in height of blood, his shining sides;
> His head, now freed, he tosses to the skies;
> His mane dishevelled, o'er his shoulders flies;
> He snuffs the females in the distant plain,
> And springs, exulting, to his fields again.   POPE'S HOMER.

F. — You have said very well; but this is not a *Definition*, it is a *Description*.

C. — What is the difference?

F. — A description is intended to give you a lively picture of an object, as if you saw it; it ought to be very full. A definition gives no picture to those who have not seen it; it rather tells you what its subject is not, than what it is, by giving you such clear specific marks, that it shall not be possible to confound it with any thing else; and hence it is of the greatest use in throwing things into classes. We have a great many beautiful descriptions from ancient authors so loosely worded that we cannot certainly tell what animals are meant by them; whereas if they had given us definitions, three lines would have ascertained their meaning.

C. — I like a description best, papa.

F. — Perhaps so; I believe I should have done the same at your age. Remember, however, that nothing

is more useful than to learn to form ideas with precision, and to express them with accuracy : I have
not given you a definition to teach you what a horse
is, but to teach you to *think*.

THE PHENIX AND DOVE.

A PHENIX, who had long inhabited the solitary deserts of Arabia, once flew so near the habitations of
men as to meet with a tame Dove, who was sitting on
her nest, with wings expanded, fondly brooding over
her young ones, while she expected her mate, who was
foraging abroad to procure them food. The Phenix,
with a kind of insulting compassion, said to her, " Poor
bird, how much I pity thee ! confined to a single spot,
and sunk in domestic cares ; thou art continually
employed either in laying eggs or in providing for thy
brood ; and thou exhaustest thy life and strength in
perpetuating a feeble and defenceless race. As to myself, I live exempt from toil, care, and misfortune. I
feed upon nothing less precious than rich gums and
spices ; I fly through the trackless regions of the air,
and when I am seen by men, am gazed at with curiosity and astonishment ; I have no one to control my
range, no one to provide for ; and when I have fulfilled
my five centuries of life, and seen the revolutions of
ages, I rather vanish than die, and a successor, without
my care, springs up from my ashes. I am an image of
the great sun whom I adore ; and glory in being, like
him, single and alone, and having no likeness."
The Dove replied, " O Phenix, I pity thee much
more than thou affectest to pity me ! What pleasure
canst thou enjoy, who livest forlorn and solitary in a
trackless and unpeopled desert ; who hast no mate to

caress thee, no young ones to excite thy tenderness
and reward thy cares, no kindred, no society amongst
thy fellows.   Not long life only, but immortality itself
would be a curse, if it were to be bestowed on such
uncomfortable terms.   For my part, I know that my
life will be short, and therefore I employ it in raising a
numerous posterity, and in opening my heart to all the
sweets of domestic happiness.   I am beloved by my
partner; I am dear to man; and shall leave marks
behind me that I have lived.   As to the sun, to whom
thou hast presumed to compare thyself, that glorious
being is so totally different from, and so infinitely superior to, all the creatures upon earth, that it does not
become us to liken ourselves to him, or to determine
upon the manner of his existence.   One obvious difference, however, thou mayest remark; that the sun,
though alone, by his prolific heat, produces all things,
and though he shines so high above our heads, gives
us reason every moment to bless his beams; whereas
thou, swelling with thy imaginary greatness, dreamest
away a long period of existence, equally void of comfort and usefulness."

THE MANUFACTURE OF PAPER.

Fa. — I WILL now, as I promised, give you an account of the elegant and useful manufacture of *Paper*,
the basis of which is itself a manufacture.   This delicate and beautiful substance is made from the meanest
and most disgusting materials, from old rags, which
have passed from one poor person to another, and at
length have perhaps dropped in tatters from the child of
the beggar.   These are carefully picked up from dung-
hills, or bought from servants by Jews, who make it their

business to go about and collect them. They sell them
to the rag-merchant, who gives from two-pence to four-
pence a pound, according to their quality; and he,
when he has got a sufficient quantity, disposes of them
to the owner of the paper-mill. He gives them first
to women to sort and pick, agreeably to their different
degrees of fineness : they also with a knife cut out
carefully all the seams, which they throw into a basket
for other purposes; they then put them into the dust-
ing engine, a large circular wire sieve, from whence
they receive some degree of cleansing. The rags are
then conveyed.to the mill. Here they were formerly
beat to pieces with vast hammers, which rose and fell
continually with a most tremendous noise, that was
heard from a great distance. But now they put the
rags into a large trough or cistern, into which a pipe of
clear spring water is constantly flowing. In this cistern is placed a cylinder, about two feet long, set
thick round with rows of iron spikes, standing as near
as they can to one another without touching. At the
bottom of the trough there are corresponding rows of
spikes. The cylinder is made to whirl round with
inconceivable rapidity, and with these iron teeth rends
and tears the cloth in every possible direction; till, by
the assistance of the water, which continually flows
through the cistern, it is thoroughly masticated, and
reduced to a fine pulp; and by the same process all its
impurities are cleansed away, and it is restored to its
original whiteness. This process takes about six hours.
To improve the color they then put in a little smalt,
which gives it a bluish cast, which all paper has more
or less : the French paper has less of it than ours.
This fine pulp is next put into a copper of warm water.
It is the substance of paper, but the form must now
be given it : for this purpose they use a mould. It is
made of wire, strong one way, and crossed with finer.
This mould they just dip horizontally into the copper,

and take it out again.   It has a little wooden frame on the edge, by means of which it retains as much of the pulp as is wanted for the thickness of the sheet, and the superfluity runs off through the interstices of the wires.   Another man instantly receives it, opens the frame, and turns out the thin sheet, which has now shape, but not consistence, upon soft felt, which is placed on the ground to receive it.   On that is placed another piece of felt, and then another sheet of paper, and so on till they have made a pile of forty or fifty. They are then pressed with a large screw-press, moved by a long lever, which forcibly squeezes the water out of them, and gives them immediate consistence.   There is still, however, a great deal to be done.   The felts are taken off, and thrown on one side, and the paper on the other, from whence it is dexterously taken up with an instrument in the form of a T, three sheets at a time and hung on lines to dry.   There it hangs for a week or ten days, which likewise further whitens it; and any knots and roughnesses it may have are picked off carefully by the women,   It is then sized.   Size is a kind of glue ; and without this preparation the paper would not bear ink ; it would run and blot, as you see it does on gray paper.   The sheets are just dipped into the size and taken out again.   The exact degree of sizing is a matter of nicety, which can only be known by experience.   They are then hung up again to dry, and when dry taken to the finishing-room, where they are examined anew, pressed in the dry presses, which gives them their last gloss and smoothness; counted up into quires, made up in reams, and sent to the sta-tioner's, from whom we have it, after he has folded it again and cut the edges ; some too he makes to shine like satin, by glossing it with hot plates.   The whole process of paper-making takes about three weeks.

H. — It is a very curious process indeed.   I shall almost scruple for the future to blacken a sheet of paper with a careless scrawl, now I know how much pains it costs to make it so white and beautiful.

F. — It is true that there is hardly any thing we use with so much waste and profusion as this manufacture ; we should think ourselves confined in the use of it, if we might not tear, disperse, and destroy it in a thousand ways ; so that it is really astonishing from whence linen enough can be procured to answer so vast a demand. As to the coarse brown papers, of which an astonishing quantity is used by every shopkeeper in packages &c., these are made chiefly of oakum, that is, old hempen ropes. A fine paper is made in China of silk.

H. — I have heard lately of woven paper ; pray what is that? they cannot weave paper, surely !

F. — Your question is very natural. In order to answer it I must desire you to take a sheet of common paper, and hold it up against the light. Do not you see marks in it?

H. — I see a great many white lines running along lengthways, like ribs, and smaller that cross them. I see, too, letters and the figure of a crown.

F. — These are all the marks of the wires ; the thickness of the wire prevents so much of the pulp lying upon the sheet in those places, consequently wherever the wires are, the paper is thinner, and you see the light through more readily, which gives that appearance of white lines. The letters, too, are worked in the wire, and are the maker's name. Now to prevent these lines, which take off from the beauty of the paper, particularly of drawing paper, there have been lately used moulds of brass wire exceedingly fine, of equal thickness, and woven or latticed one within another ; the marks therefore, of these are easily pressed out, so as to be hardly visible ; if you look at this sheet you will see it is quite smooth.

H. — It is so.

F. — I should mention to you, that there is a discovery very lately made, by which they can make paper, equal to any in whiteness, of the coarsest brown rags, and even of dyed cottons; which they have till now been obliged to throw by for inferior purposes. This is by means of manganese, a sort of mineral, and oil of vitriol; a mixture of which they just pass through the pulp, while it is in water, for otherwise it would burn it, and in an instant it discharges the colors of the dyed cloths, and bleaches the brown to a beautiful whiteness.

H. — That is like what you told me before of bleaching cloth in a few hours.

F. — It is indeed founded upon the same discovery. The paper made of these brown rags is likewise more valuable, from being very tough and strong, almost like parchment.

H. — When was the making of paper found out?

F. — It is a disputed point, but probably in the fourteenth century. The invention has been of almost equal consequence to literature, as that of printing itself; and shows how the arts and sciences, like children of the same family, mutually assist and bring forward each other.

THE FOUR SISTERS.

I am one of four sisters; and having some reason to think myself not well used either by them or by the world, I beg leave to lay before you a sketch of our history and characters. You will not wonder there should be frequent bickerings amongst us, when I tell you that in our infancy we were continually fighting; and so great was the noise, and din, and confusion, in our continual struggles to get uppermost, that it was impossible for anybody to live amongst us in such a scene of tumult and disorder. These brawls, however, by a powerful interposition, were put an end to; our proper place was assigned to each of us, and we had strict orders not to encroach on the limits of each other's property, but to join our common offices for the good of the whole family.

My first sister (I call her the first, because we have generally allowed her the precedence in rank) is, I must acknowledge, of a very active, sprightly disposition; quick and lively, and has more brilliancy than any of us; but she is hot; every thing serves for fuel to her fury, when it is once raised to a certain degree, and she is so mischievous whenever she gets the upper hand, that, notwithstanding her aspiring disposition, if I may freely speak my mind, she is calculated to make a good servant, but a very bad mistress.

I am almost ashamed to mention, that notwithstanding her seeming delicacy, she has a most voracious appetite, and devours every thing that comes in her way; though, like other eager thin people, she does no credit to her keeping. Many a time has she consumed the product of my barns and store-houses, but it is all lost upon her. She has even been known to get into an oil-shop or tallow-chandler's, when everybody was asleep, and lick up, with the utmost greediness, whatever she found there. Indeed, all prudent people are aware of her tricks, and though she is admitted into the best families, they take care to watch her very narrowly. I should not forget to mention, that my sister was once in a country where she was treated with uncommon respect. She was lodged in a sumptuous building, and had a number of young women, of the best families, to attend on her, and feed her, and watch over her health; in short, she was looked upon as something more than a common mortal. But she always behaved with great severity to her maids, and if

any of them were negligent of their duty, or made a
slip in their own conduct, nothing would serve her but
burying the poor girls alive.   I have myself had some
dark hints and intimations from the most respectable
authority, that she will some time or other make an end
of me.   You need not wonder, therefore, if I am jealous of her motions.

The next sister I shall mention to you, has so far
the appearance of modesty and humility, that she generally seeks the lowest place.   She is indeed of a very
yielding, easy temper, generally cool, and often wears a
sweet placid smile upon her countenance ; but she is
easily ruffled, and when worked up, as she often is, by
another sister, whom I shall mention to you by and by,
she becomes a perfect fury.   Indeed, she is so apt to
swell with sudden gusts of passion, that she is suspected at times to be a little lunatic.   Between her and
my first mentioned sister, there is more settled antipa-
thy than between the Theban pair ; and they never
meet without making efforts to destroy one another.
With me she is always ready to form the most intimate
union, but it is not always to my advantage.   There
goes a story in our family, that when we were all young,
she once attempted to drown me.   She actually kept
me under a considerable time, and though at length I
got my head above water, my constitution is generally
thought to have been essentially injured by it ever
since.   From that time she has made no such atro-
cious attempt, but she is continually making encroachments upon my property ; and even when she appears
most gentle, she is very insidious, and has such an
undermining way with her, that her insinuating arts are
as much to be dreaded as open violence.   I might
indeed remonstrate, but it is a known part of her character, that nothing makes any lasting impression upon
her.

As to my third sister, I have already mentioned the

ill offices she does me with my last mentioned one, who is entirely under her influence. She is, besides, of a very uncertain, variable temper, sometimes hot, and sometimes cold; nobody knows where to have her. Her lightness is even proverbial, and she has nothing to give those who live with her more substantial than the smiles of courtiers. I must add, that she keeps in her service three or four rough, blustering bullies, with puffed cheeks, who, when they are let loose, think they have nothing to do but to drive the world before them. She sometimes joins with my first sister, and their violence occasionally throws me into such a trembling, that, though naturally of a firm constitution, I shake as if I was in an ague fit.

As to myself, I am of a steady, solid temper; not shining indeed, but kind and liberal, quite a Lady Bountiful. Every one tastes of my beneficence, and I am of so grateful a disposition, that I have been known to return an hundred-fold for any present that has been made me. I feed and clothe all my children, and afford a welcome home to the wretch who has no other home. I bear with unrepining patience all manner of ill usage; I am trampled upon; I am torn and wounded with the most cutting stroke; I am pillaged of the treasures hidden in my most secret chambers; notwithstanding which, I anf always ready to return good for evil, and am continually subservient to the pleasure or advantage of others; yet so ungrateful is the world, that because I do not possess all the airiness and activity of my sisters, I am stigmatized as dull and heavy. Every sordid, miserly fellow is called by way of derision one of *my* children; and if a person on entering a room does but turn his eyes upon me, he is thought stupid and mean, and not fit for good company. I have the satisfaction, however, of finding that people always incline towards me as they grow older; and that those who seemed proudly to disdain any affinity with me, are content to sink at last into my bosom. You will probably wish to have some account of my person. I am not a regular beauty : some of my features are rather harsh and prominent, when viewed separately ; but my countenance has so much variety of expression, and so many different attitudes of elegance, that those who study my face with attention, find out continually new charms ; and it may be truly said of me, what Titus says of his mistress, and for a much longer space,

> Pendant cinq ans entiers tous les jours je la vois,
> Et crois toujours la voir pour la premiere fois.

> For five whole years each day she meets my view,
> Yet every day I seem to see her new.

Though I have been so long a mother, I have still a surprising air of youth and freshness, which is assisted by all the advantages of well-chosen ornament ; for I dress well, and according to the season.

This is what I have chiefly to say of myself and my sisters. To a person of your sagacity it will be unnecessary for me to sign my name. Indeed, one who becomes acquainted with any one of the family, cannot be at a loss to discover the rest, notwithstanding the difference in our features and characters.

THE PINE AND THE OLIVE.

A FABLE.

A STOIC, swelling with the proud consciousness of his own worth, took a solitary walk ; and straying amongst the groves of Academus, he sat down between an Olive and a Pine tree. His attention was soon excited by a murmur which he heard among the leaves. The whispers increased ; and listening attentively, he plainly heard the Pine say to the Olive as follows : " Poor tree ! I pity thee : thou now spread-est thy green leaves and exultest in all the pride of youth and spring ; but how soon will thy beauty be tarnished ! The fruit which thou exhaustest thyself to bear, shall hardly be shaken from thy boughs before thou shalt grow dry and withered : thy green veins, now so full of juice, shall be frozen ; naked and bare, thou wilt stand exposed to all the storms of winter, whilst my firmer leaf shall resist the change of the sea-sons. *Unchangeable* is my motto, and through the various vicissitudes of the year I shall continue equally green and vigorous as I am at present."

The Olive, with a graceful wave of her boughs re-plied : " It is true thou wilt always continue as thou art at present. Thy leaves will keep that sullen and gloomy green in which they are now arrayed, and the stiff regularity of thy branches will not yield to those storms which will bow down many of the feebler tenants of the grove. Yet I wish not to be like thee. I rejoice when nature rejoices ; and when I am desolate, nature mourns with me. I fully enjoy pleasure in its season, and I am contented to be subject to the influences of those seasons and that economy of nature by which I flourish. When the spring approaches, I feel the kind-ly warmth ; my branches swell with young buds, and my leaves unfold ; crowds of singing birds which never visit thy noxious shade, sport on my boughs ; my fruit is offered to the gods, and rejoices men ; and when the decay of nature approaches, I shed my leaves over the funeral of the falling year, and am well contented not to stand a single exception to the mournful desolation I see everywhere around me."

The Pine was unable to frame a reply ; and the phil-osopher turned away his steps, rebuked and humbled.

ON RIDDLES.

MY DEAR YOUNG FRIENDS, — I presume you are now all come home for the holidays, and that the brothers and sisters and cousins, papas and mammas, uncles and aunts, are all met cheerfully round a Christmas fire, enjoying the company of their friends and relations, and eating plum pudding and mince pie. These are very good things; but one cannot always be eating plum pudding and mince pie : the days are short, and the weather bad, so that you cannot be much abroad; and I think you must want something to amuse you. Besides, if you have been employed as you ought to be at school, and if you are quick and clever, as I hope you are, you will want some employment for that part of you which thinks, as well as that part of you which eats ; and you will like better to solve a riddle than to crack a nut or walnut. Finding out riddles is the same kind of exercise of the mind which running and leaping and wrestling in sport are to the body. They are of no use in themselves, — they are not work, but play ; but they prepare the body, and make it alert and active for any thing it may be called to perform in labor or war. So does the finding out of riddles, if they are good especially, give quickness of thought, and a facility of turning about a problem every way, and viewing it in every possible light. When Archimedes, coming out of the bath, cried in transport, " *Eurcka !* " (I have found it !) he had been exercising his mind precisely in the same manner as you will do when you are searching about for the solution of a riddle.

And pray, when you are got together, do not let any little Miss or Master say, with an affected air, " Oh, do not ask me ; I am so stupid I never can guess." They do not mean you should think them stupid and dull ; they mean to imply that these things are too trifling to engage their attention. If they are employed better, it is very well; but if not, say, " I am very sorry indeed you are so dull, but we that are clever and quick will exercise our wits upon these ; and, as our arms grow stronger by exercise, so will our wits."

Riddles are of high antiquity, and were the employment of grave men formerly. The first riddle that we have on record was proposed by Samson at a wedding feast to the young men of the Philistines who were invited upon the occasion. The feast lasted seven days ; and if they found it out within the seven days, Samson was to give them thirty suits of clothes and thirty sheets ; and if they could not guess it, they were to forfeit the same to him. The riddle was, " Out of the eater came forth meat, and out of the strong came forth sweetness." He had killed a lion, and left its carcass : on returning soon after, he found a swarm of bees had made use of the skeleton as a hive, and it was full of honeycomb. Struck with the oddness of the circumstance, he made a riddle of it. They puzzled about it the whole seven days, and would not have found it out at last if his wife had not told them.

The Sphinx was a great riddle-maker. According to the fable, she was half a woman and half a lion. She lived near Thebes, and to everybody that came she proposed a riddle ; and if they did not find it out, she devoured them. At length Œdipus came, and she asked him, " What is that animal which walks on four legs in the morning, two at noon, and three at night ! " Œdipus answered, " Man : in childhood, which is the morning of life, he crawls on his hands and feet ; in middle age, which is noon, he walks erect on two ; in old age he leans on a crutch, which serves for a supplementary third foot."

The famous wise men of Greece did not disdain to send puzzles to each other. They are also fond of riddles in the East. There is a pretty one in some of their tales: "What is that tree which has twelve branches, and each branch thirty leaves, which are all black on one side and white on the other?" The tree is the year; the branches the months; the leaves, black on one side and white on the other, signify day and night. Our Anglo-Saxon ancestors also had riddles, some of which are still preserved in a very ancient manuscript.

A riddle is a description of a thing without the name; but as it is meant to puzzle, it appears to belong to something else than what it really does, and often seems contradictory; but when you have guessed it, it appears quite clear. It is a bad riddle if you are at all in doubt when you have found it out whether you are right or no. A riddle is not verbal, as charades, conundrums, and rebuses are: it may be translated into any language, which the others cannot. Addison would put them all in the class of false wit: but Swift, who was as great a genius, amused himself with making all sorts of puzzles; and therefore, I think you need not be ashamed of reading them. It would be pretty entertainment for you to make a collection of the better ones, — for many are so dull that they are not worth spending time about. I will conclude by sending you a few which will be new to you.

I.

I often murmur, yet I never weep;
I always lie in bed, yet never sleep;
My mouth is wide, and larger than my head,
And much disgorges though it ne'er is fed;
I have no legs or feet, yet swiftly run,
And the more falls I get, move faster on.

II.

Ye youths and ye virgins, come list to my tale,
With youth and with beauty my voice will prevail.
My smile is enchanting, and golden my hair,
And on earth I am fairest of all that is fair ;
But my name it perhaps may assist you to tell,
That I 'm banish'd alike both from heaven and hell.
There 's a charm in my voice, 't is than music more
      sweet,
And my tale oft repeated, untired I repeat.
I flatter, I soothe, I speak kindly to all,
And wherever you go, I am still within call.
Though I thousands have blest, 't is a strange thing to
      say,
That not one of the thousands e'er wishes my stay.
But when most I enchant him, impatient the more,
The minutes seem hours till my visit is o'er.
In the chase of my love I am ever employed,
Still, still he 's pursued, and yet never enjoyed ;
O'er hills and o'er valleys unwearied I fly,
But should I o'ertake him, that instant I die ;
Yet I spring up again, and again I pursue,
The object still distant, the passion still new.
Now guess, — and to raise your astonishment most,
While you seek me you have me, when found I am lost.

III.

I never talk but in my sleep ;
I never cry, but sometimes weep ;
My doors are open day and night ;
Old age I help to better sight ;
I, like chameleon, feed on air,
And dust to me is dainty fare.

IV.

We are spirits all in white,
On a field as black as night ;
There we dance and sport and play,
Changing every changing day ;
Yet with us is wisdom found,
As we move in mystic round.

Mortal, wouldst thou know the grains
That Ceres heaps on Libya's plains,
Or leaves that yellow Autumn strews,
Or the stars that Herschel views,
Or find how many drops would drain
The wide-scooped bosom of the main,
Or measure central depths below, —
Ask of us, and thou shalt know.
With fairy feet we compass round
The pyramid's capacious bound,
Or step by step ambitious climb
The cloud-capt mountain's height sublime.
   Riches though we do not use,
'T is ours to gain, and ours to lose.
From Araby the Blest we came.
In every land our tongue 's the same;
And if our number you require,
Go count the bright Aonian quire.
Wouldst thou cast a spell to find
The track of light, the speed of wind,
Or when the snail with creeping pace
Shall the swelling globe embrace;
Mortal, ours the powerful spell; —
Ask of us, for we can tell.

HYMNS.

COME, let us praise God, for he is exceeding great :
let us bless God, for he is very good.

He made all things; the sun to rule the day, the
moon to shine by night.

He made the great whale, and the elephant; and
the little worm that crawleth on the ground.

The little birds sing praises to God, when they warble sweetly in the green shade.

The brooks and rivers praise God, when they murmur melodiously amongst the smooth pebbles.

I will praise God with my voice; for I may praise him, though I am but a little child.

A few years ago, and I was a little infant, and my tongue was dumb within my mouth:

And I did not know the great name of God, for my reason was not come unto me.

But now I can speak, and my tongue shall praise him; I can think of all his kindness, and my heart shall love him.

Let him call me, and I will come unto him; let him command, and I will obey him.

When I am older, I will praise him better; and I will never forget God, so long as my life remaineth in me.

HYMN II.

COME, let us go forth into the fields, let us see how the flowers spring, let us listen to the warbling of the birds, and sport ourselves upon the new grass.

The winter is over and gone, the buds come out upon the trees, the crimson blossoms of the peach and the nectarine are seen, and the green leaves sprout.

The hedges are bordered with tufts of primroses, and yellow cowslips that hang down their heads; and the blue violet lies hid beneath the shade.

The young goslings are running upon the green; they are just hatched, their bodies are covered with yellow down; the old ones hiss with anger if any one comes near.

The hen sits upon her nest of straw, she watches patiently the full time, then she carefully breaks the shell, and the young chickens come out.

The lambs just dropped are in the field, they totter by the side of their dams, their young limbs can hardly support their weight.

If you fall, little lambs, you will not be hurt; there

is spread under you a carpet of soft grass; it is spread on purpose to receive you.

The butterflies flutter from bush to bush, and open their wings to the warm sun.

The young animals of every kind are sporting about, they feel themselves happy, they are glad to be alive, they thank him that has made them alive.

They may thank him in their hearts, but we can thank him with our tongues; we are better than they, and can praise him better.

The birds can warble, and the young lambs can bleat; but we can open our lips in his praise, we can speak of all his goodness.

Therefore we will thank him for ourselves, and we will thank him for those that cannot speak.

Trees that blossom, and little lambs that skip about, if you could, you would say how good he is; but you are dumb, we will say it for you.

We will not offer you in sacrifice, but we will offer sacrifice for you; on every hill, and in every green field, we will offer the sacrifice of thanksgiving, and the incense of praise.

HYMN III.

BEHOLD the shepherd of the flock; he taketh care for his sheep, he leadeth them among clear brooks, he guideth them to fresh pasture: if the young lambs are weary, he carrieth them in his arms; if they wander, he bringeth them back.

But who is the shepherd's shepherd; who taketh care for him? who guideth him in the path he should go? and, if he wander, who shall bring him back?

God is the shepherd's Shepherd. He is the Shepherd over all; he taketh care for all; the whole earth is his fold; we are all his flock; and every herb, and every green field is the pasture which he hath prepared for us.

The mother loveth her little child ; she bringeth it up on her knees ; she nourisheth its body with food ; she feedeth its mind with knowledge : if it is sick, she nurseth it with tender love ; she watcheth over it when asleep ; she forgetteth it not for a moment ; she teacheth it how to be good ; she rejoiceth daily in its growth.

But who is the parent of the mother? who nourisheth her with good things, and watcheth over her with tender love, and remembereth her every moment? Whose arms are about her to guard her from harm? and if she is sick, who shall heal her?

God is the Parent of the mother ; he is the Parent of all, for he created all. All the men, and all the women, who are alive in the wide world, are his children ; he loveth all, he is good to all.

The king governeth his people ; he hath a golden crown upon his head, and the royal sceptre is in his hand ; he sitteth upon a throne, and sendeth forth his commands ; his subjects fear before him ; if they do well, he protecteth them from danger ; and if they do evil, he punisheth them.

But who is the sovereign of the king? who commandeth him what he must do? whose hand is reached out to protect him from danger? and if he doeth evil, who shall punish him?

God is the Sovereign of the king? his crown is of rays of light, and his throne is amongst the stars. He is King of kings, and Lord of lords : if he biddeth us live, we live ; and if he biddeth us die, we die : his dominion is over all worlds, and the light of his countenance is upon all his works.

God is our Shepherd, therefore we will follow him ; God is our Father, therefore we will love him ; God is our King, therefore we will obey him.

HYMN IV.

COME, and I will show you what is beautiful. It is a rose fully blown. See how she sits upon her mossy stem, like the queen of all the flowers! her leaves glow like fire; the air is filled with her sweet odor! she is the delight of every eye.

She is beautiful, but there is a fairer than she. He that made the rose is more beautiful than the rose; he is all lovely; he is the delight of every heart.

I will show you what is strong. The lion is strong; when he raiseth up himself from his lair, when he shaketh his mane, when the voice of his roaring is heard, the cattle of the field fly, and the wild beasts of the desert hide themselves, for he is very terrible.

The lion is strong, but he that made the lion is stronger than he.: his anger is terrible; he could make us die in a moment, and no one could save us out of his hand.

I will show you what is glorious. The sun is glorious. When he shineth in the clear sky, when he sitteth on the bright throne in the heavens, and looketh abroad over all the earth, he is the most excellent and glorious creature the eye can behold.

The sun is glorious, but he that made the sun is more glorious than he. The eye beholdeth him not, for his brightness is more dazzling than we could bear. He seeth in all dark places; by night as well as by day; and the light of his countenance is over all his works.

Who is this great name, and what is he called, that my lips may praise him?

This great name is GOD. He made all things, but he is himself more excellent than all which he hath made: they are beautiful, but he is beauty; they are strong, but he is strength; they are perfect, but he is perfection.

HYMN V.

THE glorious sun is set in the west; the night dews fall; and the air, which was sultry, becomes cool.

The flowers fold up their colored leaves; they fold themselves up, and hang their heads on the slender stalk.

The chickens are gathered under the wing of the hen, and are at rest; the hen herself is at rest also.

The little birds have ceased their warbling, they are asleep on the boughs, each one with his head behind his wing.

There is no murmur of bees around the hive, or among the honeyed woodbines; they have done their work, and lie close in their waxen cells.

The sheep rest upon their soft fleeces, and their loud bleating is no more heard amongst the hills.

There is no sound of a number of voices, or of children at play, or the trampling of busy feet, and of people hurrying to and fro.

The smith's hammer is not heard upon the anvil; nor the harsh saw of the carpenter.

All men are stretched on their quiet beds; and the child sleeps upon the breast of its mother.

Darkness is spread over the skies, and darkness is upon the ground; every eye is shut, and every hand is still.

Who taketh care of all people when they are sunk in sleep; when they cannot defend themselves, nor see if danger approacheth?

There is an eye that never sleepeth; there is an eye that seeth in dark night as well as in the bright sunshine.

When there is no light of the sun, nor of the moon; when there is no lamp in the house, nor any little star twinkling through the thick clouds; that eye seeth everywhere, in all places, and watcheth continually over all the families of the earth.

The eye that sleepeth not is God's; his hand is always stretched out over us.

He made sleep to refresh us when we are weary; he made night, that we might sleep in quiet.

As the mother moveth about the house with her finger on her lips, and stilleth every little noise, that her infant be not disturbed; as she draweth the curtains around its bed, and shutteth out the light from its tender eyes; so God draweth the curtains of darkness around us; so he maketh all things to be hushed and still, that his large family may sleep in peace.

Laborers spent with toil, and young children, and every little humming insect, sleep quietly, for God watcheth over you.

You may sleep, for he never sleeps : you may close your eyes in safety, for his eye is always open to protect you.

When the darkness is passed away, and the beams of the morning sun strike through your eyelids, begin the day with praising God, who hath taken care of you through the night.

Flowers, when you open again, spread your leaves, and smell sweet to his praise.

Birds, when you awake, warble your thanks amongst the green boughs; sing to him before you sing to your mates.

Let his praise be in our hearts, when we lie down; let his praise be in our lips, when we awake.

HYMN VI.

CHILD of reason, whence comest thou? What has thine eye observed, and whither has thy foot been wandering?

I have been wandering along the meadows, in the thick grass; the cattle were feeding around me, or reposing in the cool shade; the corn sprung up in the furrows ; the poppy and the harebell grew among the wheat ; the fields were bright with summer, and glowing with beauty.

Didst thou see nothing more? Didst thou observe nothing besides? Return again, child of reason, for there are greater things than these.

God was among the fields ; and didst thou not perceive him? his beauty was upon the meadows ; his smile enlivened the sunshine.

I have walked through the thick forest ; the wind whispered among the trees ; the brook fell from the rocks with a pleasant murmur ; the squirrel leapt from bough to bough : and the birds sung to each other amongst the branches.

Didst thou hear nothing but the murmur of the brook? no whispers but the whispers of the wind? Return again, child of reason, for there are greater things than these. God was amongst the trees ; his voice sounded in the murmur of the water ; his music warbled in the shade ; and didst thou not attend?

I saw the moon rising behind trees ; it was like a lamp of gold. The stars one after another appeared in the clear firmament. Presently I saw black clouds arise, and roll towards the south ; the lightning streamed in thick flashes over the sky ; the thunder growled at a distance ; it came nearer, and I felt afraid, for it was loud and terrible.

Did thy heart feel no terror but of the thunderbolt? Was there nothing bright and terrible but the lightning? Return, O child of reason, for there are greater things than these. God was in the storm, and didst thou not perceive him? His terrors were abroad, and did not thine heart acknowledge him?

God is in every place ; he speaks in every sound we hear ; he is seen in all that our eyes behold ; nothing, O child of reason, is without God : — let God therefore be in all thy thoughts.

HYMN VII.

COME, let us go into the thick shade, for it is the noon of day, and the summer sun beats hot upon our heads.

The shade is pleasant and cool; the branches meet above our heads, and shut out the sun as with a green curtain; the grass is soft to our feet, and a clear brook washes the roots of the trees.

The sloping bank is covered with flowers; let us lie down upon it; let us throw our limbs on the fresh grass and sleep; for all things are still, and we are quite alone.

The cattle can lie down to sleep in the cool shade, but we can do what is better; we can raise our voices to heaven; we can praise the great God who made us. He made the warm sun, and the cool shade; the trees that grow upwards, and the brooks that run murmuring along. All the things that we see are his work.

Can we raise our voices up to the high heaven? Can we make him hear who is above the stars? We need not raise our voices to the stars, for he heareth us when we only whisper; when we breathe out words softly with a low voice. He that filleth the heavens is here also.

May we that are so young speak to him that always was? May we, that can hardly speak plain, speak to God?

We that are so young are but lately made alive; therefore we should not forget his forming hand who hath made us alive. We that cannot speak plain, should lisp out praises to him who teacheth us how to speak, and hath opened our dumb lips.

When we could not think of him, he thought of us; before we could ask him to bless us, he had already given us many blessings.

He fashioneth our tender limbs, and causeth them to grow; he maketh us strong, and tall, and nimble.

Every day we are more active than the former day, therefore every day we ought to praise him better than the former day.

The buds spread into leaves, and the blossoms swell to fruit; but they know not how they grow, nor who caused them to spring up from the bosom of the earth.

Ask them if they will tell thee; bid them break forth into singing, and fill the air with pleasant sounds.

They smell sweet; they look beautiful; but they are quite silent; no sound is in the still air; no murmur of voices amongst the green leaves.

The plants and the trees are made to give fruit to man; but man is made to praise God who made him.

We love to praise him, because he loveth to bless us; we thank him for life, because it is a pleasant thing to be alive.

We love God, who hath created all beings; we love all beings, because they are the creatures of God.

We cannot be good, as God is good to all persons everywhere; but we can rejoice that everywhere there is a God to do them good.

We will think of God when we play, and when we work; when we walk out, and when we come in; when we sleep, and when we wake; his praise shall dwell continually upon our lips.

HYMN VIII.

SEE where stands the cottage of the laborer covered with warm thatch ! the mother is spinning at the door; the young children sport before her on the grass; the elder ones learn to labor, and are obedient; the father worketh to provide them food : either he tilleth the ground, or he gathereth in the corn, or shaketh his ripe apples from the tree; his children run to meet him when he cometh home, and his wife prepareth the wholesome meal.

The father, the mother, and the children, make a family ; the father is the master thereof. If the family be numerous, and the grounds large, there are servants to help to do the work : all these dwell in one house ; they sleep beneath one roof; they eat of the same bread ; they kneel down together and praise God every night and every morning with one voice ; they are very closely united, and are dearer to each other than any strangers. If one is sick, they mourn together ; and if one is happy, they rejoice together.

Many houses are built together ; many families live near one another ; they meet together on the green, and in pleasant walks, and to buy and sell, and in the house of justice : and the sound of the bell calleth them to the house of God, in company. If one is poor, his neighbor helpeth him ; if he is sad, he comforteth him. This is a village ; see where it stands enclosed in a green shade, and the tall spire peeps above the trees. If there be very many houses, it is a town ; it is governed by a magistrate.

Many towns, and a large extent of country, make a kingdom ; it is enclosed by mountains ; it is divided by rivers ; it is washed by seas ; the inhabitants thereof are countrymen ; they speak the same language ; they make war and peace together ; a king is the ruler thereof.

Many kingdoms and countries full of people, and islands, and large continents, and different climates, make up this whole world ; God governeth it. The people swarm upon the face of it like ants upon a hillock ; some are black with the hot sun ; some cover themselves with furs against the sharp cold ; some drink of the fruit of the vine ; some the pleasant milk of the cocoa-nut ; and others quench their thirst with the running stream.

All are God's family; he knoweth every one of them, as a shepherd knoweth his flock; they pray to him in different languages, but he understandeth them all; he heareth them all; he taketh care of all; none are so great that he cannot punish them; none are so mean that he will not protect them.

Negro woman, who sittest pining in captivity, and weepest over thy sick child: though no one seeth thee, God seeth thee; though no one pitieth thee, God pitieth thee: raise thy voice, forlorn and abandoned one; call upon him from amidst thy bonds, for assuredly he will hear thee.

Monarch, that rulest over an hundred states; whose frown is terrible as death, and whose armies cover the land, boast not thyself as though there were none above thee: — God is above thee; his powerful arm is always over thee; and if thou doest ill, assuredly he will punish thee.

Nations of the earth, fear the Lord; families of men, call upon the name of your God.

Is there any one whom God hath not made? — let him not worship him. Is there any one whom he hath not blessed? — let him not praise him.

HYMN IX.

COME, let us walk abroad; let us talk of the works of God.

Take up a handful of the sand; number the grains of it; tell them one by one into your lap.

Try if you can count the blades of grass in the field, or the leaves on the trees.

You cannot count them, they are innumerable; much more the things which God has made.

The fir groweth on the high mountain, and the gray willow bends above the stream.

The thistle is armed with sharp prickles; the mallow is soft and woolly.

The hop layeth hold with her tendrils, and claspeth the tall pole : the oak hath firm root in the ground, and resisteth the winter storm.

The daisy enamelleth the meadows, and groweth beneath the foot of the passenger : the tulip asketh a rich soil, and the careful hand of the gardener.

The iris and the reed spring up in the marsh; the rich grass covereth the meadows; and the purple heath flower enliveneth the waste ground.

The water lilies grow beneath the stream; their broad leaves float on the surface of the water : the wall-flower takes root in the hard stone, and spreads its fragrance amongst the broken ruins.

Every leaf is of a different form; every plant hath a separate inhabitant.

Look at the thorns that are white with blossoms, and the flowers that cover the fields, and the plants that are trodden in the green path. The hand of man hath not planted them; the sower hath not scattered the seeds from his hand, nor the gardener digged a place for them with his spade.

Some grow on steep rocks, where no man can climb : in shaking bogs, and deep forests, and desert islands : they spring up everywhere, and cover the bosom of the whole earth.

Who causeth them to grow everywhere, and bloweth the seeds about in winds, and mixeth them with the mould, and watereth them with soft rains, and cherisheth them with dews? Who fanneth them with the pure breath of heaven, and giveth them colors, and smells, and spreadeth out their thin transparent leaves?

How doth the rose draw its crimson from the dark brown earth, or the lily its shining white? How can a small seed contain a plant? How doth every plant know its season to put forth? They are marshalled in order : each one knoweth his place, and standeth up in his own rank.

The snow-drop and the primrose make haste to lift their heads above the ground. When the spring cometh, they say, Here we are ! The carnation waiteth for the full strength of the year ; and the hardy laurustinus cheereth the winter months.

Every plant produceth its like. An ear of corn will not grow from an acorn ; nor will a grape-stone produce cherries ; but every one springeth from its proper seed.

Who preserveth them alive through the cold of winter, when the snow is on the ground, and the sharp frost bites on the plain? Who soweth a small seed, and a little warmth in the bosom of the earth, and causeth them to spring up afresh, and sap to rise through the hard fibres.

The trees are withered, naked, and bare ; they are like dry bones. Who breatheth on them with the breath of spring, and they are covered with verdure, and green leaves sprout from the dead wood?

Lo, these are a part of his works ; and a little portion of his wonders.

There is little need that I should tell you of God, for every thing speaks of him.

Every field is like an open book ; every painted flower hath a lesson written on its leaves.

Every murmuring brook hath a tongue : a voice is in every whispering wind.

They all speak of him who made them ; they all tell us he is very good.

We cannot see God, for he is invisible ; but we can see his works, and worship his footsteps in the green sod.

They that know the most, will praise God the best ; but which of us can number half his works?

HYMN X.

Look at that spreading oak, the pride of the village green ! Its trunk is massy, its branches are strong : its roots, like crooked fangs, strike deep into the soil, and support its huge bulk. The birds build among the boughs ; the cattle repose beneath its shade ; the neighbors form groups beneath the shelter of its green canopy. The old men point it out to their children, but they themselves remember not its growth : generations of men one after another have been born and died, and this son of the forest has remained the same, defying the storms of two hundred winters.

Yet this large tree was once a little acorn ; small in size, insignificant in appearance ; such as you are now picking up, upon the grass beneath it. Such an acorn, whose cup can only contain a drop or two of dew, contained the whole oak. All its massy trunk, all its knotty branches, all its multitude of leaves were in that acorn ; it grew, it spread, it unfolded itself by degrees, it received nourishment from the rain, and the dews, and the well adapted soil, but it was all there. Rain, and dews, and soil, could not raise an oak without the acorn ; nor could they make the acorn any thing but an oak.

The mind of a child is like the acorn ; its powers are folded up, they do not yet appear, but they are all there. The memory, the judgment, the invention, the feeling of right and wrong, are all in the mind of a child, — of a little infant just born ; but they are not expanded, you cannot perceive them.

Think of the wisest man you ever knew or heard of ; think of the greatest man ; think of the most learned man, who speaks a number of languages and can find out hidden things ; think of a man who stands like that tree, sheltering and protecting a number of his fellow men, and then say to yourself, the mind of that man was once like mine, his thoughts were childish like my thoughts, nay, he was like the babe just born, which knows nothing, remembers nothing, which cannot distinguish good from evil, nor truth from falsehood.

If you had only seen an acorn, you could never guess at the form and size of an oak : if you had never conversed with a wise man, you could form no idea of him from the mute and helpless infant.

Instruction is the food of the mind ; it is like the dew and the rain and the rich soil. As the soil and the rain and the dew cause the tree to swell and put forth its tender shoots, so do books and study and discourse feed the mind, and make it unfold its hidden powers.

Reverence therefore your own mind ; receive the nurture of instruction, that the man within you may grow and flourish. You cannot guess how excellent he may become.

It was long before this oak showed its greatness ; years passed away, and it had only shot a little way above the ground ; a child might have plucked it up with his little hands. It was long before any one called it a tree ; and it is long before the child becomes a man.

The acorn might have perished in the ground, the young tree might have been shorn of its graceful boughs, the twig might have bent, and the tree would have been crooked ; but if it grew at all, it could have been nothing but an oak ; it would not have been grass or flowers, which live their season and then perish from the face of the earth.

The child may be a foolish man, he may be a wicked man, but he must be a man ; his nature is not that of any inferior creature, his soul in not akin to the beasts which perish.

Oh, cherish then this precious mind, feed it with truth, nourish it with knowledge ; it comes from God, it is made in his image. The oak will last for centuries of years, but the mind of man is made for immortality.

Respect in the infant the future man. Destroy not in the man the rudiments of an angel.

HYMN XI.

THE golden orb of the sun is sunk behind the hills; the colors fade away from the western sky, and the shades of evening fall fast around me.

Deeper and deeper they stretch over the plain; I look at the grass, it is no longer green; the flowers are no more tinted with various hues; the houses, the trees, the cattle, are all lost in the distance. The dark curtain of night is let down over the works of God; they are blotted out from the view, as if they were no longer there.

Child of little observation! canst thou see nothing because thou canst not see grass and flowers, trees and cattle? Lift up thine eyes from the ground shaded with darkness, to the heavens that are stretched over thy head; see how the stars one by one appear and light up the vast concave.

There is the moon, bending her bright horns like a silver bow, and shedding her mild light like liquid silver over the blue firmament.

There is Venus, the evening and the morning star; and the Pleiades; and the Bear, that never sets; and the pole star, that guides the mariner over the deep.

Now the mantle of darkness is over the earth; the last little gleam of twilight is faded away; the lights are extinguished in the cottage windows, but the firmament burns with innumerable fires; every little star twinkles in its place. If you begin to count them, they are more than you can number; they are like the sands of the sea shore.

The telescope shows you far more, and there are thousands and ten thousands of stars which no telescope has ever reached.

Now Orion heaves his bright shoulder above the horizon; and Sirius, the dog star, follows him, the brightest of the train.

Look at the milky way: it is a field of brightness; its pale light is composed of myriads of burning suns.

All these are God's families: he gives the sun to shine with a ray of his own glory: he marks the path of the planets; he guides their wanderings through the sky, and traces out their orbit with the finger of his power.

If you were to travel as swift as an arrow from a bow, and to travel on, further and further still, for millions of years, you would not be out of the creation of God.

New suns in the depth of space would still be burning round you, and other planets fulfilling their appointed course.

Lift up thine eyes, child of earth, for God has given thee a glimpse of heaven.

The light of one sun is withdrawn, that thou mayest see ten thousand. Darkness is spread over the earth, that thou mayest behold, at a distance, the regions of eternal day.

This earth has a variety of inhabitants; the sea, the air, the surface of the ground, swarm with creatures of different natures, sizes, and powers; to know a very little of them, is to be wise among the sons of men.

What then, thinkest thou, are the various forms and natures and senses and occupations of the peopled universe?

Who can tell the birth and generation of so many worlds? Who can relate their histories? Who can describe their inhabitants?

Canst thou measure infinity with a line? Canst thou grasp the circle of infinite space?

Yet these all depend upon God; they hang upon Him as a child upon the breast of its mother; He tempereth the heat to the inhabitant of Mercury; He provideth resources against the cold in the frozen orb of Saturn. Doubt not that He provideth for all beings that He has made.

Look at the moon when it walketh in brightness; gaze at the stars when they are marshalled in the firmament; and adore the Maker of so many worlds.

HYMN XII.

IT is now winter, dead winter. Desolation and silence reign in the fields; no singing of birds is heard, no humming of insects. The streams murmur no longer; they are locked up in frost.

The trees lift their naked boughs, like withered arms, into the bleak sky; the green sap no longer rises in their veins; the flowers and the sweet-smelling shrubs are decayed to their roots.

The sun himself looks cold and cheerless; he gives light only enough to show the universal desolation.

Nature, child of God, mourns for her children. A little while ago, and she rejoiced in her offspring; the rose shed its perfume upon the gale; the vine gave its fruit; her children were springing and blooming around her, on every lawn and every green bank.

O Nature, beautiful Nature, beloved child of God, why dost thou sit mourning and desolate? Has thy father forsaken thee, has he left thee to perish? Art thou no longer the object of his care?

He has not forsaken thee, O Nature; thou art his beloved child, the eternal image of his perfections; his own beauty is spread over thee, the light of his countenance is shed upon thee.

Thy children shall live again, they shall spring up and bloom around thee; the rose shall again breathe its sweetness on the soft air, and from the bosom of the ground verdure shall spring forth.

And dost thou not mourn, O Nature, for thy human births; for thy sons and thy daughters that sleep under the sod; and shall they not also revive? Shall the rose and the myrtle bloom anew, and shall man perish? Shall goodness sleep in the ground, and the light of wisdom be quenched in the dust, and shall tears be shed over *them* in vain?

They also shall live; their winter shall pass away; they shall bloom again. The tears of thy children shall be dried up, when the eternal year proceeds. Oh, come that eternal year!

HYMN XIII.

CHILD of mortality, whence comest thou? why is thy countenance sad, and why are thine eyes red with weeping?

I have seen the rose in its beauty; it spread its leaves to the morning sun. I returned, — it was dying upon its stalk: the grace of the form of it was gone; its loveliness was vanished away; the leaves thereof were scattered on the ground, and no one gathered them again.

A stately tree grew on the plain; its branches were covered with verdure; its boughs spread wide and made a goodly shadow; the trunk was like a strong pillar; the roots were like crooked fangs. I returned, — the verdure was nipped by the east wind; the branches were lopped away by the axe; the worm had made its way into the trunk, and the heart thereof was decayed; it mouldered away, and fell to the ground.

I have seen the insects sporting in the sunshine, and darting along the streams; their wings glittered with gold and purple; their bodies shone like the green emerald: they were more numerous than I could count; their motions were quicker than my eye could glance. I returned, — they were brushed into the pool; they were perishing with the evening breeze; the swallow had devoured them; the pike had seized them; there were none found of so great a multitude.

I have seen man in the pride of his strength; his cheeks glowed with beauty; his limbs were full of activity; he leaped; he walked; he ran; he rejoiced in that he was more excellent than those. I returned, — he lay stiff and cold on the bare ground; his feet could no longer move, nor his hands stretch themselves out; his life was departed from him; and the breath out of his nostrils. Therefore do I weep because DEATH is in the world; the spoiler is among the works of God. All that is made, must be destroyed; all that is born, must die. Let me alone, for I will weep yet longer.

HYMN XIV.

I have seen the flower withering on the stalk, and its bright leaves spread on the ground. I looked again, and it sprung forth afresh; the stem was crowned with new buds, and the sweetness thereof filled the air.

I have seen the sun set in the west, and the shades of night shut in the wide horizon; there was no color, nor shape, nor beauty, nor music; gloom and darkness brooded around. I looked, the sun broke forth again from the east; he gilded the mountain tops; the lark rose to meet him from her low nest, and the shades of darkness fell away.

I have seen the insect being come to its full size, languish and refuse to eat: it spun itself a tomb, and was shrouded in the silken cone; it lay without feet, or shape, or power to move.

I looked again, — it had burst its tomb; it was full of life, and sailed on colored wings through the soft air; it rejoiced in its new being.

Thus shall it be with thee, O man! and so shall thy life be renewed.

Beauty shall spring up out of ashes; and life out of the dust.

A little while shalt thou lie in the ground, as the seed lieth in the bosom of the earth: but thou shalt be raised again; and, if thou art good, thou shalt never die any more.

Who is he that cometh to burst open the prison doors of the tomb; to bid the dead awake, and to gather his redeemed from the four winds of heaven?

He descendeth on a fiery cloud; the sound of a trumpet goeth before him; thousands of angels are on his right hand.

It is Jesus, the Son of God; the Savior of men; the friend of the good.

He cometh in the glory of his Father; he hath received power from on high.

Mourn not, therefore, child of immortality; for the spoiler, the cruel spoiler, that laid waste the works of God, is subdued: Jesus hath conquered death. Child of immortality! mourn no longer.

HYMN XV.

THE rose is sweet, but it is surrounded with thorns: the lily of the valley is fragrant, but it springeth up amongst the brambles.

The spring is pleasant, but it is soon past: the summer is bright, but the winter destroyeth the beauty thereof.

The rainbow is very glorious, but it soon vanisheth away : life is good, but it is quickly swallowed up in death.

There is a land where the roses are without thorns, where the flowers are not mixed with brambles.

In that land, there is eternal spring, and light without any cloud.

The tree of life groweth in the midst thereof; rivers of pleasures are there, and flowers that never fade.

Myriads of happy spirits are there, and surround the throne of God with a perpetual hymn.

The angels with their golden harps sing praises continually, and the cherubim fly on wings of fire.

This country is Heaven : it is the country of those that are good; and nothing that is wicked must inhabit there.

The toad must not spit its venom amongst turtle doves : nor the poisonous henbane grow amongst sweet flowers.

Neither must any one that doeth ill enter into that good land.

This earth is pleasant, for it is God's earth, and it is filled with many delightful things.

But that country is far better : there we shall not grieve any more, nor be sick any more, nor do wrong any more ; there, the cold of winter shall not wither us, nor the heats of summer scorch us.

In that country there are no wars nor quarrels, but all love one another with dear love.

When our parents and friends die, and are laid in the cold ground, we see them here no more ; but there we shall embrace them again, and live with them, and be separated no more.

There we shall meet all good men, whom we read of in holy books.

There we shall see Abraham, the called of God, the father of the faithful ; and Moses, after his long wanderings in the Arabian desert; and Elijah, the prophet of God; and Daniel, who escaped the lion's den; and there, the son of Jesse, the shepherd king, the sweet singer of Israel.

They loved God on earth; they praised him on earth; but in that country they will praise him better, and love him more.

There we shall see Jesus, who is gone before us to that happy place; and there we shall behold the glory of the high God.

We cannot see him here, but we will love him here; we must be now on earth, but we will often think on heaven.

That happy land is our home: we are to be here but for a little while, and there forever, even for ages of eternal years.

University Press: John Wilson and Son, Cambridge.

www.ingramcontent.com/pod-product-compliance
Lightning Source LLC
Chambersburg PA
CBHW031333070726
47496CB00018B/1852